Geoffrey Howard is Area Dea Ambrose's Church, Salford. He apart from a year spent teaching he has lived and worked in the inner-city districts of Manchester and Salford all his life. He ran his first marathon at the age of forty, and leads a Manchester Diocesan Team up the highest peaks of England, Wales and Scotland in less than twenty-four hours every spring.

To
Michael Goldsmith
and
Charles (Paddy) Lynch

GEOFFREY HOWARD

Wheelbarrow Across the Sahara

Grafton
An Imprint of HarperCollins*Publishers*

Grafton
An Imprint of HarperCollins*Publishers*
77–85 Fulham Palace Road,
Hammersmith, London W6 8JB

Published by Grafton 1992
9 8 7 6 5 4 3 2 1

First published in Great Britain by
Alan Sutton Publishing Ltd 1990

ISBN 0 586 21377 5

Set in Palatino

Printed in Great Britain by
HarperCollinsManufacturing Glasgow

Wheelbarrow
Across the Sahara

CONTENTS

The author and publisher wish to thank Salford University Business Enterprises Limited for their assistance in the publication of this book

FOREWORD

Adventure comes in so many disparate forms. For some it's a grim challenge, for others an exhilarating game of risk. It can be a few seconds of sheer excitement for a base jumper leaping off a rock face or a long drawn out struggle with cold and altitude on a high Himalayan peak. Why do we undertake it, at risk of life, often in acute discomfort and exhaustion, with little if any material reward and great costs both in terms of money or lost earnings and, more importantly, in the pressures the adventure all too often places on relationships?

I know why I do it. I'm hooked, addicted to the adrenalin rush of climbing, love the feel of rock under my toes, of a giddy drop below and my own mastery of my body. Most of the time it's pure, invigorating fun, but not always. There's not much fun at over 7,000 metres. It's just hard, slow graft. It's the challenge that keeps one going, but there is also the sheer beauty of the mountains, the pleasure of companionship and the curiosity of the unknown.

When I started to read *Wheelbarrow Across the Sahara*, I couldn't help wondering how close Geoff Howard's type of adventure was to the ones with which I am familiar. I found myself being drawn more and more into the book, seeing parallels with my own experience and feelings, brought out by Geoff with honesty and a self-deprecating, yet sharp, sense of humour.

'Not much of an adventure,' I thought, 'pushing this ridiculous wheelbarrow along a much-travelled road or track with a Land Rover in constant attendance.' But it was far from being a tarmac road for most of the way; there was a real sense of danger and the physical and mental stress was undoubtedly greater than anything I ever experienced on Everest. The very fact that he could give up at any moment throughout the journey made his perseverance all the more impressive.

This isn't the standard adventure book, and it's all the better for it. It's about people, about the unfolding and strengthening relationship he had with his two 'squaddie' drivers who had volunteered from the army; it's about self-doubt and about human kindness, and above all it's the story of boundless determination in the face of adversity.

CHRIS BONINGTON, CBE

PREFACE

In these pages I relive the desert against the backdrop of my forty-seven years. Most of the events took place in the Sahara in early 1975. If I had written an account immediately on my return, I would never have seen the significance of those few weeks which were the essence of my life before and since.

I have tried to be honest about myself and others. Sometimes this has involved recording sensitive personal details, bawdy conversation and even racist attitudes. Such recording is neither approval nor endorsement. To expurgate such facts is to rewrite the story. In the case of racist remarks, their removal would collude with those who pretend that racism does not exist. There has been no conscious sweeping under the carpet of that or other difficult issues. I am grateful to Joan, Mick and Paddy for allowing me to tell the story as it was.

Geoffrey Howard
March 1990

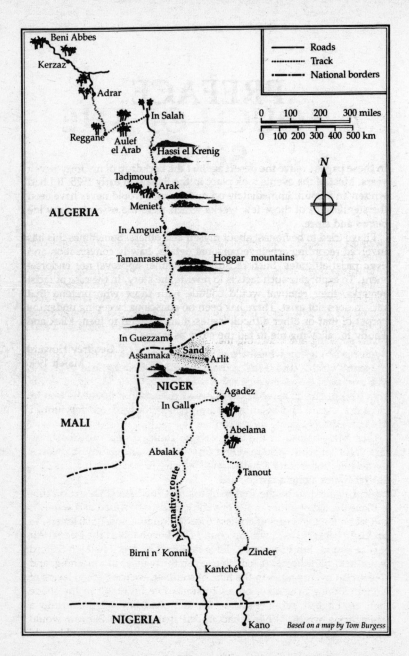

Beni Abbes

Kerzaz

Adrar

In Salah

Reggane

Aulef
el Arab

Hassi el Krenig

Tadjmout

Arak

Meniet

ALGERIA

In Amguel

Tamanrasset

Hoggar mountains

In Guezzam

Assamaka   Sand   Arlit

NIGER

Agadez

In Gall

MALI

Abelama

Abalak

Tanout

Alternative route

Birni n' Konni   Zinder

Kantché

NIGERIA   Kano

Roads
Track
National borders

0   100   200   300 miles
0   100 200 300 400 500 km

N

Based on a map by Tom Burgess

1

A TOUCH OF THE SUN

I was on my knees and feverishly cold. The sun had set behind the dunes, leaving a smoky orange cloud in a bright patch of sky. A fierce wind was coming from the east, bringing in a wintry Christmas Eve. I hauled myself up on the shafts of my Chinese sailing wheelbarrow, and stood shivering. Mick and Paddy, my soldier escorts, were camped and waiting for me fifty yards from the road. Bombadier Mick, wrapped in his duffle-coat, was leaning on the wing of the cream-coloured Land Rover, smoking and watching me.

After pushing my wheelbarrow off the road, it had keeled over the moment it hit the sand. I had righted it, and pushed, but had collapsed with sun-stroke and exhaustion. I was trying to stand, pleading for Mick's help, but he stayed put. My own rules would not allow him to assist me. Again and again, I got up, inched forward and fell, until I whimpered that I could go no further.

Then Mick helped in the only way he could. 'Come on, Geoff,' he said. 'Not far now. You're doing fine.' Slowly and gently his words coaxed me home until I had completed my first day in the desert – thirteen miles along a tarred road.

I had wanted to be the first man to cross the Sahara Desert on foot without the aid of either camel or vehicle to carry his food and water. It had taken me two years of endless trips to London, and 1,500 letters, to persuade backers that I was no crank. I had even talked the Special Air Service round. But I seemed to have deceived myself. I had left Salford fit and artificially acclimatized, able to run thirty miles in a morning, and able to run twenty miles in the heat of summer, wearing seven layers of winter clothing. Yet now, on a Christmas Eve no hotter in the shade than an English summer's day, the sun had shrivelled me into a whimpering wreck. While I had hoped that the wheelbarrow would carry my supplies two thousand miles across the desert, I found I could not even handle it on tarmac. There now seemed no chance of travelling further than the end of this road, two hundred and twenty miles south.

That night, at the end of the first day, Christmas Eve 1974, it was not the sun that was the problem. Soon after I had struggled, in a freezing wind, to put up the orange tent, it was being whitened with frost. Inside, in my sleeping-bag, I was wearing underwear, pyjamas, three pairs of socks, two shirts, a jersey, jacket, car-coat, hat and gloves, but was still shivering.

I leaned out of the tent to warm a meal and make tea but the gas jet was blocked. I felt too ill to bother clearing it, so I ate a can of cold carrots and drank salt and water to replace what I had lost in sweat. The lads' petrol stove roared above the noise of the wind. They were eating goulash and Mick was offering Paddy another cup of tea. I wanted to ask for one, but it was my aim to be self-sufficient.

After ten minutes, Mick and Paddy were listening to my snores. While I slept, those at home were wrapping presents and putting up the last of the decorations before going out to midnight communion. They would have seen my empty chair in the sanctuary. Later, when our church warden had locked up after the service; when the vicar of Pendleton and his wife had gone up to bed; when my wife, Joan, who was living with them in my absence, had laid out our children's toys – a big yellow lorry and games for Sam and face paints and puppets for Susan – and had slipped into bed, I woke and saw the luminous dial of my watch show two o'clock.

The wind had subsided and was gently flapping the canvas. I was cold and my stomach ached. Sunstroke had sapped my strength like a dose of influenza and had weakened my will to fix the gas jet, but I knew that my recovery needed nourishment. I put ice-cold water into a miniature red plastic washing-up bowl (borrowed from Susan's doll), placed it in the mouth of the tent, and dismantled the stove, often having to blow life back into my fingers and strain my eyes to see. After washing sand from the dismantled parts of the stove, I placed them on a folded towel. By three o'clock the blue jet lit up the entrance to the tent and I was groggily getting a can of sardines from the frost-covered wheelbarrow. The sardines and oil were frozen and had to be prised out, so I fried them with reconstituted potato, peas and carrots, making what was to become my most common meal.

I lay satisfied, leaning on an elbow, warming my hands on a mug of tea, looking without my spectacles at the massive out-of-focus stars and listening to a tape Joan had given me to play at Christmas. I listened over and over again to her saying, 'I know I will be missing you incredibly by now, but I think it will do us both good, though I can't see how.' I wanted to scream back that it was all a mistake, that no good would come, that I wanted nothing more than to be home.

2

I slammed off the machine sometime after five o'clock, wishing never to hear it again, and though I have kept the tape, I cannot bear to play it. All had not been well when I left, and I wanted to be home to put things right. Why, I asked myself, had I been so stupid as to come?

My reasons for the walk had never been totally clear, even to myself. My work had involved helping others to make wise decisions. Yet now I was about to risk my life without knowing why I was doing it. Just before I left England, I had struggled to analyse my motives at the request of a Sunday newspaper:

It is so easy to go through life kidding oneself that one's faith is real, that if one had all security, possessions, family and health taken away, and were made to suffer, even to the point of death, one would keep one's beliefs.

It has been easy for me to proclaim a God of love, easy to preach eternal bliss to the dying, and yet should tragedy overtake me, I can do no more than guess at my probable reactions. It is my hope that in the desert, facing loss, I may never fear to lose; enduring pain, I will never shrink from it; risking death, I may return prepared to give up my life without grudging, and having placed my life firmly in God's hands, I may never want to withhold anything from him.

And so I want to cross the Sahara Desert on foot, unaided by vehicle or camel. After almost two years' study and training, aimed at preparing myself for every contingency, I believe myself to be equipped to make the crossing.

Though not strong enough to carry sufficient food and water myself, I shall push all I require in a Chinese sailing wheelbarrow, which is easily the best man-powered machine for transporting heavy loads over soft or rough terrain.

Even with careful planning, there is still a risk. However, I cannot pretend that facing this risk simply for the hell of it and doing something nobody else has done before does not appeal to me.

I realize that what I am doing is supremely selfish. I might not come back, and if I do, I may be a different person. Whatever the outcome, it will profoundly affect Joan, Susan and Sam, and yet I go with their blessing, though not without much pain and heartsearching on all our parts. We feel sure that I am doing the right thing. Opting for security will never prove where my heart and faith are really placed.

Though selfishly motivated in part, I passionately want to help others through the walk. A short spell in Nigeria showed me poverty and hunger as would melt a heart of stone. There are millions suffering like that and I want to do something for them. I am no engineer – I cannot dig wells. I am not wealthy – I have only a little to give – but a sponsored walk as crazy as this will prompt others to help, and maybe a little hardship, hunger and thirst on my part will help me to understand the needs of the poor a little better.

If the walk proves the worth of the Chinese sailing wheelbarrow it too could help by easing the burden of millions of the world's farmers who can afford neither vehicle nor beast of burden. When I feel like giving up, as no doubt I will, they will be my spur.

At four o'clock that Christmas morning, the published reasons for my coming to the desert had never seemed more hollow, and yet whenever I have tried to replace them with something more honest, I have been unable. Maybe there was no logical reason for the expedition. After all, it was not the first eccentric thing I had done, though it was the most ambitious.

The day before Christmas 1968, when I was teaching in Nigeria, we had no bread, so I cycled on a pre-war lady's Raleigh from the mission compound to get some – a round trip of a hundred miles, mainly along dirt roads. I bought a dozen loaves (enough to give some away) and put them in a cardboard carton on the handlebars. It kept being thrown off by the corrugations on the road, but somehow, after cadging a twenty-mile lift, I arrived home just after dark.

Six months later, I went on the same bicycle to visit some friends for the day. They lived in a village thirty-five miles across the bush and over mountains. On the way back, the sun set when I was fifteen miles from home. There was no moon and cloud covered the stars. There were snakes and leopards in the bush and I had neither torch, map, nor compass. It was so dark that I could not see the ground. I rode into a three foot hole, and scrambled back up only to land in a thorn bush. By some miracle I found my way home.

That sort of thing – and similar exploits from my college days – had often caused friends to call me mad. My plans to cross the desert came as no surprise to them, but what might have surprised those who had only known me as an adult was that I had been different as a child, so different that I have sometimes wondered if I am trying to make up for a lost childhood.

— 2 —
MUMMY'S BOY

My mother said that I should have been born a girl. She used to say that I was as good as gold. I was born in 1945 at 54 Claribel Street, Ardwick, Manchester, the son of May and George Howard. My father was a property repairer. My mother had been a petrol-pump attendant during the Second World War, and was later a cleaner, lift attendant, and then records clerk in a warehouse. My parents' first child, George, had died a few days after birth. I had a sister, Ann, three years younger than me. She was always in trouble. Mother said that she should have been a boy.

We lived in a two-up, two-down terraced house which had neither bath, inside toilet, hall, kitchen nor garden. Each room was three yards square, and there was one sink, where we washed ourselves, our clothes and the dishes. Until I was four, my mother cooked on a gas ring on the table. Times did not seem hard. It was the same for everyone.

As a young child, I rarely needed to be disciplined and never answered back. If refused anything, I would not ask again. I was appalled when my friends pestered their parents until they got their way and wondered why selfishness had been rewarded. I cannot remember getting up to mischief and was only rebellious when having my photograph taken, sometimes pulling my face out of embarrassment. If left alone, I would make models from scrap, draw, tidy up the house, or polish the furniture. I spent hours sorting out stamps, checking their countries of origin in an old atlas.

I was a sensitive and kind-hearted little soul and twice put some of my pocket money into my mother's purse when she was hard up. When I was of infant school age, I spent a lot of time on her knee, and when I was a little older, though I played out, I did so less often than my friends.

I was so quiet that I was hardly noticed at school. When I was in the final year infants, we were let loose on a box of musical instruments once a week. I put up my hand to play the drums, but it was always Roy Fairweather and Tommy Sayers who were chosen. Week after week, I put up my hand. Week after week, I was given a triangle.

I was noticed at Sunday School more quickly, and the rector asked me to join the church choir. I dreaded the thought, but, at seven years old, was too scared to say so. Once installed, I was rushed off by my mother to a photographic studio to have my picture taken wearing my choir robes. It was one thing being thought of as soft, but it was another having a photograph to prove it.

My first fight came as a shock. Eric Harris and I put up our fists in the school playground. Mother had told me never to hit anyone in the face. I punched Eric's chest and arms but he hit me in the mouth. I burst into tears and said that it was unfair. From then on, I was the worst fighter in the school and avoided conflict both in the playground and on the sports field.

I knew that I was soft, but that was the last thing I wanted to be. I wanted to be like my father and grandfather. When my father was eighteen years old, he ran for the Ardwick Lads' Club cross-country team. His interest in running had begun when he had played truant from school to swim in the Openshaw Canal, two miles away. Instead of catching the tram, like his friends, he used to run there and so discovered his talent. In the winter of 1938/9 he was working for Pillings, a tiling company, on a job at Farnworth, Merseyside. He cycled to and from work, a round trip of seventy miles a day. One Saturday, after finishing work at noon, he was on his bike quicker than usual. He was running in an all Lancashire Lads' Clubs' race at three o'clock that afternoon. At ten-past two, he arrived at his parents' terraced house, had a glass of milk, and collected his shorts, plimsolls, and the light-blue football shirt he had borrowed from his uncle. After ten minutes, he was on his bike again. On his way, he called to see my mother, his new girl-friend; though he was not fancied to win, he told her he was going to bring back the winner's medal. He then had to cycle a further five miles to the start. That was fifty-two years ago. My mother fastened the medal to a bracelet and wears it to this day.

My father's parents lived twenty yards across our street. In 1903, when grandfather was fifteen (he had lied about his age, as many did), he signed up as a bugle boy in the army. He had spent eight years in India, but came back for the war. He was at the battle of the Somme and at one time spent a year living in the same trench. He was wounded twice, and gassing gave him chronic bronchitis. After sixteen years in the army, he took up boxing, going into the ring into his forties, and sometimes bringing back prizes.

I often visited him after school to massage his chest and back, sore from incessant coughing, with the embrocation liniment which he had made from turpentine and raw eggs. Most winters of my childhood, he was in hospital for weeks, fighting for his life. When home, he was fighting for breath.

I grew up thinking I was different from the male stock from which I had come. I could not use my fists and I was the worst runner in my class. The agressive male was in me from early on but was kept down by fear and shyness. It began to show itself in isolated events and then retreated. The nearer I grew to puberty, however, the more dominant my aggression became.

The first time it showed was when I was ten years old. I was ill in bed and my parents were at work, and I heard someone opening doors downstairs. I thought it was Great Aunt Mary making sure I was all right, so I shouted to her. There was no reply, only the squeak of the front-room door handle. I went to the top of the stairs, looked down, and saw the shadow of a man, who was standing at the entrance to the front room. Remembering that the police had been into school to warn us that there was a dangerous man at large, I trembled with fear, but I knew that my only chance of survival was to fight. There was nothing I could use to defend myself, only a small ceramic dog and a few comic-books. I went to the bedroom window, put my forearm flat against the glass and banged it repeatedly, gently at first and getting harder, always pulling back on impact, until it smashed. I grabbed a long shard, and, holding it like a dagger, advanced downstairs, shouting murderous threats. Downstairs, there was no sign of anyone, though the back door was wide open.

As I got older, I began to enjoy danger. I made a cannon from steel piping and a bomb out of an aerosol container stuffed with home-made gunpowder. There was never a thought of causing hurt or damage. The sound of the blast and the sight of the bomb crater and the hole the cannon had made in a sheet of steel were enough. In the school holidays, I used to play on the railway with friends. We would put six-inch nails on the track and let the goods trains flatten them into knives which we used for throwing into hoardings. Sometimes we walked along the railway viaduct to see how near we could get to the city centre without being spotted. When we were chased by the police, we dropped from the parapet on to the scrap-yard shed, and then, dodging the men, ran to the safety of the street.

Facing up to my peers did not come so easily. In February 1957, within a week of my twelfth birthday, I was throwing snowballs with friends. One of them was a tall intelligent boy, a year younger than me. He never lost a fight, and once won even after a bottle had been smashed over his head. The snowballing became less than friendly and I threatened him. He came at me, fists flying, and for the second time in my life, I could not back down. He would have won, had he not slipped on the ice and been unable to get up. I was hammering down his head with my fists. After that, if I walked away from a fight, I burned with shame. The more terrified I was, the less easily I could turn my back.

* * *

When I was sixteen, I heard Billy Graham preach at Manchester City's football ground. It changed my life and could only be described as 'being born again'. For the first time, God seemed real. In the sixth form, I started a Christian Union, but was an enigma to some of my friends. I drank, smoked cigars, went dancing, and preached new life in Christ. A couple of months before my eighteenth birthday, I met Joan.

About the same time, I offered myself to the bishop for ordination. He told me that after I had left school the Church of England would decide whether it wanted me at a selection conference the following May. While I was waiting, I took a job at Menzies bookstall on Piccadilly station, Manchester.

Alf Stones, the manager, said I would have to work Sundays. I told him I could not, as my place was in church. He asked me to try the job for a month without Sunday work and then, if I liked it, take my turn on the shift with the rest. I told him I would never change my mind but he asked me to start anyway. During my seven months there, I was hauled before the area manager many times over the issue, but I would not give in. I asked them either to stop pressing me on the matter or to sack me. They refused to do either.

Partly in preparation for the selection conference, and partly in an attempt to free myself from erroneous ideas, I began to read some philosophy. My appearance as a drinking, dance-going, cigar-smoking evangelical, having one foot in the life of Christianity and the other in that of the world, was part of the same attempt I made at work – to be true to myself and not to some ism. I did not want to submit myself to anything that could not be logically defended. I began to scrutinize my faith and eventually to doubt it and all human values, but, as I had to live in the real world, I continued to practise my faith, in the same way that I acted as if beauty, love, justice and truth existed. Doubt or no doubt, I was accepted for training, on the condition that I should first obtain a degree. The selectors advised me to apply to St John's College, Durham, which was both a college of the university and a theological college.

That summer, Joan left school and went to train as a teacher at Rolle College, Exmouth. Having seen her almost every day for a year, I mourned for her. I had passed a couple of A levels at school but now signed up at evening classes to take English and French O levels for the sixth time. The adult education centre was impersonal and unfriendly and I missed the classmates I had got to know over seven years.

Through all my insecurity, Joan's letters were reassuring, and we arranged to become engaged at Christmas. The diocesan bishop, William Greer, had ruled that engagement was out of the question for ordinands under twenty-one years old. I was only nineteen, but in early

December, I wrote to him suggesting that a general rule of this kind might not fit every case. Would he please consider me as an individual, and give a ruling soon, as I wished to become engaged at Christmas.

He wrote back, saying that I should discuss the matter with Canon Ronald Preston, one of his examining chaplains. When I went to see him at the cathedral after work, I had no idea that this kind and unassuming man was a lecturer in Christian Ethics at Manchester University, and soon to take the chair of Social and Pastoral Theology. He said that the bishop had told him to explain that engagement was not possible. I kept on saying that I wanted the merits of my case to be considered and that I was an individual. I never got round to saying what the merits of my request were, only that I wanted them to be considered, and that I needed a reply before Christmas.

Two days before Christmas, we had heard nothing and so bought the ring. We were engaged on Christmas Eve and the announcement appeared in the Manchester Evening News. The final words of it were, 'thanks to the Bishop of Manchester', though we had still heard nothing from him. It was fun challenging a bishop, but beneath the bravado, I was insecure. Joan's commitment to me, symbolized by the engagement, was what saw me through. The bishop's letter arrived a few days later: 'My Dear Howard, I am pleased to allow your engagement, on the understanding that you do not marry until after your ordination. William Manchester.'

* * *

In September 1965, I packed a tea-chest with books, clothes, mugs, coffee and a tin of milk powder and sent it by rail to St John's College, Durham. I had passed the English and French O levels and got a university place. St John's had Anglican governors, and entrance requirements were relaxed for ordinands. I had been let in with only two A levels and without a Classics O level.

The college buildings were a string of huge terraced houses winding along the Bailey, one of Durham's historic streets. Along one side of the Bailey were four of the colleges, and along the other, the granite cathedral, its green, close and cloisters. The Bailey was only accessible at one end, cut off by the river at the other, preventing through traffic and giving the colleges and cathedral environs the atmosphere of another age.

I did not much mind the traditions of the college but was dismayed that they were taken so seriously. At first, I made no attempt to react, but soon found that there was a reaction to me. I went to church one Sunday wearing jeans, and was accused by fellow students of 'doing it deliberately', of 'being an inverted snob', and of 'trying to draw attention to myself'. I told them that I had worn them quite unself-consciously, but they disbelieved me. Their disbelief hurt more than their snobbery, and goaded me into intentional anti-traditionalist acts, such as bowing to the altar at evensong in the manner of a muslim at prayer.

I became friends with another student, Richard Adams from Solihull, when he poured a jug of custard over someone's head at formal dinner. A couple of weeks later we went on a pub-crawl together – Durham's fifty-three pubs in one day – drinking half a pint of beer between us in each pub. From then on, Richard and I had fun relieving the tedium of study. When we were up late, and unlikely to get up for breakfast, we climbed through the kitchen window and helped ourselves to our share of bacon and eggs. Sometimes, we hid everyone else's breakfast in the deep-freeze or somewhere in the library. Occasionally, we walked along the parapets of Durham's five bridges, drinking a pint of beer in each of the five pubs en route.

Other students played sport, went to clubs and societies, and took out girls. We preferred our own entertainment: if we hired a punt, we ended up in the river; if we went for a walk, it was along parapets; when we wanted to get from the street to our second-floor rooms, it was often up the drain-pipe. Dinner was dull, so we livened it up. I sat in the bay of the dining-room, slid up the lower window, which almost came to the floor, and climbed out. I raced through the garden and quadrangle, and back into the college to the main electrical switch, which I turned off. By the time it was turned on again, I was in the dining-hall back in my place. In the darkness, it rained sautéd potatoes and peas, and when the lights came on, they seemed to be suspended in the air.

Facing up to fear was the chief motive behind all these pranks. As a small boy, I had been taken up the tower of Manchester Town Hall. When I looked over the parapet, I felt that I was being pulled over and about to fall two hundred feet into Albert Square. At university, I was still scared of heights. That was the thrill of walking along parapets of bridges. Other pranks faced the fear of being caught and sent down. But whatever I did, I felt that my guts were not being fully tested, and I wondered about doing something really big, like crossing an ocean. The Sahara had not yet occurred to me.

Facing my fears was part of a bigger concern. I had become obsessed with the quest for meaning, and saw the world as involved in the same quest. Like me it had failed. Its failure, I believed, had given rise to Romanticism, and now to Flower Power and the drug culture; I saw each of them as an attempt at, or a result of, escaping from reason. I found inspiration in the plays of Beckett and Ionesco, and looked for it in the writings of Camus and Sartre, but found them hard to get into. I was never much of a reader.

While I could not find meaning through reason, I failed to see that I was finding it through Joan. The weekly telephone calls and letters brought us closer together. We married in 1968 after I had graduated – two years before I was ordained, in spite of the bishop's ruling. We then took a year off to teach in Nigeria before returning to Durham for my ordination training.

After I had finished at theological college, the Bishop of Manchester offered me a curacy in the suburbs, but I persuaded him to let me work in Cheetham, an inner-city parish. My doubts were again buried, this time by work. The hours were long and hard, and our terraced house seemed always full of young people. I was able to pray, but lacked the feeling of closeness to God I had once known.

During the curacy, when we discovered that neither of us was very fertile, Joan was put on a drug. The treatment failed, which was for me mildly, and for Joan very, depressing. We were told that either one of us might more easily become a parent with a more fertile partner. All along, we had wanted to adopt children, but now Joan was saddened by her frustrated instinct to bear a child. A friend later suggested that the desert was compensation for my failure to father children: that I felt I had to succeed as a man. Others suggested that I had such a deep fear of being dominated, that I had to prove myself against the desert in the way that I had tried to stand against teenage gangs, phoney ideas, and the inflexibility of the Church. The more I have thought about motives, the less clear I have become.

What was to become clear on that first night in the desert, was that I wished that I had sorted out my motives earlier. Listening to Joan's tape recording, I had become more confused than ever about motives. I took a last look at the stars, relieved that there was no sign of first light. I would try to get back to sleep. In only half a day, the wheelbarrow had sucked from me the strength it had taken twenty-one months of training to build up. I dreaded the thought of getting up in a few hours, let alone of getting back on the road. Other than the wish to avoid seeming to be a fool and a failure in the eyes of others, I could see no reason to go on. I pulled my head undercover, shut out all thought of morning, and fell asleep.

3

RUNNING BEFORE I CAN WALK

Things were not so bad in daylight. I had slept for almost four hours more, made myself a mug of tea at about nine o'clock and carried it outside while I wished Mick and Paddy a merry Christmas. The wind was blustery and cold and the wheelbarrow and Land Rover were wet with melting frost. We were camped on a sand and gravel plain with the road running north–south, fifty yards from us to the east. Less than a mile beyond it, was a ridge of shallow dunes. There were even smaller dunes, no more than eight feet high, two hundred yards to the west. The plain stretched north and south as far as the eye could see and there was no sign of either vegetation or habitation – nothing but dust, rock and sand.

I walked over to Mick, who was crouched near the rear wheel of the Land Rover tending the petrol stove. My legs were steadier than they had been the night before but they still dithered weakly. It was difficult to believe how much effort I had put into training and preparation.

* * *

In February 1973, when I first decided to make the journey, there can have been few twenty-eight year olds who were less fit for the task. I was not quite five feet eight inches high, weighed only nine and a half stone, and found it uncomfortable to stand without arch-supports even for the duration of a hymn in church. Scholl gave me four pairs to take to the Sahara.

Acquiring fitness over the next twenty-two months was not easy. My job as a curate took mornings, afternoons and evenings, six days a week – I was given one day off – so there was no time to get fit by walking. Instead, I took up running in order to take more exercise in a shorter time. The first training run was a one-mile loop from home. I began a slow jog, but after a quarter of a mile, it seemed that my feet had gained weight and that somebody was sitting on my chest. Then a stitch stabbed my ribs and forced me to walk the next few yards. The mile took nine and a half minutes, at the end of which my dead weight pulled me, wheezing and red-faced, into an armchair. Breathing was even more difficult now that I had stopped running, and I was racked by bouts of coughing. The next morning, I was so stiff that it was difficult to climb downstairs. I trained most days from then on. Training hurt and it was always a battle to force myself out, but after six months I was managing sixty miles a week and sometimes doing fifteen miles non-stop in a hundred minutes. A further six months and I could run thirty miles with little stiffness afterwards. The main obstacle was that the only time available for training was late at night. To go out at midnight in heavy rain or frost, as I sometimes did, when I would be working next morning and when I had hardly seen my wife all day, almost broke me.

Training was not only arduous but dangerous. I lived in one of the rougher parts of Manchester, and was chased by gangs, had bottles thrown at me and once inadvertently put a gang to rout. I was running along the pavement of Rochdale Road, just after midnight, wearing, among other things, two quilted anoraks, one of which had fourteen pounds of sand sewn into the lining. The extra weight and clothing was to help me get used to the combined effect of heat and exertion, but it made me look twice the man I was! Without realizing, I found myself between two groups of youths throwing bottles at each other. I had run through the ranks of one gang from the rear, and was approaching the other, twenty-five yards ahead of me along the pavement. With bottles still in the air, those in front fled, thinking I was one of their rivals. I found myself in pursuit, not out of choice, but because I was being chased by the mob behind. The first thirty seconds were the worst. I had already run three miles, and my boots were too heavy for sprinting – besides I did not want to catch the gang in front. For a few moments, someone behind was grasping for me, but he fell back and gave up. Most of those who were fleeing dispersed down side streets and, after a quarter of a mile, the last two ran into a garden as I passed.

Assault by thugs was not the only risk. After six months' training, I repeatedly found blood in my urine, which a consultant thought indicated a kidney disorder. Both he and my own doctor warned me to stop all running for the sake of my health; their manner was so grave as to imply danger to my life. I could see no reason for panic. Nobody with such a disease could have been training so hard and felt so well. Instead of stopping, I ran even more, promising myself that if I began to feel ill, I would heed the warning. If I had done as they said there would have been no chance of being fit enough for the expedition. After nine months of tests, I was told that there was 'probably' nothing wrong with my kidneys and that I had had a bladder infection. I could resume light training but I must undergo further tests. Hospital appointments seemed to go on for ever and when I left for the Sahara, I forgot to cancel one of them.

I had also managed to artificially acclimatize myself. During August, I had learnt to sweat, going to bed with hot-water bottles, an electric blanket, a seaman's jersey, plastic underwear, and a down quilt. I went running wearing two anoraks, a seaman's jersey, and a rugby shirt, on top of plastic *and* thermal underwear.

* * *

In the first year of preparation, despite writing over nine hundred letters, I had acquired no major backers. All I had was a promise of a pair of boots from Jack Riordon, a quartermaster in the Green Howards Regiment. No one else, except the media, wanted to know. I had written to hundreds of firms asking for material support, and had asked royalty, influential people and famous explorers to lend their names to a list of patrons, but all without success.

After a year, I had only the boots, but I knew that if somebody of importance would approve the idea then the rest would follow. With this in mind, I sent my plans to the Special Air Service Regiment, reputedly the best collective authority in Britain on desert survival, and asked them to comment. I had given up hope of a reply when, after two months and three days, a letter came which began, 'We find your proposals perfectly feasible . . .'. I had a hundred photocopies made of their reply and began another support-raising campaign, including a copy of the letter from the SAS with each request.

The response was spectacular. Before long the Parachute Regiment had added their name to the backers. The Royal Air Force gave me emergency rations, advice on medical supplies, and a day at RAF Cranwell to learn how to navigate with a bubble sextant. Stuart Wilson of the Department of Engineering Science at Oxford put forward the idea of using a Chinese sailing wheelbarrow instead of the two-wheeled cart which I was considering, and one of his students, Khalid Nazir, made a wooden prototype. At the same time, Hawker Siddeley offered to make the one I would use, and other firms donated equipment and food.

Now that events were moving in my favour, it was as troublesome finding out what was needed as it was getting it. Putting a medical kit together, for example, involved consulting books, obtaining lists from other expeditions and writing to the armed forces. There were the names of all the venomous creatures in North and West Africa to be listed and the manufacturers of antiserums for their bites and stings to be contacted. Eventually, a church member who was a nurse tabulated all the medical information, and helped me to write begging letters to pharmaceutical firms. When six cartons of drugs, bandages and serums were heaped on my study floor there was the business of finding out when and how they should be administered. Then I was tested for allergies to the serums and taught how and where to inject myself.

Besides training and obtaining supplies, there was Arabic to learn, though I never got very far, French and Hausa to improve, and dozens of books to read on desert survival and the background to the Sahara. Appropriate clothes also had to be found. I chose a straw hat I had brought from Nigeria. It had a wide brim and a small ventilation hole in the top like a chimney. Such hats were worn by the Fulani, a semi-nomadic tribe of cattle herdsmen. The outer garment was an all-covering, loose-fitting, robe, made by Joan to a Nigerian design.

Schools, churches and individuals had to be encouraged to sponsor me and, periodically, information sheets had to be typed, duplicated, and sent to them. Suitable recipients had to be found for the money raised. (A programme for the repatriation of refugees in the southern Sahara was chosen, along with the Desert Research Trust, a Cambridge-based body, investigating the causes of famine. A smaller amount was to go to the theological college which I had attended and which has been host to many students from Africa.)

Hours were spent practising navigation with the bubble sextant. There were meetings with backers and the press to be organized, including trips to the seaside with newspaper photographers and television crews, who wanted pictures of me walking on sand.

Such training and preparation brought both me and my marriage almost to breaking-point. Most days, I worked into the early hours, leaving little time to spend with Joan. In spite of my working frantically for months, preparations fell behind. In early October 1974, exactly two weeks before the sailing date to North Africa, a telegram came, saying that the voyage on the Southern Ferries' ship, *The Eagle*, was cancelled. The ferry sevice was making a loss and had stopped running for the winter.

It might have been more depressing if I had been otherwise ready to leave. Many major obstacles had been overcome: a friend had loaned me £1,500, and two others, Tommy and Hilary Thomas, had given us a home after my curacy at St Luke's Church, Cheetham, had terminated. I also now had sufficient food, equipment and maps. There was, however, still no Land Rover, nor anyone to drive it. Nor was there any sign of diplomatic clearance for Algeria, Niger and Nigeria. Furthermore, my passport was lost in a postal strike in France, and the wheelbarrow was not yet ready, Hawker Siddeley having been hampered by staff shortage and technical snags.

On the day the telegram arrived from Southern Ferries, a close friend who had given me much encouragement now began to question my continuing any further. I would save myself and those around a lot of heartache by forgetting the Sahara and looking for another curacy. He was talking sense. The trip could not be postponed for ever. It would not be possible at any other time of the year because of the oncoming hot season. Travelling by any means was forbidden in the Algerian Sahara from the end of May to September, while walking would, in any case, be impossible after March. Beginning in late October and maintaining fifteen miles a day would get me to Kano, my destination on the other side of the Sahara, just in time. If the walk was to take place, it could not be seriously delayed. Anyway, I had no income other than occasional fees from the news media and they would dry up. Nor would the expedition have been possible the next winter. The trip was aimed to fit between appointments at two churches. I could neither remain unemployed for eighteen months nor begin a new job now and break off after only a year.

The logical thing would have been to admit defeat. There were too many things to do and not enough time. Yet, with an almost insane confidence, I was sure the walk was on: when I read the telegram from Southern Ferries, I had a feeling that all would be well. In spite of depressing circumstances, I was more excited and confident than I had ever been.

I am still not clear whether my confidence was the product of my faith or whether I had generated a blind optimism to prevent the facts from crushing me. When the telegram arrived, Joan and I went for a walk so that I could work the adrenalin out of my system. The Sahara had become my deity, and, though I was therefore in no position to claim any closeness to God, I arrogantly did. 'I feel so excited,' I said. 'I know God is going to do it, but I don't see how.'

'I told you before that he's throwing your plans overboard one by one. All your effort has shown him that you don't trust him. I've watched you punish yourself and we've suffered. You've worked like a maniac day and night. You've tried too hard. You've not allowed him to help you. If he wants you to go, then you'll go, and if he doesn't, you won't, so let him show you he's in control.' She was right. I would stop the frantic activity and just follow the leads that came my way.

At the outset of the plans, we had prayed for a sign of divine approval. If God would provide accommodation for my family while I was away, preferably with friends, and convince my parents that I was doing the right thing, then I would know that the trip was on. It had been a lot to ask. We had no friends in Manchester with a large enough house. Moreover, my mother, who worried even if I travelled to London, was initially distraught by the idea. I could not have gone without her goodwill, as it could have been injurious to her already poor health. Early on in the preparations, she had had an inexplicable change of heart and remained committed. Sometime later, Tommy Thomas, an old college friend, had been made vicar of Pendleton, Salford, only three miles from our home. He and his wife had offered us accommodation with them from the time my curacy finished until after the expedition. Encouraged by reflecting on these events, we walked home arm in arm.

I was later puzzled that it did indeed happen as we had prayed it would. It was not that I eventually doubted that the Almighty responded to faith, but that because I had been so bound up by the desert, so full of self-interest, so neglectful of the God I was supposed to serve, that I could not have expected any co-operation from him. Within a few days we had become bystanders, watching things happen beyond our control. My Member of Parliament, Harold Lever, in response to an earlier letter of mine, wrote to the Algerian ambassador in London and got approval for me to cross the Algerian Sahara on foot. This was despite the fact that I had already visited the Algerian Embassy to no effect after writing thirteen times.

British Airways then flew me free of charge to Paris, where the Niger authorities gave me permission to cross their territory. The passport office in Liverpool issued me with a new passport, and, though I had made dozens of requests to the army for a vehicle, BBC Radio Manchester succeeded where I had failed.

It came about when my mother made a live appeal for a Land Rover on Sandra Chalmers' 'phone-in' show. While the programme was still on the air, one of the BBC staff, Rob Frost, was telephoning the army's Adventure Training Unit in London. This unit had just received a request from Colonel Keast in the Outer Hebrides for men to be taken off his hands. The firing range which he was running was not to be fully operational for several months and he had too many soldiers to employ usefully. Adventure Training put him in contact with me and after five days Bombardier Michael Goldsmith and a subaltern had come to see me from the Outer Hebrides with a view to offering an army vehicle. As a result, Colonel Keast promised the loan of a Land Rover, trailer, and two soldiers.

The two men were to be Michael Goldsmith – the bombardier whom I had already met – and Charles Lynch, known as Paddy, a red-haired lance-corporal of the Royal Electrical & Mechanical Engineers. They would be on army pay, but I would be in command. I would also be responsible for financing the trip with respect to fuel, ferries, extra food and insurance, though several regimental charities gave donations. After seven weeks' work on the part of many army personnel, we were ready to begin.

We planned to use the north–south route through Tamanrasset in Algeria as it had the greatest number of watering points. The choice of starting and finishing places was arbitrary – the desert does not begin at a defined line. Kano, the end of the camel routes, seemed to be the obvious terminus. There were a few suitable towns at which to start but we chose Beni Abbes because the map showed it to be two thousand miles from Kano.

Getting to Beni Abbes took several days. I flew to Gibraltar on 19 December 1974, and met up with Mick and Paddy, who had taken the Land Rover, wheelbarrow and kit there on a munitions ship. We took a ferry to Tangier and drove through Morocco almost continuously for two days, arriving at Figuig on the Algerian border on 22 December. We were apprehensive about crossing into Algeria. The diplomatic clearance that Mick and Paddy needed as soldiers to pass through the Sahara had not yet been obtained. Out of kindness to me, the army had allowed them to travel without permission from the Algerians, though we were under orders not to enter Niger without confirmation of clearance. We hoped it would be waiting at the post office at Tamanrasset, the last town before the Niger border. There was still danger of Mick and Paddy being arrested as spies in Algeria, and in theory, though it was unlikely, of facing capital sentences. They had to travel with civilian number plates on the Land Rover, with civilian papers, and out of uniform, so that their military connections would not be known.

Coming into Algeria from Morocco our papers were examined by five groups of officials. Mercifully, none could read English, as all our documents showed the Land Rover to be army property. One of the checks was in what we thought was no man's land, a rocky valley with the odd bush here and there. We were stopped by what Paddy described as a gang of 'armed bandolieroed henchmen'. The leader stepped out of a hut adjacent to the road block. He wore a tatty grey uniform, peaked military cap, black moustache, and the smile of a Mexican bandit. We jumped out and met him at the rear of the vehicle and tried to show him a letter of introduction from the Algerian Ambassador to Britain, Lakhdar Brahimi. He frowned, screwed up his mouth and brushed away the letter. His comic-opera face contorted, his moustache drooped and he gripped his rifle with both hands to motion us to open the back of the vehicle.

We were obsequiously co-operative, all smiles and courtesy. Out came two tents, a suitcase, another suitcase, and a box of food. 'What's that?' he said, pointing inside the Land Rover with his rifle.

'Beer,' we answered. He forced an acid smile and held up two fingers. We almost fell over ourselves to oblige. Mick was there first and climbed onto the tailboard to pull out for the rogue two of Paddy's cans (a fact which Paddy was slow to forget). With a wave of the rifle the 'bandit' moved us on.

The final check on the Algerian side was in a small crowded office. Brown walls bore dog-eared posters of camels and cave paintings. The air was stale, clouded with cigarette smoke, and stank of the contents of the lavatory down the corridor, whose pan was half full. Travellers and officials looked weary, and we perhaps more than most: we were in our sixth hour of confusion at the border. A young, sweaty man in the usual grey uniform sat behind a large desk. 'Fill in the forms, please,' he said in French. Mick began, then paused where it asked for the name of the vehicle's owner. He wrote 'Royal Artillery Firing Ranges, Outer Hebrides'. The young official pointed to this and asked abruptly, 'What is this?' There was silence. The others in the room were unusually quiet. There was only the scratching of pens and the rustle of paper as everyone waited for the reply. 'What is this?' he said sternly, pointing. The stubble on the back of my neck tingled. I searched for Mick's eyes and found them. 'What is this?' he demanded. 'Is it the name of your company?'

'Yes,' Mick and I answered in simultaneous relief.

'Yes, my company,' said Mick.

When we were driving down from the border towards Beni Abbes, we quaked every time we saw police or soldiers. In Bechar, we took a wrong turning and drove to the gates of an army barracks. As we backed away, we disguised our panic with laughter when the guards asked what we wanted. That evening we camped on a hill overlooking Beni Abbes. At half-past twelve on the next day, 24 December, I picked up the shafts of the wheelbarrow and pushed off towards Kano on those first, torturous, thirteen miles.

4
BANDITS

Soon after nine, when I had wished Mick and Paddy a merry Christmas, I was back in my sleeping-bag. Paddy was still in his, but Mick was up. He had propped the tarpaulin trailer-cover against the Land Rover and weighted it with jerry cans to eliminate the wind that swept under the vehicle. Thus sheltered, he was making a cup of tea on the petrol stove. I heard him pumping up the pressure and singing a folk song which began, 'We don't smoke pot in Norwich City'. 'Wasn't it horrible,' he said, 'coming into Algeria on Monday? I tell you, if a helicopter had come down at that customs post, there would have been no stopping me. I'd have been in it and in those bars in Gibraltar giving it the big lips by last night.'

I heard Mick unzip the tent he shared with Paddy and hand him the tea. He zipped it up again, and I imagined him going to sit on a black plastic jerry-can to drink his own tea and have a smoke.

Mick controlled the morale. The previous evening, I could not have completed the last fifty yards without his help, but now if he had climbed on my back he could not have been more of a hindrance. He was indulging in his pet topic. He was talking of giving up. 'If I had to drive back to Tangier now, I'd do it in one go. All I'd need is a few fags to keep me awake and I'd have my foot down all the way. I wish I was back in Norwich now. Never mind, I've got a few cans. I'm gonna give it the big lips this afternoon. At half-past twelve, Mum and Dad will be on their way to my sister's in Ipswich. They'll have lunch and then at two o'clock, when they're drinking my health, I'll be drinking theirs. Dah dih dah dah, we don't smoke pot in Norwich City, doo doo . . .'

When I got up, Mick was fiddling with his radio on the Land Rover bonnet. We had no transmitter, just Mick's ordinary transistor radio with a short wave receiver. The ritual was the same as it had been the day before, adjusting the aerial, then, as he turned the tuner to the sound of whistles, crackles and snatches of foreign music, he said, 'Speak to me, London,' and, in obedience, it did.

It was the Christmas service on the BBC World Service from the parish of Dedham in Essex. We did not really listen, but it helped to put us in the right mood. We whipped up Christmassy feelings and pulled decorations and paper hats out of a hamper given by soldiers in the Outer Hebrides. We tied balloons and streamers to the tents, wheelbarrow and Land Rover and watched them being thrashed by the wind.

I was sitting on my fishing stool, wearing winter clothes, and a sailcloth robe thrown over me for extra warmth. I had had my head shaved for the sake of hygiene the day before I left England. A conical party hat was now perched on top of the grey stubble, with the elastic stretched under my chin. With a balloon bobbing against my left shoulder and sand blowing over my boots, I opened my presents – a hot-water bottle and a small canister of shaving foam from Joan, and the book of Job and a miniature of whisky from my parents.

At midday, with the tent and kit packed in the wheelbarrow, I was almost ready to begin the second day's walk. Before that, though, I opened a can of whole chicken and ripped off a leg dribbling with jelly. I had no time to steam my Christmas pudding, so I poured boiling water over it and ate it like cake. It would keep me going for the afternoon, until I could heat up the rest of the chicken for supper. Then, before hoisting the sail, I trundled the wheelbarrow onto the road.

After half an hour, flesh-pink dunes, perhaps a hundred feet high, appeared several miles ahead. The dunes that had been on the left were replaced by a sandstone ridge and the sand on that side of the road was now black. To the right, a brick-red dune stood alone among golden yellow ones. The only sign of life was a man, wearing what looked like a woollen dressing gown with a hood, riding past on a camel. The scene might have been absorbing had I not been fighting to keep control of the wheelbarrow.

Sailing wheelbarrows have been used in China for two thousand years. They are supposed to be easier to move than the western, garden variety. I had told everybody so, and the Oxford don who had suggested the design had said it was a proven scientific fact. In theory he was right. There are other advantages besides their having a sail. They are one wheel lighter than two-wheeled carts, and more manoeuvrable since they are able to turn on the spot and negotiate narrow gaps on rocky ground. Moreover, due to their large diameter wheel, they have a low rolling resistance on poor tracks and, importantly, it is the wheel, and not the person pushing, which carries the weight, since the load is balanced in a pair of lockers, one on each side, and distributed both in front of and behind the axle. It takes no effort to lift the shafts. Pushing the wheelbarrow should have been child's play, but I still could not get the hang of it.

There had been a delay in building it, so that I had only managed a few hours' practice in the streets of Salford. As I set out on that Christmas afternoon, I planned to learn as I went along. I would take it easy and avoid a repetition of the day before. I adjusted the sail at forty-five degrees to the east wind, and walked south.

If the wind had been constant, it would have been easy to lean the wheelbarrow into it. Instead, it came in gusts. The wheelbarrow, which, when loaded, was three times my weight, toppled, spinning me in circles. I was blown to one side off the macadam, then dragged back and crashed down on the other. The wheelbarrow seemed to want to shake me off like a steer at a rodeo. I hung on, having to force the shafts to the ground to slow it down. This not only strained the backs of my arms but also made the aluminium legs screech against the ground, which set my teeth on edge. Concentration was essential. Each time I looked away from the road, the wheelbarrow fell over. It must have done so thirty times before dusk.

Loading was part of the problem. A gallon container a foot out of place would put everything off balance, so each time the wheelbarrow fell, the dislodged kit had to be re-adjusted. After an hour, every joint and muscle in my body hurt. When I had breath to spare, I shouted, 'Why on earth did I come? I'm an idiot!' And looking to heaven, I complained, 'And why did you let me?' And it was not helping the poor that kept me going, but the thought of having to admit that I had no stomach. To go home would have been to face not only the critics but the people who had helped.

The sail had been a hindrance, making sport of me at each whim of the wind, so I lowered it. The mast was still waving ten feet above the ground, making the wheelbarrow top-heavy, and from sideways on there was my voluminous robe and thirteen square feet of metal for the wind to catch. I maintained a straighter course now but perpetually wanted to stop, and so had to ration myself to two minutes rest in every fifteen, and ten minutes on the hour. I sat on one of the lockers with both feet on the bar that ran between the shafts. My back was to the wind which whistled coldly in the wire frame of my spectacles and cracked the loose folds of my robe. I took a drink from one of the twenty-four plastic gallon containers which I had been collecting for two years. One was labelled 'Doby Washing Up Liquid' and another 'Barr's Orange Squash'. They now held diluted fruit juice donated in its doubly concentrated form by British Airways Catering Department.

I sat looking round. I never noticed much on the move. On the left of the road, a mile across the brown dust, was a high ridge of black rock which glinted like coal. The sky behind was a pastel-blue wall. To the right, massive pyramids of rose-pink sand blockaded the Moroccan border. The air was Alpine-clear, bringing the ridge, rocks and dunes to arm's length, like a film set.

I panned the view, looking for visual stimulation to jerk me out of my maudlin stupor. In fact, I needed to look no further than the ground below me. At three o'clock, when I had scanned every crack in the ridge, every curve of every dune, every patch of colour on the plain, I looked down and saw an ant, crawling into the wind. It was carried back on the blowing sand, but it moved unhurriedly forward. At home I might have fed it to the fish, but here I felt sorry for it and watched until it was time to move on.

When I was putting the orange-juice bottle back into the wheelbarrow, an empty plastic bag was blown out of the locker and soared towards Morocco, like a racing pigeon from a basket. I had visions of a nomad's only camel eating it and dying, so I gave chase, watching the dust from my feet overtake me. The bag was increasing its lead, almost out of view, when it arced and plummeted like a kite above the beach and was slammed against a rock.

I reached it, peeled it off sadly, wishing it could have had its liberty, and walked back with it flapping to be free. Being sorry for an ant may be excusable, even commendable, but what sort of madness takes pity on a sandwich bag? Perhaps I was ashamed of feeling sorry for myself and had to transfer the pity to something else. My self-pity was enhanced at four-thirty when I came to camp. Mick's tape-recorder was playing 'Wipe Those Womble Tears From Your Eyes'. It was a song I grew to love.

Though I was exhausted and had managed only nine miles, it had been a better day than the first. I was by no means ill, and the ground by the road was firm enough for me to get to the Land Rover without too much of a struggle.

Some time after dark, when the cans which had held chicken and plum pudding lay cold in a shallow pit, and when our plates and dishes had been scraped clean, we wrapped ourselves up and sat out of the wind, behind the Land Rover. It was the only evening for weeks that we stopped out. Since it was Christmas, it was worthwhile, but otherwise it would have been too cold.

The lads were each sitting on a black, plastic jerry-can, while I was perched on my fishing stool. The petrol stove was roaring under a steaming kettle, sheltered by three sides of an unfolded carton. Mick was perched close to it, with a bowl of hot water and suds at his feet. He had been scouring a pan, but now put it on another jerry-can to drain, alongside two clean plates. 'Do you want this soapy water, Geoff, or shall I bin it?'

'No thanks, Mick. I've done.' He picked up the bowl and tossed the water into the darkness. Paddy was sitting with his back to the Land Rover looking at the map. He beamed his torch on the suds dispersing in the sand. Mick said,

'You know, I never knew what "bin it" meant until I joined the army. I picked it up off the Manchester lads in our regiment. A right rough lot. Damned good soldiers though. You wanna see 'em on exercises. Couldn't give two monkeys!'

'Are exercises all that dangerous?'

''Course! Squaddies get killed sometimes. Ferrets are the worst. They're always turning over,' he said, explaining that Ferrets are small armoured cars. 'Then you've got the jokers who sleep under lorries to get out of the rain. The lorry sinks in the mud and that's it.' He turned to Paddy, 'Did you hear about that sergeant who walked into the back of a chopper in Northern Ireland?'

'Yes, I did.'

'You know, Geoff,' said Mick, 'half of those killed never get in the papers.' Paddy murmured agreement.

'Do you go on exercises often?'

'Two or three times a year. It's good fun really, especially in Germany. We ride all over farms and knock down fences. Farmers don't mind. They just send the bill and the army pays. I've heard of farmers slipping the lads a few marks to drive through an old fence so they can get a new one free.'

By eight-thirty, after putting the army to rights, and warming ourselves on one cup of tea after another, we were too cold to stay up. As usual, Mick checked underneath and around the Land Rover, locking everything away and tightening the ropes on the tarpaulin trailer-cover. I secured the locks on the wheelbarrow, crawled under canvas and wrote up the log and two letters. Then, as would often be the case when the wind permitted, I opened the flaps and looked at the stars. They gave me a feeling of my own finiteness, and put me in the mood for my evening Bible reading.

It was not the quantity of stars that was so impressive, though if there had been more they would have blended into a whitewash, nor was it their brilliance, though they were a dazzling variation of colour and size, but that they seemed alive. The sky pulsated with countless blinking lights.

I put my head down at nine-thirty. The time for this never became regular. It was any time between nine and one, depending on what had to be done. I usually set my alarm clock for five, ready for me to be away two hours later at dawn. After I woke, I would make a cup of tea and soon afterwards dash out with the toilet-roll. I would scuttle back, shaking with cold to read the Bible and pray. While supplies lasted, breakfast was a combination of the foods I disliked, but felt to be essential: glucose, oats and Sanatogen powder, mixed with water, milk powder and cocoa to disguise the taste. It was awful. Uncooked Quick Quaker Oats was the main constituent. It was my staple carbohydrate, eaten either as a snack or main meal – it needed no cooking, was light to carry and would not go stale, but provided energy, protein and roughage.

It took an hour to break camp – half an hour inside the tent, securing lids, folding up the canteen, and packing food, maps, writing paper, footpowder, vitamin pills and the rest, everything into its own bag – before putting my feet through the flaps into cold boots. Not many yards away, dunes and hillocks looked as if they had been dumped at random, each one rising about sixty feet above the plain. Under the night sky, they looked like slag heaps. For the first few minutes outside, I used the torch, until the blackness behind the dunes turned to a deep red. The redness flowered into a sort of technicoloured aurora borealis, beams of magenta and pink fanning across the brightening sky until everything was transfigured by a brilliant crescent above an eastern dune. Rocks, dunes, the Land Rover and I shone gold with its borrowed light.

The enchantment dissolved in seconds as the pale circle appeared and all the world became the same shade of grey. I was glad to get moving. My hands were cold, gloved as they were, and though I wore a jersey, jacket and jeans, I shivered for the first ten minutes.

I was in less difficulty than on the first two days: I no longer pushed the ends of the shafts but gained better control from between them and was able to look around without overbalancing. The road followed a wadi, a dried-up river bed, which was green with palms and which a trick of light sometimes filled with water – such mirages are natural and common in the desert. They are the same phenomenon as water seeming to appear on a dry English road on a sunny day. Occasionally, there were villages – huddles of mud dwellings, shaded by palm-trees. Plots of vegetables were fenced in by mud-brick walls to keep out the hobbled donkeys and camels which foraged in the wadi. It was rare that I saw people, though now and then I came across sheep and goats being herded by children – boys in night-shirts or girls in blue gingham, every dress made from the same roll of cloth.

Dunes, palm trees, mud-brick villages, children and animals would have made good picture postcards, but, for all its beauty, the desert was terrifying. Were it not for the narrow strip of tar, I would have been stuck hopelessly – several times I was bogged down when the wind blew me off the road.

In its native China, the wheelbarrow's narrow wheel might have sliced through the mud and found rock beneath, but here it just cut deep into the sand. I wondered what Stewart Wilson, the Oxford don who had suggested it, would have said if he could have seen me. That afternoon the wheelbarrow even stuck when I pulled it off the road for a break. It rolled into a hollow and it took me half an hour to get it one yard back onto the road. Having got there, I felt like resting, but curiosity pulled me on to my feet. There was a strange rasping noise coming from over the next rise.

It turned out to be a man shovelling sand off the road. His buttonless jacket was blown open and the wind pressed his grey shirt to his chest. The end of his black head-wrap hung loose and flapped over his shoulder, giving a clear view of his face. A dune had encroached onto the road and he was slicing away its tip, tossing it clear of the tarmac behind him. When he saw me, he leaned on his shovel until I was near enough to shake hands. Though his skin was pale, he had the lips and round face of a black African, and that African quality of showing that one does not need a reason to be happy. He was one of many people of mixed race I was to meet in Algeria. He unclipped a plastic water-bottle from his belt and held it out with a smile that was almost a grin.

'No thank you. I have plenty in here,' I said, touching the wheelbarrow.

'Where are you going?'

'Nigeria.'

'Oh, I see.' There was no look of surprise, just the nod of a deaf man trying to give the impression he can hear. He had not understood. Half an hour later, an open-backed lorry carrying the same man and a dozen of his workmates raced past, stopping quickly enough to throw them comically forward, and then reversing hurriedly to me. The men poured off the lorry, the wheelbarrow was hustled from me, and they fought playfully to have a turn. After a babble of Arabic, the tailboard of the lorry was dropped and a dozen men were lifting the wheelbarrow.

'Stop! Stop!' I yelled, flinging my arms about in a style I might have copied from them.

'It's all right. We're helping you,' said the driver. The men were holding the wheelbarrow above their heads.

'Only five miles,' he continued. 'We will take you five miles.' I hesitated and the men looked appealingly for instruction.

The pressure of administration had stopped my training before I had left England and my feet had grown soft. As I had mistakenly left my only pair of worn-in boots in Salford – I had been wearing them when I packed the kit, and changed into shoes to travel to North Africa – I now had blisters under the balls of both feet and another running from the

top of my left heel right under the foot. There were blisters, too, where
one buttock had chafed the other, and my hands and face were raw with
sunburn. My knees were blue with bruises. I had fallen many times and
could not control the wheelbarrow unless I was close enough for my legs
to bang into it. There was cramp in my neck and arms and I was so tired
that it seemed almost as if a malevolent magnetism was trying to drag
me to the ground. I wanted to cheat. Five miles would have made a
difference. I would get to camp at three, and could have had an early
night.

'Put it on the lorry,' the driver said. Two men were already up there
reaching out to guide it on.

'No, please stop,' I said. 'I must walk.'

'On foot?' the foreman asked.

'On foot,' I maintained.

'On foot?' they said, still holding the wheelbarrow high.

'Yes, on foot.' I insisted. They put down the wheelbarrow.

'Why?' someone asked. I explained, falteringly, my motives – at least,
as far as I understood them myself.

'To *Nigeria*?' said someone, in high-pitched amazement. There were
cries in French of 'Impossible! Too much sand! Too difficult!' and oaths
in Arabic that I did not understand. Then after a lecture from them on
my stupidity, each man stepped forward and shook my hand. I was a
little way ahead before they moved off. When they overtook me, they
gave a cheer so loud that they drowned the noises of the wheelbarrow
and lorry.

Their friendship continued for the next few days. The driver dropped
off a man or two at dunes that had drifted on to the road and would then
go back and pick them up when they had finished, before taking them
further south. I never found out which area they covered, nor whether
they returned home at night, nor whether there was another side to
their work. One thing was certain: unless machines were one day to take
their places, they had a lifetime's job. The trade winds have been
moving the dunes south-west for thousands of years and show no sign
of stopping, but unless they do, much of West Africa will be engulfed.
Even now, many desert towns would be buried if their inhabitants did
not transport the encroaching dunes bit by bit to the other side of their
settlements.

Each time the workmen saw me, they offered a ride and it became
more difficult to refuse, until on the sixth day I weakened. There was a
mile along which I did not walk. The blisters were hurting and the men
persuasive. I got on the vehicle but the driver had not long been in
fourth gear when I came to my senses. I was ashamed, though not
ashamed enough to walk back. I tried to tell myself that the road was

only practice for the desert. But the guilt would not go away: I omitted the incident from the log and it took me two years to own up to it.

That night I woke at half-past three and lay brooding over my lack of progress. We had come only forty-two miles in three days – fourteen miles a day. The army had said we would average fifteen, but I had hoped for eighteen and had told them so.

The West African temperature would be rising during the European spring; the longer I took, the worse it would be at the end. We had barely enough food for three months, let alone the four and a half it would take at fifteen miles a day. Nor would the £1,500 I had borrowed last that long. Insurance, ferries, food and kit took a large slice, the rest went on fuel for the Land Rover's seven thousand mile round trip. Petrol consumption was high, with the price often twice what it was at home.

We were short of batteries, too. The lads had brought four dozen for their torches and Mick's radio. I had six dozen smaller ones for the tape recorder and my torch. The tape recorder was used to send reports to churches and schools who were using the expedition to raise money for famine relief. The torch was even more essential. I made camp at sunset, and then cooked, wrote letters, and did my chores after dark. In the morning, I broke camp in the dark. At present usage I would run out of batteries before the half-way point and Mick and Paddy would run out just after.

I *had* to cover more than fifteen miles a day. I had hoped for thirty on the paved road to bump up the average before the open desert at Adrar. Just before the alarm clock rang at five, I conceived how it might be done.

Crossing the Sahara was a personal ambition and all the rules were self-made. I wanted to prove that a man using only natural supply and watering points could cross it without a camel or motor vehicle. The Land Rover had originally been meant to be no more than a safety net. Later it made economic sense to plan for the vehicle to carry things which had been given free in England but which were too heavy for me to manage for the whole way. It was a cheap alternative to buying from local merchants, but I was only allowed access to the provisions at points of safety such as towns and wells. In open desert, I was on my own. Until Mick had objected for reasons of safety, I had even planned to camp half a mile from the soldiers.

The Chinese sailing wheelbarrow was not a gimmick. If I could have done without it, I would have done. It was a tool to help me from one point of safety to another; it carried not only the tent, camping equipment, and food, but the weightiest item of all, water. But at this stage I *could* manage without it, without breaking the overall aim of carrying my own food and water. I could put everything on my back between villages because, this side of Adrar, they occurred almost every twenty miles. There was nothing against my packing a bag and loading the wheelbarrow on the Land Rover so that it could be used for the longer, more difficult sections. I could then walk much faster and push up the average daily mileage.

We were now at a point of safety, half a mile from the village of El Ouata, so I was allowed access to supplies in the Land Rover. I could begin today. There could be no early start: the lads' co-operation was needed and we always found it difficult to agree on rules. Mick and Paddy had been well briefed on most things, but in the last-minute rush they were not given full details of my self-made code of conduct. We had finally thrashed this out on the ferry from Gibraltar to Tangier.

Mick had disagreed with my proposals. He had said it was unwise to load up in villages because of thieves and dangerous to camp apart from each other because of bandits. 'Don't forget,' he had said, 'we're responsible for your safety and for the safety of the kit. If anything should happen to you . . .'

He was suspicious of the local people, and when any of them showed up he always put things of value out of sight. The thought of bandits and deep sand seemed to haunt him. He expressed his feelings so many times in the same way that when he could not see me I would find myself mouthing the words with him: 'The thing that worries me is bandits and deep sand.'

To be fair, he had spent some time in the cities of North Africa and, as one might do in similar urban areas of Britain, he had met the worst of the indigenous population. To confirm his fears, when we had been driving out of Tangier docks late at night, having only just arrived on African soil, a group of men had tried to stop us. We had been coming onto the main road at about five miles an hour when three men had blocked our exit. While one had climbed on the bonnet, another had pushed his hand through the open window on Mick's side. Mick had accelerated and the men had jumped clear.

Mick had argued his case forcefully, and I had reluctantly agreed to camp next to them. Depressingly, this meant that I was within sight, sound and smell of their superior rations, bacon-burgers, goulash, and bolognese. I had also agreed to load up out of sight, though within easy walking distance, of villages – it would be as as if I had gone into the villages for supplies, but this way meant that I wouldn't attract anyone's attention.

Tailoring the rules to make life easier was a common, but regrettable feature of the expedition. The rules were intended to simulate a solo walk, and along the most arduous sections it did – I was out there without aid – but in the region of towns and villages things were lax.

The problem of interpreting the rules was caused by the fact that, having made them myself, I was the sole arbiter. I now planned to discuss my proposed modifications with the lads before leaving camp.

While I was waiting for my companions to stir, I put water on to boil, but soon noticed that the stove had given up. I went outside to change the cylinder – the same sort as used on most small camping-stoves – and began to unscrew the burner. A gas dropping in pressure also drops in temperature – the principle behind the household refrigerator. On letting a tyre down, for example, the valve becomes cold because of the loss of pressure of the escaping air; conversely, the valve gets hot when the pressure is increased and the tyre is pumped up. As I unscrewed the burner, there was a rapid escape of gas. While I was struggling to stop it, frost was formed where it struck my already cold hand. 'Damn! Damn! Damn!' I screamed, loud enough to prompt a comment from the other tent about the vicar's strong language.

The cylinder had been partly full, but the jet was blocked. I dived angrily inside the tent to clear it, dumbfounded as to how sand could have got in. I always cleaned the stove after use and wrapped it in a tough plastic bag. Moving outside to fit the new cylinder, I noticed that I had dropped the tiny rubber washer that fitted between the cylinder and stove. I emptied the tent, shook every item, and retraced my steps outside. Paddy got up to help and we both crawled about ferreting in the sand.

'It's no use, Paddy. I probably trod on it and buried it. I'd make a new one except the only rubber I've got is in the sole of my boot.'

'Try a few layers of polythene,' he said. I was doubtful, but there was nothing else, so I tore a plastic bag into pieces, fixed these in place, and began to screw on the cylinder. A white streak of gas burst over my left hand. After struggling for a moment to stop it, I screamed and dropped the lot. My index finger was sleeved in frost and I dared not bend it for fear of splitting the skin. I gave up the idea of tea, but was able to make a washer in the afternoon with rubber from an abandoned tyre.

Before I left camp, I discussed the modified rules with the lads. They agreed to transport the wheelbarrow on those days when I was able to carry supplies on my back from one village to the next. Walking without the wheelbarrow turned out to be a success. Though it was noon when I set out, I made up time, maintaining a speed of almost five miles an hour. I hardly noticed the rucksack with its load of bread and water. It gave me a sense of liberation, being able to look around without overbalancing. The air was warm and uncharacteristically still. Palm-trees and crescent-shaped dunes seemed to waver in the heat. The road rolled over a hill and curled down among flesh-pink dunes. Seen from a hill, the dunes stretched as far as the deep blue of the horizon, above which were a few streaks of cirrus cloud. The road pitched and banked over and around waves of sand and, periodically, I met the workmen busy with their shovels.

For the next day and a half, the scenery was spectacular, especially when viewed from high ground. A sea of huge, irregularly shaped dunes seemed to tumble from blue, hazy hills over to my left. Half a day's walk further on, away from the turbulence caused by high ground, the dunes were no more than ten feet high. These smaller dunes were distinct from the level ground on which they stood, as if they had been tipped in discrete heaps by the workmen's lorry. Their surfaces were ribbed by corrugation, which ran in wavy lines three inches across, like giant fingerprints, but without whorls or loops. In the evening, when the sun mellowed and cast deep shadows, these ribs became stripes of light and shade. For that last half-hour of the day, the dunes became a deeper gold and were scored with the long shadows of palm trees, whose tops were so green that I fancied that if my arm had been long enough I could have plucked a leaf and eaten it as if it had been parsley.

Then, abruptly, for the following day and a half there was neither sand nor palm trees, just a thirty-mile climb up a canyon of broken slate and rock. The desert is full of surprises. One day you can be swamped by sand and the next climbing a hill the size of Ben Nevis. The Sahara is a new desert, and, other than water, it has the same geographical features as other major land masses. The canyon was a natural cutting through a mountain of basalt. Its sides were neither high nor sheer, just slopes of black shale rising no more than fifty feet. The road ran along the valley between them, where boulders had settled. Parallel to the canyon, but just out of sight, was a wadi, along which there was a string of villages.

Early in the afternoon, on the third day of walking without the wheelbarrow, four men appeared on the road a quarter of a mile further up the canyon. They were so still that they might have been made of granite. Two more joined them. I felt uneasy and the back of my neck was prickly with sweat, but relentlessly I kept the same pace towards them.

Eight or ten others were crouched behind the rocks. They were not the shabby workmen, but were dressed in what looked like blue and white satin. I looked back down the hill hoping a vehicle would be coming. Mick and Paddy might be on their way. They usually started out about now, and after catching me up went forward an agreed distance to make camp. No sign of them. I was alone. I wanted to drop everything and run, but I was so scared of appearing to be a coward, even to myself, that I dared not.

There was movement to the side of them, but I could not see what they were doing because of the size of the boulders. Were they regrouping? Were they trying to outflank me? My face was tingling with fear and I felt in imminent need of a toilet-roll. They were only a hundred yards away now, still as a cobra before it strikes. These were the bandits Mick had spoken of. They would kill a man to steal his clothes. Only inertia carried me forward. I could neither have deviated nor run. I could not have turned my head nor moved my hands from where they hung on the straps of the rucksack. One move and they would shoot. 'Keep on walking and talk your way out of it,' I told myself. I dared not turn round now to look for a vehicle, but I held my breath and listened for one – there was only the sound of my rubber soles on the macadam and the noise of wind.

A figure darted from his cover on to the road. My heart beat violently, almost painfully, and sweat trickled down my face. I now saw everything. The figure was a boy, dressed in clean white shorts and T-shirt, looking like an Italian child on his way to church. He was crossing the road to join his father, who was standing with a group of men on the other side. There were more children playing among the rocks, while their mothers complained to each other (I imagined) about the price of grain. They were desert folk waiting for the bus. Strength went from my limbs and I felt faint with relief.

The canyon ran parallel to the continuation of the wadi which I had been following for days. That dried up river-bed, which was out of sight over the ridge and down a thousand feet of shingle, was rich with palm-trees, and with villages. These people lived there. The wadi would rarely have been filled with water, but deep down, the soil was moist, and trees were able to drink from its reserve. The villagers ate dates from the wadi's palms, fed their sheep and goats on its shrubs, and made their homes from the mud and vegetation. They grew carrots, onions and tomatoes: the palms shielded plants from the sun, and wells provided a ready supply for watering by hand. The women, dressed in yards of a blue-and-white, shiny fabric, even looked overfed.

The men, thinner than their wives, greeted me and gathered round. A tall, old man, wearing western-style trousers, with a knee-length white robe over the top, was the only one to speak. His face was kindly, brown and wrinkled. He had blue eyes and his head was bare except for a few short grey hairs. Perhaps he was the chief. 'Are you well?' he asked.

'Very well. Are you?'

'I thank God that I am,' he said in Arabic, and continued in French, 'Where are you going?'

'Adrar,' I said, not telling the whole story. I was in no mood to be upbraided about my stupidity. I might even have had to explain where

Nigeria was. Half the local people had never heard of it. After all, it was almost two thousand miles away.

'Adrar? On foot? That's over two hundred kilometres,' he said.

'I like the exercise and, besides, I have two friends down the road in a Land Rover,' I said, implying that I would be given a lift. 'Where are you going?' I asked.

'Kerzaz.' Kerzaz was the small market-town through which I had passed, when at the bottom of the canyon two days before. I looked at my watch.

'I must go. I'm late,' I said, as if I had an appointment to keep. I was always on edge, eager to be further south. The gathering of men pressed closer to see my watch, so I held out my wrist.

'What time is it?' asked the chief.

'One o'clock,' I replied, 'so I must go.' The crowd parted, and they stood gazing up the canyon, not out of interest in me but to see if the bus was coming. It passed a few minutes later. It was not the sort I had seen in West Africa, with side-windows missing and as many chickens on board as people, but as plush as the one that had recently taken our Parish Fellowship for an evening drive around Cheshire. According to the sign on the front of this one, it was the shuttle between Adrar, the last place linked by road in the south, and Oran, a large commercial city on the coast. There was a good transport system all over Algeria, even in the desert, though beyond the road, lorries replaced coaches. On this stretch, I even saw a taxi.

5

SLANT EYES

Just before sunset on 29 December, four hours after the bus to Kerzaz had passed, I was bending over, hammering at the tent-pegs. Mick was trying to light the petrol stove. 'I bet the newspapers would like to know about this!' he said. 'What'd happen if I told them how you'd cheated?'

'I don't follow.'

'Well, there's no village here and we're carrying the barrow for you.'

'Of all the cheek! It was you who wanted to keep away from villages. Timoudi is a mile over that ridge!'

'Yes, but what about the gravy I gave you?' I wanted to hit him. On Boxing Day I *had* accepted a few spoons of gravy, but only after considerable coaxing from Mick, having refused it twice already. We had been outside the village of El Ouata – we would have been inside but for him. I now knew that I would have to put the wheelbarrow back on the road next morning, despite a relative abundance of settlements. I took the threat seriously, and dared not risk Mick causing adverse publicity.

When the tent was up, I had to prove that I had been right about the proximity of a village. I scrambled up the side-wall of the canyon and peeped over. There, down a mile of scree, were thousands of palm-trees, and, I thought, a village. According to the map it was there, but the fact that the dwellings seemed half hidden by the trees and were the same colour as the desert gave me a tinge of doubt.

I suppressed my uncertainty. It was unthinkable that Mick could have been right. Perhaps if I had allowed myself to be doubtful, I might have understood Mick's concern about the rules, and his inability to express it without aggressive confrontation. That would have eased the tension but, as it was, I was so keen to justify myself that I felt compelled to confront him. I came down the slope, trying not to smirk. Mick was still at the stove. 'Lovely view of Timoudi,' I said. 'You ought to go up.' There was no comment; instead he began to sing: 'We don't smoke pot in Norwich City . . .'

Later, I was still disturbed by Mick's comments, but it was Sunday and self-pity was always sweeter then. Sunday was my day: I could do what I liked with it. Mick had Saturday. We had never consciously allocated days to each other; it had just turned out that we had grabbed them and put our stamp on them.

Each day was different. For no particular reason, Monday always seemed a little dull. Friday was special because it ushered in the weekend. On Wednesday evening there was a sports programme on the BBC World Service, and Saturday was the day of the football results. The weekend was the high spot. I would walk during the day every day, but evenings were different from one another. If there was water to spare I would smarten up and shave, regardless of where I was, and I might cook myself a treat, kippers or pilchards. There were almost enough tins to have one or the other each week. On Friday and Saturday tea-times, we would sometimes fantasize about which pub we ought to go to and what we would eat afterwards.

But today was my day, a day for prayer and worship. As usual, after supper I played one of a dozen tape recordings of sermons by the Reverend John McArthur of Sun Valley, California. While they often helped me to gain a perspective on, and strength for, what I was doing, the one I played on this particular night enhanced my self-pity. It gave me sanctuary. I was using an ear-plug and the lads could not hear it – I had gone to church alone. I was acting like someone who puts on his Sunday best, lifts his nose in the air, and goes to worship feeling superior to those who are watching television or washing the car instead.

Mick had disturbed me more than he knew. These two hundred and thirty miles on the road should have been a time for strengthening bonds and for unifying our resolve, but I felt continually at cross-purposes with him.

The sermon did indeed make me feel superior: 'I know what the preacher means by "the concept of the body in Romans 12". Mick doesn't. He doesn't understand anything of value. He doesn't understand what it is to have real purpose, or peace. All he cares about are women and booze. He only came to the Sahara to get a sun-tan and lose weight, so that he can put on his dark glasses and show himself off in the bars back home.' I switched off the tape, realizing that I would have to listen another time to find out what the preacher was really saying.

Later that evening, when I was almost asleep, the sound of a crowd brought me back to full consciousness. My head popped outside; five young men were bounding out of the darkness from a car on the road. The headlights went off, doors slammed, and the driver chased after the others, who were almost at our tents. From their sure-footedness over ankle-twisting rocks, they were obviously young, and they were babbling in the manner of teenage boys with everyone talking and no one listening. Their babble of French and Arabic made an awful din, but within just a few feet of us they quietened. 'We would like oil, please,' said one of them in French.

'Oil or petrol?' I asked.

'Oil.'

'Diesel oil?'

'No, just oil.'

'Bin 'em, Geoff,' said Mick.

'They need oil and you won't get rid of 'em till they've got it,' I said.

'Ohhhh Kaaay,' said Paddy with a yawn, and there was the sound of opening zips.

'He'll get you some,' I said. The strangers' faces were barely visible, but from ground level (where I was leaning out of the tent) I could see that three of them were wearing football boots. 'Where are you going?' I asked.

'Béchar,' replied the one nearest to me.

'From Adrar?'

'Yes.'

'Been playing football?'

'Yes, for our college.' He explained that he was training to be a teacher in Béchar, a large town a little north of where I had begun walking. It was the most southerly westernized town, the last in which we saw television aerials. The young men had been playing football against a team from the small local college at Adrar, the town which was for me the end of tarmac and the beginning of the desert; for these city boys, it was the last outpost. 'There's no oil in Adrar,' he said with disgust.

'There's nothing else, either,' added one of the others. They all laughed. The one to whom I had been speaking was shivering audibly.

'Will your friend be long?' he asked. Before I could answer, Paddy emerged flashing a torch in our direction.

'Right, let's go to your car and see what you need.' Two of the strangers stayed near me; one of them was dancing on the spot to keep warm. The others clattered over the loose uneven rock following Paddy's understandable impatience. I was propping myself up, still in my sleeping bag with only my head outside. One of the two remaining asked me,

'Are you American?'

'No, English.'

'Oh, ho!' he said, dancing more vigorously and chanting, 'Manchester City! Manchester City! Manchester City!'

'I'm from Manchester,' I said.

'You have the best team. We all follow English football. My team is

Manchester City! Manchester City!' he said, continuing the chant which was so like those I had heard at Manchester's Maine Road ground that I marvelled when he said he had never been to England. What I did not know was that English soccer was televised in Algeria.

Paddy returned, took the tarpaulin off the trailer, and gave them the engine oil. The two who had been talking to me went with the others back to their vehicle. For a moment, I could hear their indistinct voices and the faint sound of, 'Manchester City, Manchester City . . .' Their engine fired and as it droned down the hill, toots of thanks echoed round the canyon. Paddy got into his tent and said, 'I thought they'd have offered us something for it.'

'Bastards!' said Mick.

Soon after dawn, I set off, having packed away the sail and mast on the Land Rover. The wind had taken more of my energy than it saved, and without the sail, the wheelbarrow was much easier to control. The only disappointment was that, at nine o'clock, the advantage gained by climbing for two days was lost in minutes, like the slow, laborious winding of a stiff spring which snaps and releases its energy in an instant. I had come to the top of a long hill, so steep that the wheelbarrow was almost wrenched from my hands as the descent began. It was fun, all the same, hurtling madly downhill, too fast to stop. There were no brakes, and if I had stumbled, then the bar that ran between the shafts behind me would have caught me in the back and either dragged me along or knocked me to the ground. I tried to slacken pace but the slowest I went seemed to be faster than I had ever run before. I was off-balance, falling forward, lurching with giant strides, certain that the next step would end in a nosedive. Then, abruptly, there was only the plain ahead and, in the distance, two square mud houses with flat roofs, one on each side of the road. I could just make out the figure of a boy, running from the house on the right, who was joined by a group of people from the other. They were aroused, no doubt, by the rumble of the all-metal wheelbarrow, which was audible half a mile away.

They stood with their backs to what turned out to be a mud-built shack on the left. 'Café' was daubed in whitewash on the wall and beneath it a metal plaque advertising 'Fanta'. The group – all males – were wearing either knee-length shirts or what looked like the jackets and trousers left from the last church jumble sale. I guessed they were from Ksabi, a village a mile off the road. They viewed me with the same puzzled look as I later saw on the faces of nomads miles from civilization. The questions of who I was, where I had come from and where I was going struck them with confusion. I was as awesome as an

Arab raiding-party in a Yorkshire village. They stared in silence: There were no murmurs of ridicule, no sniggers. I put down the shafts and waved with my straw hat. I wanted them to laugh, to surround me and ask for gifts. '*Bonjour messieurs! Ca va?*' But they made no response, all except the little boy, who smiled and dusted the air with his hand.

It was less than an hour from dusk, and we would have camped there had it been left to me. Instead, I moved on, leaving them leaning against the café wall. We stopped for the night a mile down the road just out of sight. Mounds of dirt, rock and sand – little hills engulfed by dunes – blocked our view so that we could see no more than half a mile in any direction. We pitched our tents leeward of one of them

I took supplies from the Land Rover, according to our agreement, as if I were actually at the café. Reloading was always lengthy. Beforehand, the wheelbarrow had to be emptied, swept out and cleaned with disinfectant and detergent, as a matter of discipline and hygiene. Then I packed sardines or beans and sausage for lunch, and meat pudding or sardines for supper, concocted a supply of the sickly breakfast mix, and restocked the medical kit, envelopes, masking-tape, notepaper, blank cassettes, toilet-paper and a plastic bag of clean clothes. Finally, I did the laundry, cleaned the eating and cooking utensils and washed myself.

As was often the case when there was little wind and a bright moon, that night I sat outside in order to save batteries. There was the loose lining of my denim cap to stitch, and a button to sew on my trousers. Then there were envelopes to strengthen with masking-tape to carry cassettes and rolls of film. Finally, I finished a recording for home and wrote up the log. Sometimes, when preparing for a long haul, I would only manage four hours' rest, but that night I was asleep by eleven-thirty and did not rise till six.

Sunrise was unglamorous and cold. Mick was up earlier than usual and we sat on jerry-cans, warming our hands on mugs of tea. 'You know,' I said, 'I've got used to the chlorine in this water.'

'We've not been putting any in.'

'Then that's why I've got the craps.' (There had been no pre-arrangement for the lads to put the purifier in the water. They had done so the first time they got water for me and I had assumed they would continue. For their part it was unnecessary as they only drank what had been boiled for tea or coffee, whereas I often drank water on its own or with fruit cordial.)

We were distracted by a lorry apearing where the road slid out of the dunes. The driver saw us and was stopping. 'Go on,' mumbled Mick. 'We don't want you around.' It moved on, as if the driver had heard. I wanted to beckon him; whenever I met local people on the road, there was never time to talk. Half an hour after leaving camp, I saw the same lorry, pulled off the road beside a derelict shack. A stocky, bearded Arab, wearing a khaki boiler suit and black head-wrap – yards of cloth wrapped round the head leaving a slit only for the eyes – jumped from the cab. I walked to him and, as he pulled down the lower part of the head-wrap from across his mouth, he introduced himself as Idris.

'Welcome,' he said. 'Would you like to stay and have some tea?'

'No thank you. I am a little late.'

'One moment,' he said, climbing up into the cab and sitting in the driving seat. He pulled a jute sack onto his lap and pointed down at my face with a dagger. 'Half for me and half for you.' He took a large, flat loaf from the bag, sliced it across its diameter, and handed a piece down to me. It was so fresh that it must have been baked that morning at Ksabi.

'Thank you very much,' I said. 'How much do I owe you?'

'Nothing. On this road all men are friends. Only the desert is the enemy.' He tucked the knife behind his seat and climbed backwards out of the cab down onto the loose stones and sand. He looked with half-closed eyes eastward into the wind. 'The wind will be even worse,' he said. 'Stay and shelter here. I have tea and bread.'

'When will the wind stop?' I asked.

'About four o'clock in the afternoon.'

'Then I must try to get further. Thank you for the bread, Idris. You are very kind. See you later when you pass.'

'Au revoir, my friend,' he said, offering his hand.

'Au revoir,' I replied. I bent my knees a little to put on the shoulder-strap and left him watching me move back onto the road. Before I had gone fifty yards, I felt a couple of grains of sand strike my left cheek. I looked at the sky, as one might on feeling a spot of rain, and saw the red dust-clouds of a storm in the east.

Climatically, the desert is violent. The temperature rockets through 50 degrees Fahrenheit between dawn and noon. This causes massive expansion of air, and demonic winds churn up dust so that one seems to be walking on the bed of a murky sea. Dust gets into everything: my white underwear became pink, and my ears were so full of it that my hearing was impaired.

The sky in the east was brown with dust, and the sun veiled. Within minutes the brown patch of sky enveloped me, as a violent storm swept across the dunes. Rather than turn back and shelter with Idris, I kept moving. Half a day saved now would mean reaching Joan and Kano that much earlier. Although I was tempted to think that such a short time would make no difference, I knew that when I got near to Kano, if I got that far, every minute would count.

To my left, the leeward side of sixty-foot dunes rose like a wall alongside the road. The wind was hissing loudly over them, whipping off their tops and spraying them into a conveyor-belt of sand, an opaque draught, streaming across the road and up and over the dunes on the other side. My feet almost disappeared in it; it looked as if I were paddling in muddy water. Above this moving carpet, the sand in the air reduced visibility down to a hundred yards.

I was ill-clad. It had been impossible to wear the straw hat all morning because the wind caught it and pulled the chin-strap – improvised from a bootlace – into my neck. Now I was in danger of losing the tightly-fitting denim cap. My robe billowed, almost lifting me off the ground, and exposed my sunburnt legs to the stinging spray. I had to hold down the wheelbarrow by sitting on it while taking off my hat, changing into my jeans, and putting on goggles and a smog-mask. Then I was off again. I was raced forward, pushed back, spun around and thrown to the ground. Though there was no sail, there were thirteen square feet of cross-section for the wind to catch. Much of the time, I could do no more than lie on the wheelbarrow to hold it down.

A white Volkswagen Beetle crawled towards me out of the fog and passed by on the left. For a second the wind was blocked and the weight taken from my hands, only to come crashing back in double measure. The shafts sprang into the air and I was dangled like a gymnast on parallel bars, before being tossed to the ground.

I was passing over a hill when Idris drove past me, hooting, and pointing to the valley where he was obviously going to wait for me. I threw myself on top of the wheelbarrow to hold it down as he passed. The desert boiled around his lorry while it rumbled down the slope. Two more lorries followed and stopped behind his. All three drivers jumped down, each adjusting his muffler to make a narrow slit across his eyes. I met them leeward of the middle vehicle, where they lent a hand to tip the wheelbarrow into a stable position. Grit swirled like drifting snow under the lorries and dropped from above, but at body height, behind the vehicle, it was much more calm. 'Where did you say you were going?' asked Idris on behalf of his friends. I was embarrassed. To tell the truth was to admit to being an idiot. But I told them.

'Where?' they bellowed in incredulous unison, pulling their mufflers from their faces. They hung their heads and shook them forlornly.

'*Pas possible! Pas possible!*' they murmured, fingering the wheel's metal rim. 'You'll not even get to Reggane and that's only a hundred and sixty kilometres into the desert.'

'The *piste* is like this,' said one of them kicking at the sand.

'*Pas* problem,' I said, not even convincing myself.

'But it is difficult for a car! You may die!'

'I'm being followed by friends in a Land Rover.'

'Then let *them* carry your wheelbarrow.'

'I must carry my own supplies.'

'But why?' I tried feebly to explain, until they began to speak softly among themselves in Arabic.

'We can give you a lift to Adrar,' said Idris.

'Thank you very much but I *must* walk,' I said. They stood wordless, like friends consoling the bereaved.

'We must go,' said Idris solemnly. Mufflers went back across faces and they took turns to shake my hand. 'God be with you,' said Idris in Arabic and, as he climbed into the cab, he turned and added, *'et bon courage!'* With the desert streaming from their wheels, they drove away my windbreak and I dived behind the wheelbarrow, now lying on its side. I put on a jersey and jacket and lay with head and shoulders propped against a locker, eating sardines and mopping the oil from the can with fresh bread.

It was blustery and there was the constant peppering by grit, but I was well protected and enjoyed watching the storm. Everything was in flux. Stones danced across the road, bouncing like heavy rain. The scene had the swirling vagueness of a painting by Turner, with the canvas a blend of sea, sky, fog and rain. There were no outlines, just moving sand and mist. The dunes were marching west. More work for the road gang! I lay for an hour until the wind subsided enough for a hill to show two miles away.

That evening, at nine o'clock, with the chores finished, I prepared for a celebration. We were less than a hundred miles away from Adrar, and it was New Year's Eve. After midnight, there would be a family get-together at my parents' house; I still wanted to take part in it, however far from home I was. It had been held every year since I was five, and I had only missed it once, the year I was in Nigeria. I took a mug of water to clean my teeth, shave, and take a bath. I cleaned my teeth without paste, before pouring water into the miniature bowl and shaving. Next, I bathed myself with a soapy cloth in the appropriate hygienic order.

With a change of underclothes and socks, and aromatic cream on my ears and nose, it was like childhood bath-nights, with clean sheets and 'vapour rub'. I set the alarm clock for a quarter to midnight, and settled down for a couple of hours sleep. The clock failed to ring, but, inexplicably, I woke with thirty seconds of 1974 left. I snatched my miniature of whisky and lifted it towards the raised glasses at home, before stepping outside to watch those stars to the left of Polaris which would be blinking over Manchester.

There would be hugs and kisses, wishes of 'Happy New Year!', pork pie and trays of drinks. There would be somebody saying, 'Well I'm glad to see the back of last year,' and someone else wishing the new year to be as good as the last. There would be tales of family heroes, dead and gone, and there would be the quiet looking round the room wondering who would be the next to go. And, as I stooped to get back under cover, I recalled that there would, even from the sanest, be a concession to superstition that would be gone by the morning, a belief that the beginning of the year foreshadowed the character of the rest. I knew that it did not, and could not, but for the next week I found myself despairing as if it did. Normally I am a good sleeper, but that New Year's Night I lay awake for hours, with cold, sexual fantasy or worry. The tent might blow away, I might get bitten by a snake, or I might not be able to pay back the £1,500 I had borrowed to finance the trip. I woke up frightened at having my knife and pill-bottles in the tent in case I should end my life during my night's sleep.

The first day of the year began with dispiriting hills and seven miles of slow gradient. Every few minutes I found some reason to stop: to take off my sweater, to put on my robe, to change from boots to training-shoes and back again, to eat some oats, to take my temperature, to redistribute the load inside the lockers and, when I had no other excuse, simply to rest. The slow gradient ended when the road climbed the steepest incline I had yet encountered. The first yard took all the effort I could manage, creeping a toe's length at a time, my rubber soles slipping on the loose stones, as the wheelbarrow pushed me back to where I had been and we fell over. I righted the wheelbarrow with effort, turned it round, and pulled it backwards up the same yard, but no further.

The only way forward was to zigzag. I leaned almost horizontally into the harness, my nose two inches from the wheel. At each turn of the zigzag, the wheelbarrow toppled, and when I was tacking into the wind, grit, picked up by the wheel was blown into my eyes and mouth. Somehow, after half an hour, I was at the top looking back at the sign which warned *'Rapide Descente 300 metres'*. Morale always rose after a struggle; I would never have to go over the same ground again. This time it seemed I was wrong; across the next valley was another cliff, except that the sign at the top read *'Rapide Descente 500 metres'*.

Camp on New Year's Day was a trial, too. The lads had pitched their tents behind some small dunes and it was a struggle to get there. I cursed them. Paddy was digging the rubbish pit, but sand kept blowing back into it like teeming insects. Mick was heaping piles of spaghetti bolognese on to two plates. I opened the lockers to pull out the kit but found that the top had come off a water container and half a gallon had spilt, soaking the tea bags and bursting the envelope which carried my documents. Vibration was the cause. It scoured cans and batteries and took the surface off the inside of the wheelbarrow, blackening food and equipment with metallic dust. Lids sometimes shook loose, and jumbled kit was powdered with salt, cocoa, oats, foot powder and sand.

When I had just erected the tent, Paddy laid aside his empty plate, strolled over, opened a locker and, with an expression of humorous disgust, peered inside and said, 'What d'you keep in there? Pigs?'

'How'd you guess?' I said, pulling my aluminium dishes from the wheelbarrow. They were thick with dried food and grime. Mick exclaimed,

'Ugh, Geoff, they're evil. I hope you're gonna wash 'em.'

'Can't spare the water, but by the time I've finished cooking they'll be sterile.'

'No wonder you keep getting the craps.'

'It would have helped', I mumbled under my breath, 'if I had been drinking chlorinated water.' I put the dishes inside the tent and was half-way to following them when Mick asked, 'Want some spaghetti bolognese, Geoff?' I turned round in the tent mouth and sat down with my feet outside to take off my boots.

'No thanks. Got to keep to the rules.'

'It'll get wasted,' he said. 'I'll have to bin it.'

'Then it'll have to get wasted.'

'If I left the can just over there you could say you found it.'

'No thanks.' I zipped up the flaps, not daring to show my anger. I still do not know whether Mick's approach to the rules, trying to get me to break them one minute, and pointing an accusing finger the next, was a friendly tease or not. The effect that evening was that it hurt, especially as my supper was delayed for over an hour by blocked jets.

Next morning, the jets, and my mood, were worse. Before dawn, I was in the sleeping-bag, propping myself up on an elbow, Bible in one hand, torch in the other, flicking the beam periodically to the right of my legs, where the small aluminium pan and stove were struggling to boil water for tea. Now and then the faint popping of the jet stopped and I restored the dim-blue circle with a match. After fifty-five minutes there was the gentle tapping of bubbles. Tea was almost ready. I packed away my Bible in its plastic bag and, as it was now light enough to see, switched off the torch. A tea-bag, a spoon of Marvel milk-powder, and the green plastic mug was steaming triumphantly by my side.

Paddy used to say that tea was a morale booster. Indeed it was, especially in the morning. It kept out the cold and gave strength and comfort beyond its natural powers. While leaving it to cool, I reached over for the map; the mug was caught by my sleeve, fell forward with a gurgle, and emptied. The sleeping-bag began to soak up tea from the steaming groundsheet, and I screamed, 'Damn! Damn! Damn!' as I beat my fist in the warm puddle.

'Something the matter?' asked a sleepy voice.

'Yeah, Mick, Yeah. I'm going round the bend.' I did without tea – a case of having to.

Before setting off, when all had been packed away, I unwittingly slipped my clip-on sun-glasses into my back pocket. As I lay under the wheelbarrow to tighten the grub-screws on the suspension, there was a sharp snap. I hauled myself up, shouting abuse at my stupidity. I pulled the now broken glasses from my pocket: one lens was split, so I fixed the halves in a crude frame of electrical tape.

Difficulties were always tempered by contact with people. Whether it was talking to travellers or just listening to the lads, whether I felt warmth or animosity did not matter. Attention was diverted from my ills. The next twenty-four hours were especially rich in this respect.

By three-thirty, I had done eighteen miles and was hoping to manage twenty-two. The going was easy and the temperature pleasant. The hill that was waiting for me across the next two miles of nothingness was typical of those I had climbed that day – no more than a hundred feet high, with a gradual slope. All the same, I had sore feet and was feeling sorry for myself. In the middle distance, undulating sand hid the road, though not a tiny green Land Rover moving along it. After a minute or two, the vehicle drew up and Manfred and Gloria, a German architect and his wife, jumped out. They were stocky, blond and in their late thirties. 'Happy New Year for yesterday,' said Manfred. 'We read about you in our newspaper.'

Gloria pulled a glossy magazine from their Land Rover and handed it to me. I did not understand German, and was not interested in the photograph of myself at the top, but bottom left, was a small black-and-white snapshot of Joan and the children. Joan was smiling, she had her hand on Susan's curly, three-year-old head, and Susan herself was trying to force a menacing kiss on little Sam. Though I had forgotton to bring any photographs with me, this one seemed empty. It was a cold fossil; the people in it could have been of strangers. I was suppressing my feelings, and was often to see the photograph in the evenings when I closed my eyes.

'Is there anything you need?' asked Manfred.

'Could you post some letters for me?' I handed back the magazine and gave him a bundle of mail.

'How about some cigarettes?' he asked. I did not smoke but I hesitated to reply. Mick was short of them and I was deliberating whether to get them for him.

'I'm sure you can use them,' Manfred said, as he thrust them into my shirt pocket.

They were typical of the many Europeans we met who were tired of conventional holidays. Soon after Manfred and Gloria had gone, when I was hurrying to make up time, a second German couple jumped out of another Land Rover. They were older, rounder and darker skinned. Each fired an eight-millimetre cine camera at me from opposite sides of the road. The man was excited and let out raucous laughter, sounding like a cross between a throaty American and a macaw. I instantly disliked him. I was in no mood to stop, and continued past as if I thought they wanted to film me from behind. They ran after me, shouting, but I could barely hear because of the noise of the wheelbarrow.

The man's hand grabbed my shoulder and jerked me round. They patted, pawed and shook me while they jumped up and down. 'We write about you in de nyawspepper! De first one! De first one to do it!' That was confidence – the first man to carry his own food and water across the Sahara, and I had not even left the main road yet. I told them that I was late and walked off.

Four hours later, three miles on, the lads and I were in our tents. I was eating supper in the dark to save batteries. Food always tasted better when I could not see it. Often, when I switched on the light to make sure that the dish was scraped clean, I was disgusted at the mess I had been eating. Previous days' food and grime always made a meal look unappetizing, though it never affected the taste.

Mick spoke up from the other tent. 'These fags aren't bad. Decent couple Manfred and Gloria. Better than the other two cowboys from Hamburg. Did you see 'em, Geoff?'

'Yeah, but I got away as fast as I could,' I said.

'Manfred and Gloria said they'd met them and were trying to shake them off,' Mick replied. A gust of wind flapped the tents. 'I can't believe this wind,' Mick continued. 'I've tried five organizations to get it to stop, including the Red Cross and the Salvation Army. I'll have to try praying to Mohammed. I've not got me bronzie. All I've got is slant eyes to keep the sand out.'

'Why not try a space blanket?' I said.

'I'll try anything.'

'It should keep you warm. They keep in 98 per cent of radiated heat. I'm getting out for a pee in a minute, so I'll get one out of the Land Rover if you throw the keys.'

A space blanket, so called because it is a product of space research, is more efficient than an ordinary blanket. It is a thin sheet of plastic, covered with a shiny coating of the metal alloy, virilium, and folds up to the size of a handkerchief. Though it is meant to be used to keep out the cold, we had brought six of them to cover the tents and reflect away the sun's heat, and to signal for help if needed. We had never imagined we would put them to their intended use.

I went to Mick's tent, opened the zip and reached inside. An orange circle of light, the beam from his torch, darted round the tent walls, there was the jingle of keys and I felt them cold in my hand. There was enough light from the sky for me to see the padlocks. I unfastened them and hooked the heavy, clanking chains to the tail-board to take its weight. 'Throw me a bar of chocolate, as well, will you Geoff? It's in a tin in the nearest carton on the left.' I was envious. Chocolate was part of army rations, not mine. I wanted a space blanket even more, but I could not take anything from the Land Rover for myself until the next settlement.

I lifted the tail-board, secured the locks, opened the vertical zip of the lads' tent, and poked the goodies and keys inside. 'Thanks Geoff. If this wind doesn't stop, I'll go silly. I'll get boozed out of my mind when I get to In Sha-la-la [Mick's name for In Salah].' There was a noise of a parcel being unwrapped as Mick unfolded the space blanket. After two minutes, he called out, 'Hey Geoff! This is good news – I'm warm already.'

The next morning, when I had been on the move for half an hour, I came across a shack to the left of the road, looking like two different sized cartons glued together side by side. Four robed men were idling beneath the 'café' sign, which was daubed in white on the mud wall. The proprietor, a young man, even skinnier and shorter than I, with bulging eyes and half a gold tooth, was standing in the doorway wearing an oversized European suit. 'Have you any bread?' I asked.

'Yes,' they replied in ragged unison. The proprietor led me into the windowless gloom. For a moment, until I took off my sun-lenses, I could see nothing. The walls were unpainted and the ceiling had bits of flaking mud dangling from it. There was no furniture, only a large mirror, once part of a wardrobe door, leaning against the wall. A glass cabinet sat on the counter, crammed with dusty trinkets, leatherwork and tins of sardines. I pointed to three red, leather bangles, decorated with turquoise beads – presents for my daughter Susan and my two nieces. He put them on the counter and asked, 'Tea or coffee?'

'Coffee, thank you.' He reached behind and took an aluminium teapot from a camping-stove and poured black coffee into a half-sized tumbler. On the shelves behind were stringed instruments made from wood, leather, and large, hollowed-out seed-pods. They, too, were dusty, and looked like exhibits from a museum. 'What are those?' I asked, expecting an Arabic name with which to impress my friends.

'Guitars,' he said.

'How much?'

'Five.'

'Give me the one with the full set of strings, and two cans of sardines.' There were voices outside and then two heavily-built Algerians came striding in, each wearing an astrakhan hat and a sheepskin car-coat. There was much laughter, directed, I thought, at me. I began to total up. 'Two dinars each for the sardines, five for the guitar.'

'*Non! Non! Non! Monsieur,*' said the little man. 'Not *five* but *fifty.*'

'Too expensive!' I said, and I pushed the instrument back and paid for the rest. The two customers thought this hilarious; as I turned to leave, and saw myself in the mirror, I joined in the laughter. I had been haggling like a nomad, while they, dressed like English salesmen, were ready to pay without question. Still laughing, they shook my hand and bade me, '*Bon courage,* stranger.' I stepped into the sunshine, forgetting the bread for which I had gone in.

6

MIND GAMES

A mile down the road from the café, my lower left shin began to hurt. I was learning to shut out the daily discomforts, however, either by looking around, or by playing mental games. Though the Sahara is often monochrome and denuded, it has the same topographical shape, river beds, mountains and plains as when it was fertile. It is like a line-drawing in a children's painting-book, waiting to be animated with colour and detail. Flat expanses of sand conjured up images of the savannah it had once been: giraffes picking leaves from high branches, an antelope grazing, and young zebras running in circles while their mothers eye a drowsy lion in the long grass. The cliffs which had proved so difficult bordered a valley a mile or more across, the bed of what had once been a great, meandering river. It put me in mind of the vast River Niger further south, which brings fish and game to villagers all along its course. My mind games were not always concerned with the past; sometimes they involved transforming my surroundings into a fantasy landscape. In the river-bed, islands of rock stuck up above the imaginary water level. One, almost enveloped by a dune, became a dinosaur with spines down his back. Newly-forming dunes broke the surface like whales rising to breathe. The desert sand sometimes seemed to be made up of pellets of dried yeast, road-workers' grit, or face-powder.

I was beginning to feel at home in the desert. From my previous life in England only close family connections mattered. I tried to recall friends' telephone numbers as an exercise, but astonishingly, though I had only been away from home for fifteen days, could only manage my own, my sister's and my mother-in-law's. When I eventually did get home, though, I remembered most of those I had forgotten as if I had not been away.

That day, the stony, arid soil was uninspiringly flat and showed little sign of life, apart from posts every ten kilometres giving the distance to Adrar. 'It's now five to ten,' I thought. 'From this post to the next is $6\frac{1}{4}$ miles. At four miles an hour, the next one will arrive in $93\frac{3}{4}$ minutes, at $28\frac{3}{4}$ minutes past eleven. Since I know from experience that a post is visible from a mile and a half, it should appear in the distance at $6\frac{1}{4}$ minutes past eleven.' Arithmetic not only took my mind off the leg, but also spurred me to keep up a pace of four miles an hour. It worked well and the sighting and arrival were both within two minutes of the estimates. On getting there I calculated when I would arrive at the next post, where I promised myself lunch.

At lunch-times, I was given to mental lapses. I would sit down on the fishing stool, ready to eat, but then I would be up and down, in and out of the lockers, getting the fork I had forgotten, or the knife to peel the carrot, or even the carrot itself. I might get up for one thing and put back another by mistake. It rarely took less than seven minutes to organize the few things I needed, so that day I rehearsed mentally as I went along: 'Choose the best place to stop. Back down the camber. Press the legs of the barrow into the sand but keep the wheel on the road so that it doesn't get stuck. Take the wire fastener off the lid of the locker. Walk round, take out matchbox and place fasteners in it for safety. Replace matchbox. Take out fishing stool. Expand it and throw it onto the ground on the other side of the wheelbarrow. Take out orange-juice container and fork. Close left locker. Walk round and open right locker. Take out can of beans and sausage . . .

I rehearsed this over and over again, but when I stopped – and the story was usually the same – I relaxed and limped around, opening each locker several times in confusion. That day, I not only forgot the can of fruit and the opener when I sat down to lunch, but was up and down, putting on more clothes and trying to find the most sheltered spot in relation to the wheelbarrow. As usual, once I had put down the wheelbarrow, I had stiffened up and been able to think only of aches and pains. Apart from what I felt, it seemed that my brain became dulled when I stopped moving.

I had been asked by Professor John Mills and Dr James Waterhouse of Manchester School of Medicine to record my temperature every waking hour. They were using me as a guinea-pig to investigate the hourly variation in mental efficiency of those with irregular sleeping patterns, such as airline pilots or globe-trotting diplomats. They were seeking to establish the link between blood temperature and someone's relative mental ability, whereby if you know one you can estimate the other. Just before bedtime, until an hour after getting up, a person's blood temperature is low, and there is a resultant decrease in mental efficiency. Even if a person stays awake all night, the pattern is unchanged. Readings will be low during the night and higher during the day. Shift workers and international travellers take several days for their systems to readjust, with the consequence that their low temperature when awake results in poor mental performance and a feeling of disorientation.

The researchers had given me an electric thermometer, a stalk of red plastic, to put in my mouth. Before taking my temperature I was neither allowed to breathe through my mouth for ten minutes nor to take food or drink for half an hour. The thermometer was connected by a spiral of red wire to a small meter in my pocket. Though originally designed for the other end of the alimentary canal, it was ideal for my purposes; it was virtually unbreakable and gave accurate readings in half the time of an ordinary clinical thermometer. Despite not strictly working shifts, I recorded abnormal temperatures, probably – though it is not proven – because I had missed so much sleep. When I stopped walking, my temperature dropped below normal, which might explain my confused state. Readings were only normal when I was walking, perhaps because of the tendency of exertion to increase body temperature. At home my temperature had followed the expected pattern, but here readings were so low when I was resting, even at midday, that I often kept the thermometer in my mouth for fifteen minutes in the hope that it would rise.

That evening, after supper, I was too tired to write up notes, so I lay thinking over the day in order to make it easier to write them up in the morning. My eyes were open, just able to discern the tent staked out over me. I recalled an old man I had seen that afternoon, standing by a well. I tried to remember if there had been a dog with him, but it was difficult to concentrate. My ears were burning, and my left shin throbbed as if it did not know I had stopped walking.

It took an hour to sort out the jumble of thoughts. It was always easier to listen to Mick and Paddy than it was to think. They had been having their usual discussion about food. Paddy asked Mick if there were any sweets.

'I'm damned hungry. Have we got any stickies?'

'You're always the same. You don't need all that food you eat.'

'But I'm used to three big meals a day. A good breakfast, dinner and tea, and here I'm only getting one decent meal a day. I'm wasting away.'

'You're like all squaddies. Eat three good meals a day, give it the big lips at night and then go and eat a Chinese or fish and chips.'

'No I'm not. I'm not eating half as much as I did on camp and I'm starving.'

Conversation lulled for an hour until I was almost asleep, then Mick said, 'D'you still feel hungry?'

'Hungry? I've told you! I'm starving!'

'Go and get a packet of biscuits out of the Rover will you?'

'Oh, it's too cold.'

'There's a tin of pork we could have as well,' said Mick.

'No, we couldn't, could we? No, we couldn't waste it.'

'It wouldn't be a waste.'

'Ohhhh, I'll go,' groaned Paddy. There was the rustle of sleeping-bags and clothes. Mick was getting out too.

'Hey Geoff, here's a travelling chippy. What do you want? Hang on, he's out of fish. Will you have a pie?'

'What sort?'

'Meat and potato or steak and kidney.'

'Steak and kidney.'

'Have you got any change?'

'Yeah, hang on.' I reached out an arm in the darkness and found my pile of loose coins, placed, as usual, to the left of the groundsheet. I tapped them blindly to sound as if counting them out.

By morning, the slightest weight on the leg was unbearable. I had what I suspected to be 'shin soreness', inflammation where the tendon meets the bone, and for which rest is the only cure. To walk was to risk breaking it, but there could be no more than an overnight stop before Adrar, the end of the macadam and the last supply point before open desert.

I ambled intentionally slowly, hiding my wrist-watch in my pocket, in case I damaged the leg further through impatience and hurrying. In spite of taking my time, the wheelbarrow fell over every couple of minutes, when balancing required the left leg to take the strain. I was cold into the bargain, and when I was dropping my shorts, I over-balanced because of the painful shin, and soiled myself and my clothes with diarrhoea. Back on the road, the pain in the shin was severe and only distractions, natural or contrived, kept me going. I sang the childrens' song 'If you're happy and you know it, clap your hands', which required hand-clapping and foot-stamping after each line. The humour of letting go of the wheelbarrow while clapping, and of trying to stamp one foot while walking, without injury to the other, dulled the pain. At other times, the surroundings helped to take my mind off it. An Arab's flowing robes and racing camels gleamed white against the ochre dirt. Then the road swung left of a forest of palms, where man-made trenches flanked the road and cradled young trees, and on past a mud-brick café, and the village of Sbaa, with its pyramid tower and mosque.

Despite the scenery, however, my shin felt as if it was in a red-hot clamp, with someone turning the screw. I could not take any more. I clambered onto the wheelbarrow, to pray for a healing miracle, laying aside my glasses and hat. I put my head in my hands and prayed until

I felt right, but I knew that feelings would not buy God. 'Forgive me,' I prayed, 'for trying to bribe you with emotion.' There now seemed no need even to ask for help; my needs were known, so I waited for a cure. I remembered Joan, as a nineteen-year-old student. Just before the end of term she had strained her back at college. The doctor had told her that she was unfit to travel, but she came home anyway. The journey had made her worse, and when she reached my parents' house, she collapsed in pain on the settee, from where she was unable to get up. After encouraging ourselves to trust God, we prayed, and she sat up, cured. While I was thinking of this, there was a murmuring in the inflamed blood vessels, a surging as healing bubbled through. 'Thank you,' I shouted, and leaped with joy into the air.

I screamed with pain. My legs folded, both knees hit the ground, and I scrambled, in a rage, back on to the wheelbarrow. Having recognized that emotion does not buy God, I now fell into the trap of believing that the right method does. 'I know where I went wrong,' I thought. 'I didn't rebuke the evil in the name of Jesus.' With both hands gripping the shin I commanded: 'In Jesus' name be healed!' I trusted God and leaped, but hit the ground in agony. After ten minutes, I lifted the shafts in a temper and pushed off in more pain than ever, singing, 'I just don't trust you any more, Lord. Why did you cheat me and let me down? I just don't trust you any more.'

Five minutes later, an Arab in a small blue van stopped and gave me a few kilos of tangerines. They seemed to be a peace-offering from above, as if God were apologizing. He seemed to be saying, 'Listen Geoff, there are some things I can do for you and there are some things I can't. Don't expect me to cover the sun, to flatten mountains and sand dunes or to heal your leg. Some other time, yes, but not on this walk. Believe me, I am with you and you will get to Kano, but not with the help of a God who cheats for you. You know the golf sketch where the vicar prays and his ball is miraculously deflected into the hole. Well, I'm not like that, so don't expect me to clear *this* course with my magic wand.'

In my job, I had expected the sick and the dying to trust God, and I had come to the Sahara hoping to discover whether I myself would keep the faith in adverse circumstances. If God had removed all obstacles, I would never have known. From then until the end of the trip, every time I thought I had had enough I would repeat, 'This is what the trip's about. This is what it's all about.'

In spite of rationally accepting hardship, I would have done almost anything to be rid of the pain, which by now dominated every thought. I would have taken pain-killers but for the danger of numbing the leg and overworking it. There were no bandages large enough in the wheel-barrow to make a cold compress, so I poured water on my sock where it touched the inflammation, but the water filled my boot and left the sock barely damp. I tried every trick to ease the pain, both shorter and longer steps, walking stiff-legged, then on my toes and then on my heels. In fact, the way I had instinctively started to limp turned out to be the best: a short step on the left heel with the leg stiff and a long springing step on the right. I tried running but gave up after two paces, and then went from meditation to mental arithmetic, calculating the length of each step by counting them for each revolution of the wheel. Next, I tried thinking of cold drinks and old friends, but the pain hung on. The joint and muscle were all right. The inflammation was where there had been only skin and bone before. There seemed no other explanation than a hair-line fracture. Thoughts of gangrene and amputations terrified me until, after seventeen miles, I reached camp, where Mick was waiting to make me forget myself.

After dark, when I had eaten and was lying counting the throbs in my leg, we heard the hoot of a car-horn and roar of an engine. 'If any of those Coventry supporters comes this way asking for petrol,' shouted Mick, 'I'll tell 'em where to go. They beat us today. And talking of supporters, you'd better lock your barrow. Rangers beat Celtic and those Cath'lics will be on the rampage. Hey, Geoff, d'you think the Chinese take-away in Adrar would deliver a couple of chop-sueys?' (There was no restaurant, Chinese or otherwise, in Adrar, apart from the hotel dining-room.)

At dawn, with Adrar thirteen miles away, I set off to reach its safety without the wheelbarrow, using a six foot pole as a staff. The lads would stay put and do their washing, though one of them would drive into town at lunch-time and bring me back if I had not already managed to get a lift back myself. They wanted it that way in order to save making and breaking camp. The following day, Monday, we would all drive into Adrar, I having already walked that section. We would pick up supplies and I would continue with the wheelbarrow from where I had left off.

Walking was nearly impossible. As hard as I tried, I could not make use of the staff, so I carried it, hobbling like a stage imbecile. After half an hour, when the drone of an engine approached from behind, I had to bring every muscle into play to maintain a normal walk. If the driver had seen that I was hurt, he would have stopped, and I was not up to explaining why I could not accept a lift. I kept control until the car had overtaken and was out of sight.

Without the wheelbarrow, more styles of walking were possible and I even tried hopping. The staff and right leg propelled me for forty yards until the leg gave way and the injured one, without a thought, took the strain and I ended up on my hands and knees ranting and raving. I was most comfortable using the previous day's shuffle but with an added stoop. I tried to meditate to stimulate my faith but gave up. As a way of dealing with a crisis this seemed repugnant – a bit like a child only turning to his parents when he or she wants something. God was there and there seemed no need to pray or sing hymns either to transport me away from the present reality or to ward off danger by attracting God's attention. So I made a joke-offering to God and sang satirically, with all the insincerity I could muster, the song which begins, 'This world is not my home. I'm just a passin' through.'

This led to a real Sunday morning's devotion, singing new stanzas to the song I had started a few days before: 'Thank you for sore legs; thank you for the pain; I wanna thank you, Lord. This is what it's all about; this is why I came. I wanna thank you, Lord.' I sang, pondering whether my thanks were as spontaneous as I had thought or whether I was just too scared to complain.

Another musical diversion was prompted when I saw electricity pylons striding towards, and then alongside, the road, like evenly planted trees. They sent Respighi's music, *Pines of the Appian Way*, marching through my head, to which I gave bass accompaniment with my hat. When I put the staff between the denim cap and the wind, the turbulence vibrated the peak with the noise of a bassoon. While the leg craved attention, I strained to forget it, even using rubbish as a distraction. With Adrar now five miles away, flotsam and jetsam were increasing, so I began to make a mental inventory of all I passed – six sardine cans, two bottles, the greater part of a tyre, too many small pieces of rubber to count, a five-litre can and the cylinder head from a car engine. Finally, my mind was distracted by thoughts of home.

* * *

My watch showed that Joan would be in church, her eyes and ears on the preacher, her hands turning the pages of a picture-book for Susan and Sam. Our children had brought us a lot of happiness. We had adopted them while I was preparing for the desert. Before learning about our infertility, we had already planned to adopt 'hard-to-place' children, and so, with little prospect of natural children, we applied for adoption all the sooner. We fostered Susan with a view to adoption, knowing that there was a possibility of a tug-of-love. Unless someone had been prepared to take the risk, she might have spent her childhood in institutions. She was a year old and her mother had wanted her to be fostered while she got herself sorted out. She hoped to get a new home and take her baby back. When she visited us with her boyfriend and said that she would be able to take Susan in a few weeks, we had to disguise our emotions. Joan showed love and courage. We knew that if the mother asked for her back, we would have to give her up cheerfully, even though Joan and Susan were inseparable. The child was insecure and frightened, unable to let go of Joan for one waking moment. Joan did the laundry, washing up, and housework holding her with one arm. Susan was so frightened of being alone, that she would not go to sleep, in case we left her. One night we did not sleep at all. After six months, against expectations, Susan's mother requested adoption.

Before the legalities had been completed, early in 1973, I went to a local youth club to show slides of my work as a missionary. Aided by nostalgia, I made up my mind, there and then, to return to Nigeria on foot. Joan was not surprised. I had been talking about it ever since our time out there. I would walk north to south, with the wind on my back, and raise sponsorship for the sort of people I had met in Nigeria. When preparations for the desert were under way, we were given another child, four-month-old Sam. His mother asked to meet us and when she did, she held him and wept. After a few minutes, she handed him to Joan and agreed to the adoption. Two days before the hearing, she reversed her decision and asked for him back. Two months later, she changed her mind again, in our favour. When we got to court, we waited six hours in the corridor, to be told that the papers were not in order. For the first time in the affair, Joan broke down. No doubt the thought of my departure added to the strain. The adoption went through a month later.

* * *

It was after I had been deep in thought for a long time, stooped forward, that I looked up and saw Adrar, like the celestial city, its towers and palms floating on the mirage of a lake. The duller buildings blended with the desert, but others shone pink, blue and gold, edged with ornamental plasterwork in white.

The nearer I got, the slower the town seemed to come. I was like a thirsty man watching raindrops fill a bucket. And when it did arrive, I knew that Kano was still one thousand, seven hundred miles away over mountains and dunes, almost as far from me as Manchester, my home, where, as I turned ruefully north, I wished I had stayed.

Having reached the centre of the town, I hobbled back to the north of it, where I had seen vehicles waiting for the filling station to open. They were still there and I was sure that one of them would be going my way. Two of them later were, but ignored me. I was expecting the lads soon, anyway, as they were coming to pick me up if I had not arrived by lunch-time and it was noon already.

It was too cold and windy to sit and wait, though, so I limped back the way I had come, embittered at having to walk unnecessarily. To the right, there was open ground, with the circular mud walls of wells which were inexplicably ranged in a line at ten metre intervals. Small boys used them as goal-posts, while a trail of adults crouched behind them among baked piles of excrement. I walked on past a dead cow and the arrow markers for the airstrip. By two o'clock, Adrar was three miles behind me and there was no sign of the Land Rover nor of any other vehicle. I was cold and hungry – in eight hours I had only had three tangerines – and I throbbed from toes to groin.

A cyclist appeared over my right shoulder, struggling against the wind to reach me. He was skinny, a little older than me, with his western-style clothes in tatters. He was going to Sbaa on an old black bicycle, the sort English policemen used to ride. Tied to the pannier with rough string was a small hessian sack, the week's rice for the family, and a loaf, their Sunday tea. When he had dismounted, he broke me a piece, though I had not complained of hunger. I am ashamed to say I took it, despite suspecting that his family might go short. No one can teach the desert folk about kindness.

It was half-past two before he pedalled on but I could go no further. I sat on a large stone, shivering and looked north appealingly, shouting, 'Mick! Paddy! Where the hell are you?' A bright-red saloon car zoomed past from the south and shot me to my feet with my arms waving wildly. I fell over but carried on waving from on hands and knees and saw the car stop two hundred yards away. I tried to run, desperately hoping the driver would wait but, even better, he turned to come back for me. I stood leaning on the staff, grinning and throwing an arm in the air as he approached, but he and his companion never so much as looked as they sped back to Adrar. It was, I concluded, someone having a driving lesson.

Back on the stone, I yelled 'Stupid! Stupid! Stupid!' as I drove the staff angrily into the ground between my feet with the action of a woman pounding corn. I swung it round my head, brought it down savagely into the sand, and watched the wind carry off the dust. A little calmer, I began to write on the ground with the stick, 'Howard is a nut', but was distracted by a tiny blue van in the south and was determined not to let it go by. I stood in the middle of the road, conscious of my effrontery, flagging it down with a bundle of banknotes. The driver stopped and welcomed me aboard. He wore a white T-shirt, jeans and black head-wrap. A man in a grubby white robe was in the passenger seat. I squeezed between them and turned round to greet a woman and six children in the back. They and their dog were sitting cramped on sacks of flour. 'Put your money away,' the driver said, 'Don't you recognize me?'

'Yes, of course,' I said doubtfully. 'You gave me the tangerines.'

'That's right, but I have been your friend for many days. Do you ever hear vehicles honking at night?'

'Yes, often.'

'That's me, saying good-night,' he laughed. Twenty pleasant minutes retraced the morning's steps and I stood beside the Land Rover waving goodbye and listening to the blue van's familiar toots as it continued north.

I shuffled towards Mick who was standing twenty yards off the road by the rear of the Land Rover. I paused for a moment to shout farewell to the driver, but when I turned, Mick had his back to me, leaning inside the rear of the Land Rover. I felt like hitting him on the back of the head with a rock. 'Where've you been? You could have picked me up. You said you'd come after lunch!' I said, a good deal more calmly than I felt. He turned round, offering me a hunk of bread and margarine with cheese on top – real luxury. I had neither margarine nor cheese in my rations.

'We thought you'd be having a job getting there so we gave you plenty of time. We planned to come at four o'clock. Hope the bread's OK. We'll be eating properly later.'

'It's fine Mick, thanks,' I said, unable to feel angry any more. I had reached Adrar, so I was able to accept help from the lads. Paddy handed me a mug of tea and I sat down on a jerry-can.

'Cheers, Paddy.'

'Will you be doing your washing now?' he asked.

'Just as soon as I've finished my tea and had a bath.'

Without a word, he took the staff I'd been using, drove it into the ground with his sledge hammer, secured it with guy ropes and tied a washing line for me from it to the Land Rover. Meanwhile, Mick was peeling potatoes, carrots and onions, which he had bought when he had made an advance visit to Adrar the day before.

I sat holding the mug, looking in the direction from which I had walked. Along the horizon were the palms of Sbaa. Nearer, just a few yards away, were our tents, their mouths pointing away from me, out of the wind. I laid the sturdy Ministry of Defence plastic mug on the sand and then hopped round to the front of my tent to bring out my dirty washing. The flaps were pegged half open to let the air into my sleeping-bag. Other mornings it had been rolled up and put in a plastic case within minutes of my getting out of it.

As I stooped to reach into the tent, I paused. Everything inside was covered in a quarter-inch layer of powdery sand, which the wind, contrary to its direction, had blown inside. Incidents such as this, and there were many more than I have recorded, could have worn me down had I not taken an almost fatalistic view. I looked at set-backs as if they were predetermined, as if a fixed number of them were waiting for me and once one of them was overcome the number to come decreased.

Now that I had reached a town, there was an elaborate routine to undergo. I would take a stand-up bath in Mick's washing-up bowl, wash all my clothes, clean every item of equipment, and wipe the wheelbarrow, lockers and the groundsheet with disinfectant. There were reports and letters to write, tape recordings to family, schools and churches to finish.

It was not much extra work to sweep out and clean away the dust, but it did mean, yet again, dismantling the stove. This proved to be a blessing, for this time I noticed a piece of fabric, like the backing of a sticking plaster, wedged in the tubing that connected the cylinder to the burner. This had obviously been there since manufacture and had caused the blockages I had blamed on sand. After removing it there was no more trouble from low pressure.

Cassette tapes and rolls of film had to be posted the following day in envelopes that were tough enough not to burst and yet could be easily opened by customs officials. No envelopes that I had brought were suitable, so that night I made several of them, as I regularly did, strengthening ordinary ones with sticky tape, and making reusable fasteners out of wire from abandoned tyres.

After we had eaten, I lay half inside my sleeping-bag refixing the broken sun-lenses with tape. The lads were in their tent, reading, when Mick broke the silence.

'Are there any decent shops in Kano, Geoff?'

'Quite a few compared with the one-eyed places we'll be going through. You're in civilization when you get to Nigeria. It's the richest black African country and Kano's got a million inhabitants. There are hotels, a Barclays Bank, a Coca-Cola factory and loads of clubs.'

'Can I get a decent suit there?'

'I'm not sure. They sell suits, but African tastes differ from yours. I think you should be able to.'

'If there's bandits along any of these sections,' he said, 'we'll skip 'em and you can tack on the extra mileage by walking round Kano a few times.' I could never have agreed to such a plan, but was pleased at Mick's change of mood. He was, at last, looking foward to Kano instead of looking back. As for me, I was apprehensive. Tomorrow, I would have my first real taste of desert. There was no tarmac beyond Adrar.

7

THE CRUCIBLE

By ten-fifteen the next morning, 5 January, we had loaded the wheel-barrow on to the trailer and were driving to Adrar, along the section I had walked the day before. Mick had bandaged my leg an hour earlier and I was enjoying the comfort of the ride, my mind on the task ahead. We had been told by travellers that the stretch of desert from Adrar to Reggane would be the worst part of my journey. What would I be doing in a week's time? Resting in Reggane? Or catching the ferry for Gibraltar? Those words of Idris, 'Pas possible,' and his hangdog look would not leave me alone.

That was not all. The two and a half weeks I had been away from home seemed like years. The camels, palm-trees and sand were all commonplace now, as if all I had ever known was Algeria, as if Joan was only an acquaintance of my fantasies. I wondered whether I had slipped out of her consciousness. I was hoping to collect a reassuring letter from the post office. Things had been tense between us throughout the two-year preparation period. While I had been around, it had been easy to smooth things over, but now I was at her mercy. Was she enjoying the release from all the strain? Perhaps she was getting on a little too well without me. It was this nagging feeling that was driving me to Kano and had increased my daily average to 19.6 miles. It was this that had caused the shin injury, pushing me on when I could have taken things more slowly. It was this that had prevented me from resting half a day here or there, from starting late in the morning and from stopping early in the evening. Every hour mattered: I had to see her as soon as possible. We had not seen a town to speak of for almost two weeks. There was good enough reason, especially with the leg injury, to rest for a couple of days, but, with Joan in mind, my plan was to collect my mail, buy food, take on water, have a cup of coffee at the hotel, and be off towards Reggane. Even such a short break would reduce my daily average to 18.3 miles.

From the Land Rover I could see the awful brown flatness. I was sure I remembered the oil drum we had just passed. Yes, and there was the first of the three dead cows. I thought it funny how I kept seeing dead cows but no live ones. We passed the airstrip, wells and garage, drove into the town, along a street tarred down the middle but with sand for a pavement, and stopped.

Adrar was clean, and there were none of the African smells offensive to western noses – just the opposite. The air was sweet with the smell of bread from the bakeries which seemed to be on every other street corner. There were no beggars, no obviously destitute people, nor was there any decaying rubbish in back streets. Everywhere was clean and tidy. There was little to repel a European, yet it was with wide eyes that I saw a 'Trans-World Tours' motor coach taking its pale-skinned passengers through the town. There was nothing here for the average tourist, nothing for my friends Jim and Mary, who go off every year on a package tour. Where was the chemist's shop to buy a tube of sun-tan lotion or a sticking plaster? Where could they eat steak and chips, buy their favourite drink, or be entertained? There was a hotel, where you could buy an alcoholic drink, but there was only one variety of beer, which you would have to drink from the bottle at five times the English price.

The hotel restaurant – there was nowhere else to eat – could serve you with tea, coffee, bread, sardines, lettuce, carrots and potatoes, but nothing else, certainly not a meat dish – there was no fresh meat in Adrar. As for entertainment, a Welsh village on a Sunday would have had more to offer. Hooded Arabs and the occasional donkey gave the streets tourist appeal but such scenes were also common in the more picturesque oases further north. Apart from the few ornamental buildings, it was an unattractive little town, built from mud. There was a dull uniformity about the place. Everything about it was grey-brown – houses, donkeys, sand and peasants' heavy robes. Nor were there any colourful bazaars, though there was a market where I later bought fruit, vegetables, eggs and three small glasses, the sort from which Algerians drink their coffee.

We called first at the post office, set in a square edged by trees, wells and the concrete façades of offices flying the red, white and green national flag. Mick went into the post office while Paddy walked along the square to the hotel. I used up the film in my two cameras before following Mick inside. The interior was a large, square room. Two dusty fans, which I suspected had not moved since the French walked out in 1962, hung idly from the high ceiling. There was neither a window nor a door open: customers and staff sweated visibly and there was the smell of a sports changing-room. A notice on the left wall warned desert travellers to report to the police before embarking. A broad counter divided the room but there was no glass partition between the solitary counter-clerk and the handful of customers.

There were no mothers with push-chairs and family-allowance books, no grannies collecting their pensions. The customers were all men, heavily robed, standing in groups or leaning on the counter with no apparent desire to be served. Only Mick, who had gone in ahead of me, looked eagerly over the counter towards the office staff doing their paperwork. The clerk ignored him but now and then shouted in Arabic and a customer came forward to collect a form or a tattered bundle of money. It was rumoured that banknotes were never withdrawn from circulation but simply frayed away.

While I waited, I took the films out of my cameras and put them in the home-made packets. After ten minutes, Mick was asked for his passport and was then handed a sheaf of letters, all in the same size of envelope, all addressed in the same neat hand of his father. The clerk turned to me and I gave him my passport and put down eleven packets and envelopes on the counter for posting. After looking in a drawer, he handed the passport back. 'Nothing for you.'

The Land Rover cruised out of sight at two o'clock. Mick and Paddy had left me just south of Adrar. They would wait five miles ahead, not daring to go further because of my leg. It took a few minutes for me to balance the load. Soon after I had moved off, a massive column of dust appeared in the east, headed by a battered green lorry, the sort the Eighth Army might have lost. The lorry, which was coming from the local gravel-pit, drew up, and the Arab driver put out his head: 'Where are you going?' he asked in French.

'Reggane.'

'It's a hundred and sixty kilometres away!'

'I know.' He screwed his fingers against his temple and drove on. Yet, as I moved forward, I began to think that I was not so stupid after all. This was open desert, and there was not a dune in sight and it was firm underfoot. There was hardly any sand, just a scattering of blackened stones over baked clay. There was neither grass, bush, nor palm-tree. There were no houses, no people, no hills, and not a rock bigger than a cricket ball. This kind of desert is known as *reg* and covers vast areas. The Tanezrouft reg, further south, is larger than Great Britain and Ireland together. Firmness was all that could be said for it. Vehicles had scored a shallow trench, a foot deep and as wide as a narrow road. Tyres had thrown the dirt into parallel ridges, knee-high on either side. The track was like a tin roof, with corrugations running across it at right angles six inches deep. The wheelbarrow rose and fell with every step and occasionally became stuck in a hollow. The rumble that had thundered from the wheelbarrow on tarmac was now replaced by a creak as it rose, and a thump as it fell.

I had tied a three inch strip of webbing between the shafts, which I used as a harness. It ran across my chest, and over my shoulder, and I leaned into it to gain control. The corrugations bumped the harness into my shoulder and sent the shock down to the shin, which was strained further because I was unable to tell at which angle to put down my foot. In spite of this, the going was better than I had dared to hope. Now that the leg was bandaged and had rested almost a day, it was not as painful, and I was able to manage the five miles to camp in two hours.

Though the landscape was flat, it seemed, both visually and from the effort it was taking to move the wheelbarrow, that I was continually walking up a hill, but when I looked back, it was as if I had just walked down one. The earth curved up and around me wherever I went, as if I were at the bottom of a dish, and no matter how far I travelled I could get no nearer the rim – like a spaceman hurtling, as he thinks, towards the edge of the universe, only to find it unfolding before him and closing in behind, so that he is always at the centre.

Heavenly bodies taunted me, encircling the crucible, performing their daily stunts of scorching and freezing, and bringing about the oddest sights. At mid-morning, when the ground became hot and the air wafted up in varied densities, the refracted light produced mirages: the horizon flooded in every direction so that the edge of the 'dish' was lapping with water. Towards noon, the mirage drew nearer, to about half a mile, as if I were on an island trapped by the in-coming tide. Later in the afternoon, it ebbed, and by about four o'clock it had disappeared.

More than once, a distant grey tower bobbed in the water. It wobbled and contracted, becoming shorter and fatter, before trembling into the yellow shape of the Land Rover. When it drove away over the ochre expanse, it broke into pieces and dissolved in the air.

Though mirages are natural phenomena, the illusion of my standing in a dish was an involuntary product of the imagination. The desert was flat, mile after mile. Its only feature was a scattering of red shale; as a reaction I began to superimpose pictures. Just as someone deprived of sound, sight and tactile stimuli will invent wonderful and sometimes horrific experiences, so I could not prevent my imagination from running away with itself. One minute I was a ploughman; the next I was scrambling to get out from under an interrogator's lamp. I was sailing the Pacific, or a character in a surrealist painting; often I was walking over the red shale past one football pitch after another, with goal-posts stretching as far as the eye could see, like white crosses over the fields of Arnhem.

These inventions not only relieved the boredom but gave escape from pain. At times I went almost mad, talking gibberish, pulling faces, and singing in mock Latin. In the presence of Mick and Paddy, I acted normally, but when I was alone, and especially in difficulty, the gates which allowed me to escape from convention were opened. The corrugations of the track were half-filled with grit so that the wheel lost momentum in each hollow and at times I thought of myself as an engine-driver, pushing my train back to the station, always careful not to trip over the sleepers. In saner times, I found myself watching the wheel. Small stones, sticking to the rim, became dislodged and at one point were tumbling down the curve as quickly as the wheel was rising, giving the appearance of effervescence. Now and then, I was brought back to reality by the bleached bones of a camel or a black coil of wire, the skeleton of an abandoned tyre whose rubber had perished.

Next day, to avoid the corrugations, I decided to walk parallel to the track but there were stones everywhere the size of golf balls. These made the wheelbarrow bounce and unless I hurried, the wheelbarrow easily toppled. I had to race to keep up the momentum but I was forced to rest five minutes in every twenty.

Just before noon, I began to feel ill and slumped exhausted over the wheelbarrow. My head was turned sideways, cushioned on an arm, my heart beat loudly, and the sun was hot on my back. Sweat trickled from my temple into my eye; I blinked and blinked again. Something colourful hovered in front of me. A butterfly was flapping around the wheelbarrow looking for a fragrance to match the colour of that great metallic flower. I guessed that she had been blown far from her oasis, and now there was no landmark other than the wheelbarrow, not a tree, not a blade of grass, not a ripple on the plain, nor a rock bigger than my fist. A moment later the wind lifted her away. She went in wavering loops, following the interminable stream of sand towards the coast of Senegal, sixteen hundred miles away.

By five-thirty, I had met up with the lads and, content at seventeen miles, stooped in the twilight to hammer home the twenty-eight pegs. I loved to stop for the night but dreaded the effort of making camp. Out from the wheelbarrow came bundles and boxes to place inside the tent along the walls, leaving room for the sleeping-bag down the middle. The tent-pole bag was torn, so I put it on one side with the sewing kit. Off came my robe, straw hat and boots, and on went my sweater, jacket, denim cap and suede shoes. I lay with my feet toward the open end of the tent, unfastened my canteen and boiled what was left of a cabbage I had bought in Adrar. It went down well, with dry bread to mop up the water. The food and rest gave me back my strength and I no longer felt ill.

I almost always cooked inside the tent, following the example of the Polar explorers – I figured that the danger was minimal. Moreover, it took twice as long to cook outside, with the wind often blowing out the light. Inside, the stove kept me warm while I cooked or whenever I made a mug of tea which was three or four times a night.

When I had eaten the first course of cabbage, and the second of meat pudding, potato and carrots, I poured cold water into my used billycan and put it on the lighted stove. I was about to prepare a dessert of mashed potato, flavoured with an Oxo cube. Just then, Mick and Paddy, who were sitting in the cab of the Land Rover, saw amber headlights flickering behind the northern horizon. They jumped out excitedly and I picked up my pen to record what they said.

'It's at least three miles away,' said Mick.

'I think it's more,' replied Paddy.

'I hope it's Brits. I'll bum some airmail envelopes from them.' (Mick wrote to his parents every day and had brought insufficient airmail envelopes. It was usual for him to weedle a few from any European who stopped.) 'There's two vehicles, not one,' he said. The water was getting hot and becoming clouded with the residue of the last course, so I crumbled two Oxo cubes into it and stirred.

'There's three, er, no. It's a convoy! It sounds like whoofers [diesel lorries] to me,' said Paddy.

'I hope it's not a military convoy after us,' said Mick. The labouring engines could be heard groaning like a battery of tanks. My torch showed small bubbles in the murky water on the base of the pan. The fragments of Oxo cube were dissolving into brown swirling streaks and the bubbles grew and began to rise.

'One, two, three, four,' Mick paused, 'five, six. They're cars,' he added excitedly. 'I'm going to put the Rover lights on. I don't want 'em mowing down the tents in the dark.' I stirred the potato powder into the liquid and would have begun eating but it was too hot.

The vehicles drew alongside and I could see their amber lights through the canvas and hear slamming doors and excited friendly voices. 'Geoff, are you coming out?' asked Paddy. 'Some of these people would like to meet you.' I put a lid on the dish, wrapped it in a towel and went out. Cars and small vans, with only disrepair in common, were head to tail, headlights burning, a few yards away. The party was French and German. Young men and a couple of women, one of whom was over fifty, stood in small groups chatting. Most were teachers bound for Gao in Mali. They were getting there the cheap way and combining adventure with the bonus of having their cars with them at the end. There was not a tent between them and some had no sleeping bag. They either slept in a car or on the ground with a blanket, though in two days they would be far enough south for the nights to be warm.

Paddy introduced me to the leader, a man of forty who earned his living taking convoys across the Sahara. I told him that we were leaving the present trail at Reggane and going through In Salah and Taman-rasset. 'I don't envy you going through Tam [Tamanrasset] in this weather,' he said. 'It's 1,700 metres up.'

'It'll be warmer by the time we get there. I've chosen that way because the longest distance without water is two hundred and fifty miles, compared with at least five hundred the way you're going.'

'Any idea how far Reggane is?' he asked.

'Sixty-three miles.'

'That will take us four hours, getting us in at midnight. There's a wall there that we can shelter behind.' Suddenly, the group burst into laughter. A young man was pushing the empty wheelbarrow – and not very successfully. The leader, anxious to press on, cleared his throat and shouted the order. Mick, who seemed to have disappeared, got out of the driving seat of the leader's car and a young attractive French woman emerged from the passenger side to stretch her legs. Mick's efforts had been rewarded. He ambled towards us smirking, tapping a packet of air-mail envelopes on his palm.

When they had gone, I settled down to the potato and made a mug of tea. We could hear the groan of their engines for so long that we thought more vehicles were approaching. In fact, we saw no one else until Reggane.

I mended the tent-pole bag and listened to another sermon before switching off my torch. I could not sleep but lay on my back staring at the blackness, listening to the wind and one of the lads snoring. Darkness twisted things. I was back in the post office at Adrar, empty-handed and imagining Joan to have died or to have found another man. Sleep came in snatches. I woke to manoeuvre a rock under the groundsheet, then to put cream on my burning ears, later to pull my knees up to my chin to get warm, then to eat some dates, and finally when I was called out by diarrhoea.

Long before dawn, I was propped on an elbow, with a warming mug of tea and a few verses of Romans. Then, as I gathered kit and loaded up, I watched the sky, no longer black but grey, as it was heated gently from below. Grey warmed into red like hot iron, then into pink, until the lower sky glowed like that above a blast-furnace at night. When the sun finally appeared, the reds and golds dispersed, swallowed up in daylight.

It was one of the best days I was to have. At the end of it, I was tired but glad, making camp after twenty-three miles, the farthest I had managed on or off tarmac. It had been an unspectacular grind with little let-up. My head had been thrust forward and eyes half closed. I lived outside myself, trying to forget the shin, and think only of the post office at Reggane.

After dark, I got under cover to cook my supper. Paddy was in the Land Rover cab and Mick was in their tent. We had not seen another vehicle all day. 'I can't stand all this traffic,' Mick said. 'We were stuck in a jam for an hour today. I'm going to ask the Minister of Transport to have traffic-lights put up on this stretch.' I heard Mick unzip his tent and get out. Then there was the continuous splash of water on the ground.

'I hope you're well away from my tent while you're doing that,' I said.

'Hey the Naffy wagon's here. What d'you want, Geoff?'

'Bottle of Scotch, please.'

'They're out of Scotch. Will gin do?'

Paddy was still in the cab. He often sat there in the early evening to read a book or map. Paddy and I shared the neurosis of spending longer than necessary calculating where we would be on what date if we maintained that day's speed. This time, the cab-door creaked open, there was a crunch as his shoes hit the ground, and there was excitement and humour in his voice. 'At twenty miles a day we should reach Tam by February thirteenth, and if you're not there by then, Geoff, we'll be there without you.'

'What, only February thirteenth! I should be there before then. My visa for Niger begins on my birthday, February the twenty-second. I want to be at the border by then and that's two hundred and fifty miles after Tam.'

Paddy climbed back into the cab and I unfolded a map. Reggane was forty miles away, with a bit of sand just before it, but nothing serious. I had to do twenty-three miles tomorrow and then, if I let the lads carry the wheelbarrow into Reggane on Friday, I could run the final seventeen miles.

When roads, buildings, telegraph-poles and trees are in view, it is easy to judge distances, but in the desert, where in the morning and evening there is not even a haze to blurr distant outlines, it is nearly impossible. Sometimes, especially when the sun was low and blinding, I could not tell whether a dark shape was a rock a hundred yards away or a crag at three miles.

It was always disappointing to sight the Land Rover and anticipate being in camp in a few minutes and then have an hour to walk. It was with the idea of learning to judge distances that I set out the next morning. The plan was to look back at intervals after leaving camp to see how long it took for various features of the Land Rover to disappear, so that I would know how much longer there was to walk when they reappeared in the evening.

After five minutes, the Land Rover looked a hundred yards away, but must have been four hundred. Every detail was clear except for the number-plate. Ten minutes seemed to make little difference, with the jerry-cans still discernible on the roof-rack. After twenty minutes, almost a mile away, the fine details had disappeared. It looked much smaller, but its outline and colour and the orange of the tent were still clear. Thirty minutes and the tent had gone. An hour and there was a speck of yellow on the horizon as tiny as an aphid. One hour and twenty minutes and it had slipped over the curvature of the earth, or so it seemed.

By two o'clock, I had walked fifteen miles and was sitting on the wheelbarrow forking out the last sardine, when Mick and Paddy arrived. Mick jumped down in his shoes and shorts, looking quite bronzed. 'Piece of cake, eh, Geoff?' he said, referring to the going underfoot.

Though it was easier than I could have hoped, my pride and self-pity would not admit it. I managed to restrain myself from snapping back, 'Piece of cake! You try pushing this thing fifteen miles in a morning! It's bouncing all over these stones and my leg's killing me, especially when I put my foot down unevenly, which is about every step. I'm stinging all over with sunburn and I can't even move my head to look at my wrist-watch without getting cramp in my neck and shoulders.' But I kept my thoughts to myself and said, 'It'll do me. If this is difficult, I should eat the easy bit after Reggane.'

'How many miles d'you reckon today, twenty?' asked Paddy, who was stripped to the waist and had a knotted handkerchief on his ginger mop of hair.

'No, twenty-three.'

'Well, you're doing the walking.'

'See you about five, then,' I said. And they drove off into another amazing wall of water.

My task *was* 'a piece of cake', comparatively. It was the best going I could hope to see, but just beyond that wall of water, minutes away, the ground became lacerated with gulleys, as if a maze of streams had scored the ground and had been filled with sand. Within a yard, the wheel had stuck and sunk six inches. The load, as heavy as three sacks of cement, seemed immovable. Leaning forward into the harness and pushing with all my might, I could not move. Eight miles further on were Mick and Paddy – I had two and a half hours before sunset to reach them.

A sustained push was useless. I tried rocking the wheelbarrow back and forth, then jerking. Finally I had it. With an almighty tug-of-war heave, with my back almost horizontal and shoulders pressed hard into the cross-bar, I crossed the first patch of sand. Then we rumbled over ten yards of hard ground to the next.

Time and again: Stuck! Stuck! Stuck! The land was not flat now but undulating, rising no more than a few feet in various shades of brown and gold as far as the eye could see. Every few yards there were depressions filled with sand, each of which took minutes to cross. Between them, the slightly higher ground was firm and unbroken.

For navigation, I had been lazy and followed the *piste*, which was now a trench of sand. After a while, it forked and pursued parallel courses. The worse the surface became, the more the *piste* divided, each trail trying to seek out better ground. The hard shale was now gone and the flat lake had become a choppy sea of sand and rock. The *piste* disappeared and I stood lost in a maze of tyre-tracks, which shot in every direction. I left the wheelbarrow, stood on a bulge of rock and shielded my eyes. To the east, across miles of barren brownness, there were dunes floating in an azure sky – another spectacular mirage. And yes, to the south, among the sand and rock, there were tyre-tracks converging. I made my way towards them, and found two trails running side by side through the sand. The one on the left seemed best. Lorry wheels had dug furrows in it, uncovering rock at the bottom. That lasted only a minute though, so I tipped the wheelbarrow on its side and hauled the dead weight to the second track, which proved even worse than the first. I could never tell how good the ground was until I had tried the wheelbarrow on it.

After an hour, I hurt all over. I wanted to lie down and die, but the thought of the situation at home was caught like a hook in my brain, pulling me against my will towards the post office at Reggane. By four o'clock, I knew from the morning's reckoning that I should have been able to see the Land Rover. The ground became firm for a few hundred yards and I ran, my eyes taking in every dot on the horizon, looking for that familiar yellow speck, but I missed seeing a sandy hollow right under my nose. I tripped and toppled into the dust.

There was sand everywhere between the knee-high crags, so I climbed on one of them for a better view. The evening 'tide' had gone out and I could see for miles. The track fizzled to nothing ahead and there was no sign of the Land Rover. I was lost!

8

THE REAPERS

In September 1974, there were no gowns to be seen in Cambridge. The students were not due for another month, though the streets and cloisters were crowded with tourists, who were outnumbered only by their cameras. I was walking a little quicker than the flow, past Bermuda shorts and floral shirts, making my way, with my briefcase, to the University Department of Biology to see John Larmuth, Director of the Desert Research Trust. The trust was researching into the possibilities of alleviating famine through cultivating desert. John Larmuth had tentatively offered the use of the trust's Land Rover for my trip and I was going to discuss this with him.

He was in his mid-thirties, tall and thin, with searching eyes and hair cropped like a Buddhist monk. Around his room were rock samples, a blackboard, office furniture and a tray of soil which was 'baking' under a fierce light. After introducing myself, I walked over to it. 'Simulating the desert?' I asked. 'The soil looks pretty poor.'

'You know, seedlings survive better in stony soil. They're kept cooler and don't dry out as quickly,' he said. He strolled over to the blackboard. 'Moisture retention is a key factor,' he said. 'The desert and the sea have more in common than poetic imagery. In the sea, living things fight to keep water out. In the desert, the problem is keeping it in. You've seen a gerbil haven't you?' I nodded. 'Well, it gets all its moisture from seeds and dew. If its breath were as humid as ours, it would die within days.' He made a drawing of a gerbil's mouth. 'The roof of the mouth is hard and rippled,' he went on. 'As it breathes out, the water vapour condenses on the cool, horny tissue. When it breathes in warm, dry air, the moisture on the roof of the mouth evaporates and is inhaled. The evaporation cools down the mouth in readiness for breathing out.'

'Well,' I said, 'I don't want to take too much of your time, so how about the Land Rover?' He motioned with his arm to the middle of the room.

'Have a chair while we talk.' We sat in two old, well-upholstered armchairs. 'What would you do if you couldn't get the Land Rover back because of floods?' he asked.

'Floods! Now that's hardly likely, is it?'

'You'd be surprised. When it rains, it rains!' I had no answer, and began to sink lower into the chair. Though I had worked out every detail for me and the wheelbarrow, I had not given much thought to the Land Rover. 'I'll tell you what,' he said. 'You can borrow it if you can find a guarantor. The Land Rover doesn't belong to me and I've got to make sure that those who've given money to the trust don't have it wasted.'

'I can't give that sort of guarantee. If we had anyone who could put up the money then we'd buy our own and resell it at the end.' As we talked, I felt that if I had pressed him he would have loaned it to me anyway, but the Land Rover was necessary for the research programme and it would have been irresponsible to put John's work at risk.

The remainder of my time with him was spent picking up tips on desert survival. 'The chief thing to remember,' he said, 'is that when you lose your fear you're in real danger.'

* * *

Now, after I had been walking for only seventeen days, I had almost forgotten those words. Having seen taxis north of Adrar, and then a couple of days ago, a convoy which had not so much as a compass, I had begun to think the desert not so terrible after all. I had become slack.

Because of the track, navigation had been easy and I had been leaving my sextant in the Land Rover. This sort of complacency could have cost me my life. Furthermore, the best map I had for this region was twenty-two miles to an inch. Though I had small scale maps at three inches to a mile for some areas they are not produced for all the Sahara, nor could I have afforded the hundred pounds they would have cost if they had been.

At four-fifteen, there was one hour of light left and still no sign of the Land Rover. The fatigue had been flushed away by fear. Fifteen minutes earlier, I could hardly walk; now I was running. I charged over rocks and taking a run at sand, found that the wheel would skate for short stretches. I drove hard, never allowing the momentum to drop. On and on, instinctively south, south-west, one eye on the ground, and the other on the angle of the sun. The last eight miles had been the worst up to that point, and yet I had gone faster than ever before.

I had food and water for days and Reggane was only twenty-five miles away, but I was terrified, with no control over my body. I was tired and thirsty and my shin was ablaze, but I could not stop: on, on, on – through a pool of sand – past one dead cow and then another – race across shingle to hit more sand and sink deep – turn backwards – heave, jerk, shout – firm ground again – race into sand – kick the wheelbarrow for its stupidity – stop, heave – trip and fall – get up and heave again – fall face down – spit sand – up and on again. And there was still no sign of the Land Rover.

The map showed Reggane to be off the main *piste*. Paddy would have seen the trail better than I. He often rode 'shot-gun' on the roof-rack. I was terrified that, while he had taken a branch off the *piste* towards the town, I might now be heading towards Mali, a waterless eight hundred miles away.

The desert was cut in all directions by sandy scars, and there were tyre-tracks everywhere but with no hint of general direction. I was now moving south-west, dazzled by the low sun. I refused to pray, telling myself that doing so would demonstrate a lack of confidence in God. This was no more than bravado since I charged blindly on. The ground was soft but fear ploughed the wheel through it, until at last I saw the Land Rover, silhouetted on a spit of amber.

The danger had passed; I no longer needed the overdrive. Muscles sagged. Blood drained from them. It had been impossible to stop my body from charging but now it was impossible to fight off the fatigue. Though I was floundering, I did not much care. My legs dithered weakly and I was breathless. Sweat was dripping from my nose and chin and streaming from under my arms. It seemed odd that my skin could be so wet and my mouth so dry. I drank three pints of water and then eased the wheelbarrow backwards onto firm ground and trundled on in the certainty of my safety. As I drew nearer, however, I was nagged by a feeling which was soon confirmed. What I could see was not the Land Rover but a rock. This time I could not have cared. There was no fear, only exhaustion, no flush of adrenalin, just acceptance.

The sun hung dazzlingly low, casting deceptive shadows. I could barely see ten yards because of the glare, and it was no use trying to look far ahead. I picked my way forward waiting for the sun to set. I would then pitch my tent and have the night to weigh up the situation.

Suddenly, I stumbled across flat, hard ground, a track so firm that it might have been paved. I did not see it until I was standing on it. Then, a few moments later, at twenty-five minutes to five, the trail dipped steeply for thirty yards, and there was the Land Rover at the bottom.

It was the usual evening of preparation before reaching a town – wash, shave, letters and tape-recordings. Mick was on form. He was getting into his sleeping-bag when he yelled, 'Oh, I've burnt my bum today . . . and if that fish and chip wagon doesn't come I'll tell him what he can do with 'em. Come on Sally Army! I want my hot pies!'

At seven-thirty next morning, I put on my running shoes and green army jeans and began jogging the eighteen miles to Reggane. It was a steeplechase over rock and sand, like crossing mussel beds when the tide is out. To make matters worse a kilogramme of oranges and documents bounced in the pocket on my left thigh, reviving pain in the shin which had almost healed.

At nine o'clock, after twelve miles, I came to a slippery escarpment, a cascade of sand tumbling five hundred feet to a plain which, in spite of a slight haze, I could see stretching some sixty miles south and west. Below, in the middle distance, buildings and palms lay in clusters several miles apart. Ahead, to the left, tin roofs glinted on another plateau, which rose at a distance of eight miles away. Pylons strode down from it, past a settlement and a water-tower on the plain due south of me and lost themselves in the haze to the west.

After glancing at the military map and checking with the compass, there was no mistaking Reggane. It was the tin roofs on the other plateau. I skidded down the escarpment in high spirits and made a bee-line for the town. The valley floor was sand embedded with coloured stones. Here and there logs surfaced from it like the inclined hulls of sinking ships. I stopped to dislodge one of them, hoping to carry it and make a camp-fire that evening. When I got my hands under the protruding portion I realized there was no point in heaving. I simply fingered the bark and examined the end grain. The colour was perfect, the bark wrinkled and grooved, but to the touch it was unmistakably stone, a monument to the savannah that once had been.

As the plain rose towards the plateau, I saw two poles in the ground; with a rag flapping from each they looked like wind socks. Drawing nearer, I realized that warm air had twisted their outline – they were two men using scythes, no, garden rakes. The two young Tuaregs wore the voluminous light-blue *ganduras* or smocks, baggy green trousers, indigo head-wraps and the long swords of their tribe. The Sahara is home to the Tuareg and they can be found right the way across it from Algeria to Nigeria. They have the reputation of being fearsome warriors. I had seen them in Kano clutching their swords as they slept in shop doorways where they were employed as night-watchmen. They were said to be fearless swordsmen and able to shoot a man between the eyes at a hundred paces. Here they were dragging pebbles off the sand into small heaps. They had neither transport nor water-bottle.

'*Bonjour*,' I said. 'How are you?'

They did not say a word but looked me up and down. If they viewed me with suspicion then I was much puzzled about them. It was the way they put me on the right track that made me wonder – guiding angels in the Bible have a habit of appearing as two young men.

'Reggane?' I questioned, pointing to the plateau. The taller of the two took his weight off his rake and pointed in the other direction.

'Reggane,' he said.

'No, Reggane,' I retorted, wishing to be sure and pointing to the plateau. He was irritated by my disbelief and pointed forcefully in the same direction as before, shouting, 'Reggane!' I followed the direction of his arm, and by ten-thirty, had arrived and was standing in an empty square of faceless mud buildings. Nothing moved. There was something odd. The men gathering stones and then this awful stillness. Out among the dunes, quietness could be tranquil, but here it was as eerie as an empty theatre. I fancied I could hear the cold laughter of market traders and the chant of children's games. Five pied wagtails landed silently on the white-hot sand on the far side of the square. Then the breeze caught a red and green flag on the Ministry of Agriculture to my right. Perhaps the two men I had met worked from there, harvesting stones!

Next to it was the post office and the door was wide open. I dashed, almost ran, inside but there was no one there. It was a small, dusky room and everything was wooden and old. Cardboard folders of stamps lay haphazardly within my reach. I could have helped myself. I leaned across the counter and tapped with a coin. 'Pardon!' I shouted. Out across the square, two men appeared and went into a doorway opposite. Could they be the ones I had met? Fear often played tricks with my perception and now it seemed as if I was losing my grip of reality.

Suddenly, the 'other-worldliness' vanished as a cheerful young man dressed in white shirt and trousers bounced in as if on springs. He clasped my hands and bowed rhythmically while greeting me in Arabic.

'Are you in charge?' I asked.

'Yes,' he said, releasing his grip.

'Have you any mail for me?' I asked, handing him my passport.

He began to read it page by page, showing amusement, but remaining on my side of the counter. Another man, unshaven and somewhat older, came in, his over-long robes trailing on the floor. The younger said in Arabic what I assumed to be, 'Hey, have you seen this?'

Together they thumbed through it. I was in no mood to stop them so long as I got my mail. A third Algerian wearing European dress walked in and stood behind the counter. His hooked nose and moustache looked like the plastic variety that would have come off with his thick-lensed spectacles. He never smiled, and moved slowly as if ill. '*Monsieur*, what do you want?' he asked.

It transpired that the other two had nothing to do with the post office and knew hardly any French. The clerk held my passport four inches from his face and strained to read it.

'Excuse me,' I said. 'It's upside-down.'

He pulled a drawer from under the counter and, taking letters from it unhurriedly, held each one up to his eyes. 'Nothing for you, *Monsieur*,' he said, putting the last letter back in place.

My envelopes for posting were lying in a heap on the counter. I scribbled on the back of the one to Joan, 'Reggane l0.1.75 – still received no mail. Hope to arr' In Salah 18.1.75.'

Reggane was a soulless place, little more than a hamlet inhabited by a handful of people and the wind. There was a bar with no booze and a store, of sorts, where we bought some of almost every item we recognized, including carrots, processed cheese and chocolate, which tasted like cocoa-flavoured sugar. Reggane's salvation was its bakery, petrol-pump and water supply – an eighteen inch diameter hole with a stream at arm's length below. By now Mick and Paddy had arrived and we took turns, along with an old man and a little girl, to scoop out basins of water.

The Land Rover dropped me off on the edge of the town, surprisingly on a tarmac road, and I arranged to meet the lads nine miles further on. It was a pleasant afternoon and my thoughts were on In Salah one hundred and eighty miles away.

There are two chief routes south through the Algerian Sahara, each about two hundred miles from the other. One begins at Algiers, and the other at Oran. Reggane was on the route from Oran, and we were about to transfer to the route from Algiers, along a one hundred and eighty mile dog-leg. Using sections of two routes made the journey longer but minimized the distance between wells.

In Salah would be the biggest town for a thousand miles. There we hoped to buy fruit, meat, sugar, sand-ladders and inner tubes. At In Salah we would leave the north-easterly dog-leg, no longer with the wind in our faces, and join the trans-Sahara route from Algiers, along with tankers for Tamanrasset, and tourists for West Africa and beyond. It was a beautiful thought and we spent hours talking about it.

The sand took up many different colours to the right, while high up on the left was a cliff-face – the wall of a plateau – where the rock had been whitewashed and hollowed out as someone's home. I trundled along the valley, keeping the curve of the plateau to my left and watching the distant Land Rover, which seemed to be going too far south. According to the map we were supposed to leave the road and take an easterly track up the plateau. Since the scale was twenty-three miles to an inch, it was possible that a deviation of two or three miles would not be marked, but that could not account for the tarmac. We had been told there was none on our route. Another mile revealed a track going up to the plateau and a sign pointing straight ahead to 'Hamouda' – a village which was not on any of the maps. I guessed that in the absence of a sign to In Salah the lads would have kept going towards Hamouda, so I followed.

To the right, there were placards in French saying, 'Keep to the road. Military exercises in progress.' Beyond them, two grey Land Rovers chased each other in clouds of dust. To the left, barbed-wire coils enclosed a deserted barracks.

I was contemplating going back to Reggane, but if the map was wrong, then that would mean that I would have to walk back this way. Just then, a tanker drove up from the south and the driver confirmed my suspicions. I was going through a military zone towards the Tenezrouft route and Mali. The track I wanted was unmetalled, three miles behind me. It branched off opposite a small village, a satellite of Reggane, almost where I had begun walking. As I turned back, I regretted not having asked the driver if he had seen our Land Rover. There was not much hope of sending a note with a southbound traveller. The tanker was the only vehicle I had seen all day.

The first sign of the village was the graveyard. There were no walls, just rough stones the size of dinner-plates marking each grave. No flowers, no marble vases, just empty plastic buckets and washing-up bowls. Beyond the graveyard was a jumble of dwellings and a school, a rectangular building with a tin roof. On the other side of the road, a sign nailed to a wooden stump pointed up the escarpment and read, 'In Salah'. It was easy to miss, especially with the village to divert one's attention.

I trudged over the soft earth, in among the houses, and stopped outside the one-room school, where a crowd of boys had gathered. There was a moped leaning against a mud wall a few feet away. 'Whose is that?' I asked. There was a brief silence. 'Don't you speak French?'

'A little,' said a small voice. 'But look, our headmaster, he speaks it well.' Along came a young, athletic black African in a red track suit and white plimsolls. Instead of explaining what I was doing, I gave him details of the expedition typed out in French. He sat beside me on the wheelbarrow, smoking a cigarette and reading. Then I told him that my friends had gone off in the wrong direction and that I was willing to pay the owner of the moped for taking a message to them.

It took a long time for us to reach an understanding. He wanted to know how I knew that they were nine miles towards Mali and seemed to be bothered that I was only guessing. 'What happens if they are not there? Is he to drive on and if so, how far? Does he get paid even if he doesn't find them?'

Eventually, we came to an agreement and the headmaster sent a boy into a nearby house to get the owner of the moped. He was a slightly-built student called Abdulla, here on teaching practice. His clothes were better suited to the air-conditioned discothèques of Algiers. After a brief conversation with the headmaster, he zipped up his brown leather jacket and pulled his head-wrap across his face. A few moments later, he was pop-popping south with a note for Mick and Paddy in the back pocket of his corduroy jeans. I had suggested in the note that, as it was then three-fifteen, rather than their breaking camp, one of them should drive back and take me to where they were for the night and back to the village next morning.

I sat on the wheelbarrow and sank my teeth into a fresh loaf. Dry bread was the norm. The hungry-eyed children pushed nearer. 'Give me a present,' said one of them. The words were scarcely out before one of his taller companions clamped a hand round the back of his neck and with a dusty, unshod foot kicked his buttocks, exposed through his torn shorts. The bully threw his victim to the ground and shouted arrogantly,

'Give *me* a present.'

'What sort?'

'Money.' Then others joined in.

'A pen, please.'

'Sir, a pencil.'

'Some bread.'

'A book, please.'

'Yes, a book.' I jumped off the wheelbarrow and pulled out the only literature I had to spare – details of the expedition in English.

'These are all I have, but they are in English.' They snatched them from my hands while the boy who had asked for bread asked again. I gave him a fist-full.

'Please sir, a pen,' said another, followed by a chorus of the same cry. I had one ball-point pen with me and a few in the Land Rover. I took the pen from the wheelbarrow and pointed with it to a pylon by the road, a hundred yards away.

'The first boy to reach that pylon gets the pen.' Only three boys understood and I got them to explain in Arabic to the rest. Each stood at the ready, one eye on the pylon, the other on my raised arm. Suddenly, a man, as if mad, ran among them like a fox among chickens, snatching and swiping the air with hands and feet. The children dispersed in seconds and the man, breathless, pulled his hood back over his head and turned to me.

'I'm sorry about the children,' he said. 'They're a terrible nuisance.'

'But I like them,' I protested. It took several minutes to gather them back and put them under starter's orders. A heavily-built boy without shoes shot into the lead in his red nylon socks. He kept ten yards in front of the pack, his robe inflated to twice his size. Then, proudly and smiling, he slowly walked back for the presentation, his friends dancing round him patting him.

'*Merci, Monsieur*,' he said, removing the pen's blue top and writing on his palm.

'Give *me* a pen,' asked the bully with a scowl. Just then, the Land Rover caught our attention and we all turned towards the road.

I was not angry or upset so much as concerned by the lads going so far in the wrong direction. Not only had it been obvious from the map that they were ninety degrees off course but they had been on tarmac for nine miles after being told that the track in In Salah was dirt from its start. Mick still seemed to be looking for an excuse to return home, so I chose not to make an issue of the blunder. In any case, next day we suffered a blow which almost put a premature stop to the walk.

We had driven back to the village and had just turned off the road on to the In Salah track. Mick and I were sitting beside Paddy, who was driving, when there was a loud bang. We were thrown forward against the dashboard as the Land Rover crashed to a halt. Paddy jumped out and seconds later leaned into the cab through the open doorway. 'It's the rear off-side wheel. There's an eighteen inch split in the inner tube and,' he paused, 'you're not going to like this, the bolts holding the split rim have all sheared. The wheel's clean in two.'

'What does that mean?' I asked.

'The wheel's made in two parts and bolted together so that you can change a tyre without levers. All the bolts have snapped.' Mick and I jumped out and joined Paddy, who was by now crouching meditatively over the broken wheel. It looked like a simple repair job to me and I thought the gloom on Mick's face was part of his act.

'It can be mended, can't it?' I asked.

'No,' said Mick. 'Not without high tensile bolts and we don't have any. I think we're gonna have to bin it.'

'No,' Paddy snapped. 'We don't bin *anything* until In Salah on the *return* trip. It'd be suicide to drive without a spare. We can fix it temporarily but it'll take an hour.'

Some of the children came running over from the village. Mick turned, waving his arms wildly at them. 'Clear off! Buzz off! Get lost!' he shouted. They had failed to understand my French but they understood his English and 'buzzed off'.

Including those on the trailer, there were seven intact wheels. With Mick's help, Paddy set about removing one bolt each from five of them and bolting together the sheared rim. Having five instead of six bolts on some of the wheels was a risk we did not like taking. The roof-rack alone carried half a ton of water, fuel and spares, and the Land Rover was fully loaded inside to the extent that the leaf springs were flattened. Mick and Paddy were careful drivers and it was hard to imagine what further precautions they could take to prevent the even weaker rims from shearing again.

It was unthinkable to begin walking before knowing the repair was complete, so I sat glumly on the wheelbarrow which we had lifted off the trailer. It was half past ten in the morning, twenty-four hours after arriving in Reggane and I had not yet left. A day longer to wait for a letter! A day longer to Kano! The army had said I would manage no more than fifteen miles a day. I secretly hoped for twenty-one. In spite of only thirteen miles on the first day, nine on the second, a day's rest at Adrar, and another here at Reggane, the average was still eighteen.

I ate three small carrots and was half-way through a can of sardines when I noticed a sea shell in the sand almost beneath me. A tourist probably dropped it, I thought, but when I looked closer there were more of them, far too many to have been left by a traveller. I was excited at the thought of finding fossils eight hundred miles from the sea, but I chastized myself for being so stupid. In an area with such rapid changes in temperature as to erode hard rock into sand, soft shells would not have survived. For a few moments, I wondered if the sand and shingle had been brought from the coast to be used as a road surface, then I doubted my sanity in thinking that anyone would bring sand to the Sahara. Besides, other than tyre marks, there was nothing man-made about the track. I strode well away from the Land Rover but there were cockle shells everywhere and a few needle whelks, like minute unicorns' horns less than half an inch long. When I arrived back at the Land Rover I met Abdulla, the student teacher, who had been attracted by the breakdown. He was in the most Arab of all poses, sitting on his heels, his feet flat on the ground and his arms folded across his knees. 'Abdulla,' I said, pointing to the ground, 'who brought these shells here?'

'Nobody,' he said, not taking his eyes off Mick working on the wheel. 'They are everywhere. This area was under the sea. Later it was forest. Not like it is now; it's not rained for twenty years.' His voice wandered on in the dull, matter-of-fact tones of someone describing his own environment. He was far more interested in Mick working on the wheel. He sounded as enthusiastic as I might have been if talking about paving stones in Manchester.

The last time that sea had covered that area was between a hundred and a hundred and thirty million years ago. I picked up a shell to take a closer look. It looked as if it had just been brought home by Susan from Blackpool. My mind wandered. If those shells had been preserved then the sand and shingle in which they lay could not have been eroded by the sun and wind. If that had been the case then the much softer shells would have disintegrated first. The sand, shingle and shells were a prehistoric beach, preserved somehow over millions of years – and it took a breakdown for me to discover it.

9

THE OMEN

It was a still, warm Sunday morning on 12 January, the twentieth day of my walk. The low sun touched the gentle white curves of the plateau with gold and bathed them in undeserved serenity. The wheelbarrow was on its side, half the contents spilled out, and I was picking myself up. It was the eleventh or perhaps only the tenth time I had fallen that morning. 'Let me give up,' I screamed to heaven. 'Why won't you let me give up?' Yet it was not God that kept me going but my critics. I could hear one of them, an old paratrooper who had fought in the desert.

'*You'll* never make it. You've no idea!' I had to prove him wrong. Yesterday, after the breakdown, those fourteen miles had been bad, but this was worse. It looked good to the eye, it felt firm underfoot, the Land Rover had no problems, but the wheelbarrow seemed designed to plough a furrow. It looked like shingle but it was a sprinkling of pebbles on compacted sand.

I was part way across a basin between two outcrops of rock. The wheelbarrow had been stuck, almost to the axle, but when it came free I toppled with it. I tried to dust the grit off my forearm where it adhered to the sweat. Then I swung on the end of the shaft and righted the wheelbarrow. The way ahead was over a mound of sand. I waded over it, trying to drag the four hundredweight on its side, and when all else failed, I beat it with my fist, kicked and cursed and pleaded with it to try harder. I was whipped on against every natural instinct.

It was all the harder because I could have given up at any moment. I was not a man fighting to live but I was a boxer on the ropes, praying for a miracle that would save him from almost certain defeat. To throw in the towel would mean the end of misery, a shower, clean sheets, good food and reunion with my family after the months I had spent in training camp. But I doggedly believed that things would change, that they could only get better, yet when I reached the outcrop I wailed with despair. Exhausted and confused, I came, cap in hand, busking for help and half sang, half cried 'What a friend we have in Jesus'. On the other side was another dust bowl identical to the last.

I had to retrace my steps and double back around areas that proved too soft only to find that everywhere else was as bad. My method was to look ahead as far as the eye could see, work out the route mentally, then, leaving the wheelbarrow, test the ground in small sections and mark the way with my feet. This meant that I walked further than recorded. For the most part, the Land Rover milometer was my measure, but there was never a day when I did not walk more. In trying to keep the wheelbarrow upright as I walked, I moved along a wavy line. Furthermore, I often took detours to avoid sand which the Land Rover had gone through using its four wheel drive. On one occasion, when the Land Rover was only half a mile away, I had to go three miles to reach it. Perhaps this was rough justice for my having ridden that one mile on the workmen's lorry on the sixth day.

It took an hour to cross the basin, jerking the wheelbarrow backwards along the maze I had marked out. When it was easy enough to push forward, I was almost horizontal, with my nose an inch from the wheel, which paddled sand into my face. On soft ground, the familiar rattle was replaced by the occasional noise of tearing metal. Sometimes the wheelbarrow was stuck so firmly that the aluminium honeycomb began to rip from the rim as I pushed.

When I got to higher ground, I sat on a long, flat slab of white rock in a salmon-pink sea. A green bush billowed from a crack in it like a sail. I and my tracks were the only sign of life. The *piste*, marked by oil drums, was completely out of sight, over a mile away to the north. I peeled a carrot and opened a can of sardines. Sunday was the only day when Joan's routine was sufficiently fixed for me to know what she was doing. As I began to eat, her lunch would have been in its final stages and Susan, our three-year-old, anxious to leave the table. A mince dish with potatoes and fresh vegetables! Apart from the tins of Hunter's puddings, I had not tasted meat since I started the walk.

Sweat began to dry and strength seeped back into my limbs. I was relaxed and much recovered when a nomad appeared from behind a crag fifty yards away and looked down on me. By now I was eating some of the bread from Reggane. It was rock-hard and dry as a biscuit. Bread never went mouldy in Algeria, which meant that so long as I was prepared for a good chew, I could always buy enough to last to the next village.

The nomad was standing quite still, looking down on me. I was expecting his camels to follow him and understood that he would not come further before they were in view. He seemed familiar, so familiar indeed that it took time to sink in. He wore a white robe and hat like mine, a little odd as they were of Nigerian design. Something prickly crawled up my spine to the back of my neck, and my stomach tightened.

Metal-frame spectacles! Puma training shoes! Moustache! It's me! I slapped my face and pinched my thighs till they hurt.

The wraith turned slowly to his right and disappeared behind the crag. I put down my lunch and followed him in frantic pursuit. The sand where he had stood was undisturbed, and there was neither sight of him nor his camels. Having felt pain, I knew I was not dreaming, and I wondered if I had gone mad, though the fact that I had hallucinated, and had shown myself to have such a naïve view of God, would be sufficient proof for some. After the shock, I was warmed by the idea that the visitor was Jesus or an angel, and then terrified by the thought that it was an omen of my death.

Whether the ground actually became firmer or whether I was spurred on by fear I do not know, but I began to make better progress. I picked up reasonable speed and had just about regained my composure when a hand appeared on my left shoulder from behind! The wraith had caught me up. I gathered my courage, and turned, prepared to look myself in the face. Instead, I saw a smiling, though breathless, New Zealander.

'You walk at some speed,' he said. 'What a job I've had catching you. We read about your trip in the paper before we came on holiday and now we're on our way back through Reggane. Your friends told us to follow the *piste* and we'd be sure to meet you head on. We'd gone miles, then saw your tracks going in the opposite direction, so we doubled back.'

'Yeah, the *piste* was too churned up. I've been south of it all day.'

'I stopped just behind you but before I could get out of the car you were well away. I shouted but you didn't hear, so I had to chase you.'

'Would you mind doing a deal? I'll give you two oranges if you let me take your photo.'

'Yes, but you don't have to give me the oranges. You can take the picture anyway.'

'Come to think of it I'd have given you the oranges even if you'd said no.' He pointed over his shoulder with his thumb. 'My camera's in the car. I'll only be a minute.' A minute or two later he drove up in a battered English saloon car with a bumper and two door handles missing. His wife, four-year-old son Nicky, and baby were inside. I would never have risked travelling with a family in such a car.

'It's not mine,' he said, getting out. 'Mine's too good for the desert. I've swapped it for a couple of weeks. Mine's up north with a friend.' His attractive wife got out wearing too little for my ease. Looking in her direction was an embarrassment. Every time she spoke, I was forced to look and was conscious of staring. Nicky held a beer bottle out of the rear window.

'Look what I've got,' he said. 'A vase.' I had seen hundreds, perhaps thousands, just like it, sticking out of the ground, but I had never stopped to look at them. Dark-green and pear-shaped, it was shiny on the side that had been buried, but the exposed parts had been 'frosted' by the blast of sand.

Moments later they had taken my picture and were on their way. Their danger was greater than mine. Engine failure north of Reggane and they might not be found alive.

By the yellow light of weak batteries I wrote: 'Today maximum effort, minimum progress.' It had been a relief to reach camp but had taken all the will-power I could summon to put up the tent and cook a meal. I had wanted to curl up in my sleeping-bag on the ground. The fact that food and water were running out due to slow progress, demoralized me still further. There was no chance of supply before the village of Aulef el Arab, forty-two miles away.

When the jobs were done, I switched off my torch and lay on my back listening to a gerbil skidding up and down the tent under the fly-sheet. Mick and Paddy were rummaging in the back of the Land Rover. 'Shine that torch over here, will you? It's like Slack Alice's side-show. Roll on In Sha-la-la. I'm gonna give it the big lips when I get in those bars. I wish that Watney's van would hurry up.'

'Never mind your Watney's van! Where's my *Penthouse*?' moaned Paddy. I was in no mood for jokes either. The vision of my ghost was playing on my mind. I was uneasy in the dark and would have turned on the torch except that after only one fifth of the journey I had used half my batteries. I would buy candles at In Salah.

I was comforted by the little natural light that seeped through the canvas. I could just see my hand when I held it out. I rubbed it over my face, fingering the stickiness. With only two gallons of water left there was no chance of washing and I would have to cut my consumption by half. I would eat tinned vegetables, being sure to drink the water in which they had been canned, and I would conserve body fluid by eating little or no protein. No sardines, meat, beans or oats until Aulef. Even after Aulef, the only food I had with any meat content, the meat puddings, and beans and sausage, were down to a dozen tins each. That would mean more wretched soya protein and oats. I slept badly and had a dream that was to confirm my fears about the ghost. I was arrested for riding a bicycle without a rear light; I woke as an enraged policeman took me by the throat.

Psychic awareness ran in my blood. It was an affliction rather than a gift, and I was to be healed of it two years later by what I believe was the power of Christ. In the past, when members of my family had dreamt of policemen, it had meant that someone was going to die. It was significant that the policeman had gone for *my* throat. It seemed that a malevolent spirit was out to get me. I wondered if I were going mad. God seemed remote but I appealed for his protection and received a measure of assurance, though I felt that I was followed by an evil presence. It was as if I were surrounded by snarling dogs held back by chains. There was always the fear that a chain would snap or that I would step too near.

I got up feeling bilious and with a burning headache, wobbling from the previous day's struggle, as if I were finding my legs after a long illness. I cut through shallow, sandy hills, but the struggle was anaesthetized by day-dreams. I was pushing the wheelbarrow in our church's annual street parade, the 'Whit Walks'. In front of me, two teenage boys were carrying a floral tableau with the words 'God is Love' written in pink carnations, and little girls dressed like bridesmaids were holding the ribbons attached to it. At the head of the procession, the Burnage Silver Prize Band was playing 'Onward Christian Soldiers'.

I was still conscious of the desert upon which this scene was superimposed. My parents and Joan were on the crowded pavement near an ice-cream cart and a streamer seller. Near them, one of our neighbours, with her hair in curlers and wearing her pinafore, leaned on her broom. 'You're doing very well,' she shouted, 'but don't you think you've had enough? We're all very proud of you. Why don't you give up? Four hundred miles isn't bad. No one can call you a failure.'

'Don't listen to her,' cried Terry, the young bus-conductor from next door. He was at the kerbside, in uniform, ticket-machine and all. 'Keep going for Heaven's sake. Don't give up now.' My conflicting thoughts argued with each other from pavement to pavement.

'Why don't you come home?'

'Get a move on! Get those knees up!'

'Are you all right?' asked a quieter, more immediate voice. 'Can I help?' Two Frenchmen were standing on the sand beside their little van.

'I'm OK, thank you,' I said.

'Your friends asked me to measure how far you have come. Nearly five kilometres,' said one of them. I remember little about him except that he had a black beard flecked with grey, and gave me oranges. As he was driving away I noticed a bottle jutting from the sand near where his van had been. I pulled it free and found it to be sand-frosted and pear-shaped, like the one Nicky had shown me. A present for Joan.

By then the worst of the day was over and things became easier, as I later recorded:

Frenchman stopped. Black/grey beard, kind eyes. Told me I'd come 5 kilometres. Three miles in three hours. Sang 'Hallelujah Chorus' and the Rolling Stones' 'You can make it if you try'. Stopped at 1100 for dates and an orange. Nothing to drink all morning as yet. Approaching the crags we've seen for a couple of days. Undulating scenery, sandy patches. Occasionally would hear the cart rumble as the ground became firm. Thanked God I could see all my friends, relatives, all the old ladies, Joan and the kids in my daydreams. Felt v. contented but tired. 1230 lunch, carrots, dates, dry bread. Boys drove past 7¾ miles in 5 hours. I said make it 14. After lunch going progressively easier, went back on to *piste*, sandy but rocky at bottom of tyre-tracks. For an hour huge cloud came and covered sun. Whose prayer was that? Collected four sand-frosted bottles. Shoulder chafed by strap. Also difficult to look down at watch. When I move my head awful neck cramp. Socks and shoes full of sand. Kept on stopping to empty them. Came between two crags, blackish sand. When I saw L.R. today at finish I yelped for joy. Arrive at camp 1545 but completely knocked out. Opened can of mixed veg, used water to steam the pudding Paddy gave me at Reggane. Now using same water to heat veg' and carrots. Will now drink it. Glad of arriving early, need light for writing. Thankful that worst is over. Should reach Aulef day after tomorrow . . . Diarrhoea embarrassing. Written letters and report. Long chat to Mick thr' tent walls. Says they've enough food. Now try to sleep. 2200 hours.

I woke at two o'clock lying on my kit and again at half-past three, doubled across the tent. Diarrhoea, which I had now had for five days, finally drove me from my bed at six-thirty. The day was the easiest since Reggane and I came to camp after twenty miles feeling strong, with Aulef only two hours away. Mick was standing naked drying himself, his yellow washing-up bowl at his feet. 'Don't do that to me,' I said. 'Get some clothes on. I've not seen the wife for a month.'

'I couldn't give two monkeys,' he said, making ballet leaps out of sight behind the Land Rover.

After putting up the tent, I sat outside, took the bandage off my shin for the last time, and undressed, before washing myself with a mug of water. Sweat had made my skin sticky, and had glued rivulets of sand to my spectacles. It had so impregnated my string vest that when it had dried I almost succeeded in standing it up like a birdcage.

It was twilight and a brilliant new moon was gliding down the bright end of the sky, followed by a cascade of stars. Everything – wind, sand and stray paper bags, disappeared over that western horizon. Just my luck to be travelling east.

At dawn, the canvas hung still. I had just woken and could hear my pulse. The red second hand was coming up to six-thirty, 14 January, and

I was counting thirty-eight beats a minute, slower than ever, half the rate of two years ago. I had never been fitter or stronger.

Within half an hour of breaking camp, I came over the brow of a hill – compacted earth with pockets of drifted sand. On the other side, the track dropped sharply for a quarter of a mile where, to its right, was a dome of sand about 150 yards in diameter. Around its base, palm-trees were growing and there were a few houses built of clay. A sign by the side of the *piste* showed it to be Timoken, an unmapped hamlet, though there was no sign of any people. Soon afterwards, I stocked up with the sweet-tasting water of an oasis, the banks of which were encrusted with salts and shaded by palm-trees.

The most difficult leg this side of the half-way mark was over. As I walked, I began to dance and improvise a song: 'They said you'd never make it, la, la, la.' It escaped my notice, and was to my embarrassment, that the Land Rover was driving alongside. Paddy's ginger mop was poked out of the window.

'We'll go into Aulef,' he said. 'You carry on towards In Salah and we'll see you between half-eleven and twelve.' The Land Rover turned right and after half a mile disappeared under spinach-green palms. I followed tyre-tracks north for a couple of hours until they fizzled out. The traffic that had caused the furrows a mile back could not have come this way.

I checked the map against what I could see. It seemed to tally. The plain was composed of salmon-coloured powder. It gradually rose to my left, but remained level ahead as far as distant, hazy mountains. I went on, confident of my compass, but becoming less so, and found myself in the middle of a disused airfield, among landing markers, gutted buildings and a wrecked radar scanner. It was already half-past twelve and unlikely that the lads had taken three hours buying bread. I had lunch and then sat on the wheelbarrow swatting flies, neither willing to go further out of my way, nor to return, just in case I was on the right track. Had I been in a vehicle I could have gone back, but on foot it was not worth risking the wasted energy.

Half-past one and the breeze carried a faint vibration, almost too low-pitched to be heard. I surveyed every inch of the horizon but the sound died, leaving me to pin my hope on every rustle of the wind. The faint drone returned. It was like the sound of a tractor ploughing on the next farm. I shook my sand-filled ears by the lobes and listened. Nothing, except the hum of a dozen flies. I popped the red plastic thermometer in my mouth and sat checking the map. Being sure I was on course did not convince me I was going the same way as everyone else.

That was one of the problems of using the *piste* and a sextant. The desert routes were well worn and usually easily followed. Navigation by the sun and stars almost always took the same course as the tyre-tracks. Now that they appeared to diverge a problem had arisen.

I was not, at that moment, too worried about being lost. I could have navigated to In Salah, regardless of the *piste*, unless I stepped on a cobra or got my throat cut, but it was no use getting there alone. I yelled at screaming pitch, 'Mick, Paddy, where the hell are you?' Inactivity fed my anxieties. There had been sufficient hardship to take my mind off Joan, but as I sat there alone and well rested, I could not help worrying.

For a few seconds, the wind picked up, stirring the dust. A tangled ball of dried grass raced back towards Aulef like a whippet bound for home. The noise returned and grew louder. The Land Rover was pitching and rolling over the southern brow like a small seagoing craft. Paddy jumped from the cab, his knotted handkerchief white against his reddened skin. 'D'you reckon we're on the right track, Geoff?'

'We're going in the right direction but I don't know where the *piste* has got to.'

'We can't be far off. Let's bash on. You've done thirteen. How many more?'

'Six. Anyway, what kept you?'

'The law,' said Mick. 'We had forms to fill in, *and* he touched us for fags into the bargain, *and* we had to get water from the well.'

The *piste* soon returned. In fact we had never lost it. There had been such a wide expanse of firm ground that a trench had never been worn. Having reached Aulef and taken on water, that night was a pit stop. My grease gun had broken, so Paddy used his to service the wheelbarrow. I washed my billycans for the first time since Reggane, and cleaned the kit and groundsheet with disinfectant. By ten-thirty I was in the tent mending my shorts.

'You should have seen the depth of that well today. Must have been a couple of hundred feet deep,' said Paddy from his sleeping bag.

'Yeah, *and* we had to fork out fags for the water. I can't wait to meet an Arab on the Underground asking the way to go. I'll tell him. I've gotta get my own back. I did it once with a Kraut I met on Piccadilly Underground. I was just home from Germany and he asked me the way. I sent him right in the opposite direction. I know it was silly, stupid and childish, but, boy, I got a kick out of doing it. Roll on In Shal-la-la. Where's that fish and chip wagon? This is the second time he's missed. D'you reckon we'll hear anything about the visas at In Salah, Geoff?'

'I doubt it.'

'NFI! NFI! I wish those buggers at Bulford would pull their fingers out.'

'They said they'd send the visas to Tam, but what bothers me is how they can do that. The visa has to be stamped in your passport, and they can't do that while you've got it.'

'NFI!'

'What's NFI mean?' I asked.

'The "N" stands for "not" and the "I" stands for "interested". Please yourself what the "F" stands for. Anyway, if there's no visa I'm gonna live it up for a couple of days, then put me foot down and not take it off till I get to Gib. What's Tam like anyway?'

'Never been, but they say there's loads of hotels, bars, Turkish baths and that sort of thing. Americans fly in, have a shilling camel ride and go home saying they've done the Sahara.' We talked until the early hours, and consequently I overslept. I set off to the sound of Mick trying to tune into his sports programme. All he could get was jamming noises.

Things went well for me, though. It was my best day for a week across wastes of compacted sand and grit. There was no sign of life or vegetation, though the evenness of the landscape was interrupted here and there by low hills and crags. The going was good and in the morning an Arab gave me a soft fresh loaf the size and shape of a strong man's forearm. The afternoon was cool and easy under a patterned lace curtain of cloud. It would have been perfect if half a gallon of water had not leaked into my rolled-up sleeping-bag.

That evening, when I was putting up my tent and preparing my meal, Mick was singing and seemed exceptionally cheerful. 'What about that then, Geoff?' he said. 'City drew two–two with Manchester United in the League Cup semifinal!' I was unable to share his joy, not particularly because my home team had been held to a draw, but because I fell headlong into the tent, throwing a pan of boiling rice everywhere.

The following day took me over more stark hills and across empty plains and plateaux. When I was half way up an escarpment, I saw a signpost at the top, too distant to read. It was the free-standing sort that might have stood outside a country pub. In getting to it, even using the zigzag technique, I fell repeatedly. Time after time my boots lost their grip and the load pushed me backwards down the scree. The robe had tripped me each time I had stooped low enough to exert sufficient force, so I had taken it off. The sun took advantage of my bare skin and drew from me rivers of sweat. If ever I needed a country pub it was now. Yet, as I inched forward, the sign became clear. It read, 'The White Horse'. I was reluctant to trust my senses but the sign was unmistakable. I would order a pint of cold beer.

As I came over the brow, there was nothing but a windswept plateau. Some joker had daubed the pub sign on the reverse of a notice which looked back the way I had come. It read in French, 'Dangerous Cliff'. I smiled, mopped my face, and sat on a rock to toast myself with two pints of chlorinated water. Roll on In Sha-la-la! I could hardly wait to get in those bars.

The plateau was a vast wilderness of sand. There were many tracks all going the same way, each searching for a firmness absent from the rest. In the quest for solid ground, I struggled from one parallel route to another until I was stuck, north of them all. The going looked even worse ahead, so I left the wheelbarrow and scouted around. I felt liberated without the load, as if I could fly, and I found the cruel surroundings suddenly beautiful. In the hot, quivering air, the bright-peach floor was rippling like canvas, and the sun was bouncing like heavy rain at my feet. No longer the rattle of metal. Every scratch and whisper was loud like the crackles in the silent moments of a film. Whistling nostrils, the gentle swish of the robe and a crunching like snow beneath my boots.

As I turned to go back, the wheelbarrow was far away, perhaps half a mile, the black and yellow stripes just discernible. It had been painted that way to make it stand out – the opposite of camouflage. A tiny, forsaken insect. Behind it, across an empty mile, a ridge looked at itself in a mirage lake. Beyond that a cloudless sky.

Suddenly I felt all alone. My metal companion, my life support, was no longer beside me. Just me and open space. The vastness was closing in, choking me like asthma. It was agoraphobia but felt like claustrophobia. I jogged, sprinted towards my inanimate friend and when I got there I was so relieved I wanted to cry. Camels, vehicles, even wheelbarrows give equanimity in the desert. Without them there is little to which to relate. There are many tales of madness overcoming travellers whose cars have broken down or whose camels have died.

After two hours, I reached firmer ground but became concerned that I could not see a four hundred foot escarpment which, according to the map, should have been less than a mile ahead. All I could see was the blue sky and miles of undulating grit scored by tyre-tracks. When the Land Rover drew up, Paddy was looking perplexed. 'Where's this escarpment we're supposed to be approaching?' he asked.

'I did wonder,' I said, 'but it won't be the first time the map's been wrong.'

'With a scale of twenty-two miles to an inch, the escarpment should be massive,' he added.

'I know,' I said. 'It should be filling the skyline. The other map shows the *piste* dipping south through a village. No sign of that either.'

'Nothing much we can do, except bash on,' he said.

'How's the craps, Geoff?' Mick chipped in.

'About the same.'

'I've got 'em,' he added, 'and Paddy was sick during the night.'

'Well, there's plenty of pills in the Land Rover.'

'I'm OK now, thanks,' said Paddy. 'We'll push off and see you in a couple of hours.' Ten minutes later the escarpment was at my feet. I was not at the bottom of a cliff but at the top, looking down across another dusty plain four hundred feet below. It stretched for miles and became lost in blue haze and mirage lakes. The symbol for the escarpment on the map was as small as a greenfly and easy to misinterpret but we would have to be more careful in future.

The track switchbacked and twisted down the escarpment to the valley below. I ran, letting the wheelbarrow have its rein. It was a clattering, perilous descent, during which the wheel rim became seriously loosened, and the kit thrown into a jumble. Salt, oats and water-containers lost their lids and disgorged their contents among my clothes and papers. To add to my injuries that day, Mick was in a sombre mood – Norwich City had been beaten by York.

Next morning it was unusually still and warm, with a light covering of cloud. The *piste* was crossed now and then by gullies of sand and ran along the foot of the escarpment, which towered several hundred feet above it to the left. Provided I could hit the patches of sand quickly enough and keep the momentum, the wheel would skate across. I charged at them, yelping encouragement to the wheelbarrow, and patting it when it had done well.

The stillness at dawn had been but a prelude. Mid-morning, we were overrun by a storm. The wind, like a deluge of muddy water, lashed grit and small stones from the cliff above. I went on, protected by goggles, smog-mask, gloves and thick clothing. I was making heavy weather of it but dared not rest for the cold. We were under the shadow of flying grit, the sun no more than an aura of gold.

At one o'clock, without warning, the wind dropped, dust settled, and I was under a pleasant sky. The driver of a passenger lorry stopped to give me some bread and carrots. In return, I gave him one of twelve tiny mouth-organs that Hohner had given me. He puffed at it, producing not a discernible tune but a catchy rhythm, while attempting a dance not unlike the Irish clog variety. Ten or more passengers – all men, some in western dress and others in robes – gathered round singing and clapping. I told them I was late, picked up the shafts and left them to it.

Half an hour later, I was in a forest eating the bread they had given me. Stone pillars, a yard thick, lay scattered and broken, like fallen Greek columns. The prehistoric trees looked as if they had been felled the day before, but they were as sterile as hot bricks from a kiln and probably one hundred and thirty million years old. I sat on a log among the shadows of creatures now extinct and others long since departed for pasture in the south.

The next day took us past the quarter-way mark, and brought us within seven miles of In Salah. From camp we could see the silhouette of its palm-trees, framed by dunes on either side, which, as daylight faded, were decorated with pin-points of silver light. Mick shouted above the noise of the petrol stove. 'Look at that view! Roll on In Sha-la-la. I wish I was in those bars tonight.'

I could not wait to leave this north-easterly dog-leg either: no more walking into the wind; no sand for five hundred miles. Instead, the rocky tourist route to our half-way mark, Tamanrasset – the end of backwater villages, and, I hoped, of the long silence from home.

The next morning, 21 January, the tent was wet with dew, the first time for weeks. I had worked until one in the morning, finishing reports and letters, writing a shopping list, and packing films and tapes. It had blown a gale in the early hours and I had been up with my torch at three o'clock to attend to the guy-ropes and check that the washing was still on the line: it was, but it had become red with dust. I had not slept much and was up before dawn. After drinking a mug of tea, I packed away the tent and set off, watching the trees float nearer as the pale sun thawed the earth.

As trite as it sounds, I had forgotten what greenness was until I saw those palms. The desert had been sterile, free from odours, except my own, and void of sounds, except those of the wind and the wheel-barrow. But now a donkey brayed and the faint chant of women drifted with wood smoke from the town. The track forked with no sign to show the way. I chose the deep shade of the palm grove where the high foliage sprinkled drops of sunlight on the path. The air was still, warm and damp, as thick and scented as molasses, rich with the smell of plants and animals.

A stream bubbled along the side of the track, watering shaded plots of carrots and onions. Women, dressed in black, like nuns, were on hands and knees at the water's edge collecting fodder for their live-stock into baskets, singing as they worked. Boys and old men drove donkeys, which carried baskets of sand from where it had blown into the town at one end, to be taken off by the wind at the other. Birds chattered among the vegetables and splashed in the water. Too soon, I was out on the other side, dazzled, like a man leaving a cinema in the afternoon. Just a few yards away were dunes spiked with palms. In the safety of the oasis their beauty was overwhelming – a tour operator's paradise.

By comparison, the town was drably monochrome. It was different from Adrar only in that a main street, with post office and government buildings, replaced the square, but otherwise the sepia buildings were less than my expectations. The post office was the grandest building. It was the same square room as in Adrar, the same crowd of mustachioed Algerians, with their sallow skins and monks' habits. At nine-fifteen, a middle-aged counter-clerk appeared. He ignored the customers and began totting up cash and postal orders. Mick had arrived before me and was almost at the front. We had nodded to each other, but the near silence and the many people standing between us would have made conversation impolite.

Was there a letter from Joan? What might be in it? I was trembling a little, more anxious than if I was going to have a tooth out. The hands of the wall clock seemed to stand still.

10

WHEN YOU'RE SMILING

When I was in the sixth form, the headmaster announced that the school was to hold a carol service – the first one in my six years there – and I began to drum up support for it. Most of my form agreed to go, until one of our number, Bob Berry, came into school with tickets for the Christmas Dance at Fairfield High School for Girls, scheduled for the same night. This was stretching my Christian duty to its limits. Fairfield girls were class! So was their school, set out of town in an eighteenth century Moravian settlement. We had never had a chance to get near the place before. Ours was a technical school, bordered by a railway line and two busy roads and scented by the Openshaw Brewery. I was a Christian but my dreams of heaven had never been so blissful as the thought of those girls. Still, I had to do my miserable duty.

By the evening of the service, I had had an idea: my father would pick me and a few friends up afterwards and drive us to the dance in his old Bedford van. We duly arrived at half-past nine to find the dance in full swing. We walked in, as arrogantly as the Mafia, expecting there to be dozens of girls ready for us to charm, but the early arrivals had got the pickings! There were more boys from Audenshaw Grammar School than there were girls, and the girls were all over them!

I left my friends looking bemused and stalked around the hall looking in every corner. There were only three girls spare. One of them was quite pretty. She was slim, almost too slim, she had high cheek-bones and short, fair hair, not quite blonde, and wore a little make-up and a dark-blue, short-sleeved, Courtelle dress. She accepted my invitation to dance and, while we moved around the floor, told me she was in the lower sixth, being a year younger than me, and was hoping to be a biology teacher. Her name was Joan Gill. She went back to her place for the foxtrot and some old-time stuff, but the rest of the time we danced. She was intelligent and good looking. I later discovered that she was not acquisitive, would never defend her character, was not judgemental and would unswervingly do what she felt was right, and yet she was neither pompous nor priggish. Importantly, she shared my faith. I did not want to let this girl go.

Within the next fortnight, we met five times, sometimes in the morning, visiting espresso coffee bars in Manchester and walking for hours through snow and slush. After a couple of dates, I knew that I wanted to marry her. I had seen friends commit themselves to each other, cocksure of their relationship, only to find things going sour. I knew that our relationship was different, but they had all said that. I had wanted to talk with her about marriage but I did what I thought was the mature thing and kept quiet. I was only seventeen and she sixteen, but after a month – it seemed like a year – I could hold back no longer. Aware of our immaturity, I said, 'When we're grown up, will you marry me? You don't have to answer now. Think about it.'

'I'll think about it,' she said, and then she smiled and said, 'I've thought. Yes, I will.' Did she now regret that decision, I wondered? She had not even had second place. I had not intended to neglect her, but had been dedicated to parish work. A knock on the door, a call on the phone and anyone could have had my attention. That is part and parcel of a clergyman's life, but when free time had come, the Sahara had taken it all.

When she had been upset by my neglect, I had been unable to convince her that I loved her and accused her of being tiresome. She was a guileless and loving woman, the sort who would be faithful, even out of misplaced loyalty. She believed in doing what she felt to be right, regardless of the cost. Yet I had had a second dream, the night before Aulef, in which Joan had begun to reject me. In it, she had come to her senses and realized that there was more to life than being a drudge. It showed our marriage to be in a much worse state than I had ever perceived it to be. In it, I had seen her with a tall, dark, young man, though I had not caught sight of his face and did not know who he was. I had been convinced that the dream was the result of my guilt. It was a comment on my state of mind and not on Joan, but the more I had tried to dismiss it, the more uncertain I had become. Had I pushed her too far? Then there was her strong womanly instinct to become pregnant and bear a child. Was there not pressure on her to find a more fertile man? My anxiety was distorting Joan's character beyond recognition.

* * *

The post office clerk worked unhurriedly through piles of papers, while three Scandanavians came in and talked quietly in a corner, followed by two French. I checked the clock with my watch: ten o'clock – I had been waiting three-quarters of an hour. The man behind the counter stood and singled out Mick. I was next. I could not believe it. He was pointing across the room at me. He had seen my passport and was dealing with mail first. My heart was thumping. There were three letters, one each from my sister, mother and Joan.

I had craved for a word from home, but now I had it I headed down a back street to the bakery, clutching the prize I had not the courage to open. I bought vegetables, oranges, dates, thirty tins of sardines and fifty candles. Mick and I ended up in a bar, 'giving it the big lips', while Paddy stayed outside filling the jerry-cans from a hose. The unopened letters were still in my pocket. 'So, no sand-ladders and no inner tubes,' said Mick.

'It's odd about sand-ladders. The textbooks say they're a must and yet we've been unable to get them either here or at home. And I haven't seen a single vehicle carrying them either,' I replied. The young barman leaned over the counter and looked down at my feet.

'You want to sell?' he asked.

'The boots? No, sorry.'

'Have you tape-recordings?' he asked. 'Cassette music with guitar? Elvis Presley? The Beatles?'

'I have some pop music.'

'You sell?' he asked. I turned to Mick.

'Do us a favour – get a couple of cassettes from the Land Rover. We'll swap 'em for plonk.' Mick returned with the cassettes.

'We're in luck. There's a couple outside heading north. They'll sell us their spare inner tubes.'

'How much?'

'Twice the price we'd pay at home, but who's arguing?' I bartered for the wine and then went out to meet them.

'Hi,' I said. 'Where've you travelled from?'

'Agadez,' said the man, with a strong English accent.

'Are you British?' I asked.

'Good Lord, no!' he said, in perfect English. 'Belgian. We're conference interpreters.'

'Which route did you use?'

'Tam, In Guezzam, Arlit.'

'Arlit,' I said. 'That's pretty sandy, isn't it?'

'Not at all.'

'I've heard that before,' I said. 'You've got four wheel drive.'

'Yes, well, there is some sand about a hundred miles south of here between Tadjmout and Arak, but the rest is very good.' He laughed and stamped his foot, 'It's firm all the way.' His new Land Rover should have robbed him of any credibility but I began to be persuaded. 'Look,' he said, 'we were in Arlit only six days ago. We don't forget that quickly.'

'How about water?' I asked. 'Is there any between here and Tadjmout?'

'Oh, yes,' he said with delight. 'At Hassi el Krenig.' His wife spoke up.

'It's very beautiful. There's a lovely spring.'

'But be careful,' he said. 'It's infested with cobras and scorpions.'

'I've seen the *hassi* on the map but it's way off the *piste*,' I said.

'Only two kilometres, and it's well signposted.'

'How about tarmac? How far does that go south of here?'

'Sixty kilometres.'

'More than I thought!'

The tarmac served me well. By evening I had begun the four hundred and thirty mile haul to Tamanrasset. I was in bed, eighteen miles south, my share of a bottle of wine in one hand, and Joan's thirty-page letter in the other. My worst fears were unfounded but she and everyone else was missing me greatly. Susan, our daughter, was having more tantrums than usual and my parents were playing my Christmas tape every day. Otherwise there was much to cheer. I almost knocked over the candle laughing at my sister's letter. Heightened feelings of joy, mingled with sadness and an intense headache, gave me little sleep for a second night. I was up long before dawn, eager to be on the move.

We had a spare wheel for the wheelbarrow which we had been carrying on the Land Rover. The one we had been using until now was a sandwich of sheet aluminium and honeycomb foil, materials used to make aircraft floors. The rim was held in place by six pairs of angle plates, which were bolted together through the wheel on one face and through the rim on the other. The bolts had been elongating the holes in the honeycomb, thereby loosening the rim. The previous night, Paddy had fitted the spare wheel, which was made of a different design. It had eight steel spokes, an inch and a half wide, welded to a rim and hub.

The tarmac ended six miles short of where the Belgians had promised, then the 'hard, rocky' *piste* described with a stamp of the foot became hills deep in soft grey ash which looked like powdered asbestos. The track subdivided round and over mounds of the substance, which were shaped like a succession of slag-heaps tipped one against the other on the top of existing low hills. I concluded that the substance was natural as it went on for twenty miles.

Every few minutes lorries from an army base passed, enveloping me with the dust, making me close my eyes and hold my breath. I arrived at camp looking like a cement worker. The powder had got into the wheelbarrow, into my hair and clothes, and had stuck to my skin. Each time I coughed or blew my nose I found evidence of that day's walk. I resolved to rise early and to get going before the lorries. I blew out my candle at ten-forty and fell asleep, only to be woken soon afterwards by Mick trying to get the result of the Manchester United versus Norwich City replay on his radio.

The mountain of ash came to an end at ten o'clock the next morning in an exhilarating descent. I took advantage of it and raced half a mile down to a broad expanse of mud-flats, where I tipped the wheelbarrow onto its front corner while I consulted the map. The mud-flats were six miles across, surrounded by hills. It could have been Derwentwater in time of drought – a flat, almost circular, expanse surrounded by hills. On the far side of the mud-flats, below the opposing hills, there was indeed water, marked on the map as an intermittent lake. My route was to the left of it.

I righted the wheelbarrow but it would not go forward. I jerked it backwards in case it was in a rut, but it was not that simple: six of the eight spokes had sheared from the rim and were splayed out, jamming against the frame. The damage had been done when I had run downhill, but it was only when the wheelbarrow had been tipped on its side that the spokes had moved out of place. I kicked them back into position and wrote a note to Mick and Paddy which I tucked into the pouch of my robe: 'Come as soon as you can. Wheelbarrow broken. I should be left of the lake.' I crept forward hoping that the wheel would hold. But for the smooth flats there would have been little chance. After an hour, an Italian truck driver offered to deliver the note for me. After a further hour, I had reached the hills and dared go no further in case the uneven ground sheared the remaining two spokes. The lake had shifted north-east, and had proved to be a mirage.

The rules allowed Paddy to repair the wheelbarrow only when I had reached the safety of water, which meant getting to the lake, and if that proved brackish, going on to Hassi el Krenig, the spring mentioned by the Belgians. I could abandon the wheelbarrow so long as I walked to the *hassi*, so I took from the locker the things I would carry by hand: two pints of water, two oranges, a map, a compass, and a carrot given me by the Italian truck driver. I would not go on until the lads arrived.

It was a sultry afternoon. I was sitting watching the 'lake' when, suddenly, the Land Rover drove out of it, like an army landing-craft. The vehicle seemed only two hundred yards away, but was in fact a mile and a half, and though moving, neither made a sound nor appeared to get nearer for two or three minutes – it was as if I were watching through a telescope.

Mick and Paddy took the wheelbarrow and arranged to meet me twelve miles on, at Hassi el Krenig. I stuffed the oranges in my pockets, picked up the water-bottle, and followed.

There was camaraderie in the desert. Travellers stopped to greet each other, regardless of race or nationality, each ensuring that the other wasn't lacking anything essential. The British, with notable exceptions, had not learned this. That afternoon, a dark-blue Land Rover, with GB plates, passed within five feet of me, at little more than walking speed. The driver and the woman with him turned their heads when I raised a friendly hand. Within a further hour three separate foreign drivers had offered me lifts and warned me of cobras, scorpions and bandits.

It was now twenty-past five and I had walked twenty-eight miles since dawn. The track meandered between hills which were close at hand and rose sharply to about two hundred feet, thus preventing my seeing very far into the distance. I passed a dried-up well, but there was still no sign of the picturesque spring. I should have been there half an hour earlier. The sun went down and the breeze brought goose-pimples to my arms. I was without warm clothing. In the half-light, I became uncertain of the way. The track forked either side of a hill. I breathed curses at the Belgians and their 'easy to find' and 'well-signposted' *hassi*.

The map was useless, so with a prayer, I went doubtfully left. I had tried to be well equipped for navigation, written many letters, made long-distance telephone calls and trips from Manchester to London to get bubble sextants, protractors and compasses, spent a day at RAF Cranwell learning how to use them, and weeks practising to achieve a navigational accuracy of two miles. But now I was lost on a piece of track used by tourists whose Michelin maps were eighty-three miles to an inch. I was not carrying a sextant: it was too heavy and anyway the *hassi* was not on the navigational chart. This was the third time I had been lost and I felt foolish and scared. The moon was up and daylight nearly gone; I had eaten the oranges and had no water, only a compass round my neck, a map and what I stood in.

The lads had not been able to find the *hassi* either and had driven on a few extra miles in their search. Paddy had had a hard afternoon playing the vulture, picking at and sawing up abandoned vehicles, collecting metal to repair the broken wheel. He had made eight right-angled brackets and used them to bolt the spokes back to the rim. Now, at dusk, his work complete, he scrambled up a stony bank with his binoculars and looked north. There I was, on course, not far away. He climbed back down and then I heard three signal blasts of the Land Rover horn. I knew I was safe.

The next morning, I rose with reticence in the cold pre-dawn wind, and trudged with the repaired wheelbarrow over shallow hills. There were no dunes but it was rough going over compacted sand and grit. An hour of it was enough to drive away all memory of the good times. My pride became hurt when a motorized caravan passed without stopping. As my curses followed it, it lurched to a halt, broken down. The driver was too busy to speak but his hitch-hiker companion gave me a bar of soap. At the time, I wondered why.

Soon after I had left them, the *piste* became easier, down a decline towards a distant strip of hills which looked blue through the haze. By one-thirty they had grown as large as Highland mountains, and the trail had slipped between them. To eyes blinded by the wind, the green-and-purple rock looked shaggy with the hues of heather and bracken and, in my imagination, I was under water at the bottom of a loch. Xerophytes, leafless bushes which were the image of water weed, floated skyward from the scree, and shoals of nibbling birds drifted over them.

Long before camp was due, I rounded a corner and saw the Land Rover detached from the trailer, kit littered yards around and Mick and Paddy standing among it. I steered between the boxes. 'I've not done twenty-three, have I?'

'Yeah,' Mick replied sarcastically.

'Have you broken down?'

'No, we're binning half our load.'

'Come on, what's happened?'

'The tow-bar housing has sheared, so we've got to dump the trailer.'

'What happened?'

'I dunno. We were going at our usual twelve miles an hour when it just tore away.'

'I'm really narked at that Captain Whatsisname,' I said. 'When I went to Bulford for the final briefing he told me that the trailer they'd sent from the Hebs was nearly new. He said, rather than risk damaging it, he'd swapped it for an old one. That's a lovely way to get rid of your junk! I bet the Hebs didn't know about it.'

The trailer had been carrying heavy items – compo, spares, petrol, water, and oil – all of which would have to be transferred to the vehicle or jettisoned. Paddy began by servicing the engine and then pouring the remaining four gallons of unused oil into a hole. Next went my sand-frosted bottles and rock specimens. All unnecessary weight was abandoned. While the lads worked, I pitched my tent and heated up a can of Scotch herrings I had been saving for a special occasion. Mick was singing outside: 'When you're smiling, when you're smiling, the whole world smiles with you. . . .'

'D'you reckon we'll get it all on?' I shouted.

'We'll manage,' answered Paddy, 'but somehow we'll have to put some weight onto the front springs. The back ones are almost inverted, not to mention the strain on the split rims.'

'Are you gonna load up the cab?' I asked.

'Nah! I'm gonna strap boxes of compo on the front bumper.'

Later, talking through the tent walls, we composed a telegram which we would ask a traveller to send to my press agent: 'Trailer dumped. Towing assembly sheared, 88 miles south In Salah. Also both barrow wheels seriously damaged. Makeshift repair. Progress otherwise good. Morale high. Contact Hebrides. Geoff.' The long hours of work always affected my appetite. At home, I had eaten about a kilogramme of food a day, while here I was eating three. Normally, I took no sugar in drinks and rarely ate desserts. I had thought it unimportant that the crisis in supply of 1974 had prevented my bringing sugar from England, but now I craved for high-energy food. Jam, sugar, and dry potato powder, when I managed to get them, were all eaten straight from the container with a spoon.

In the morning, the wind made sport of me until, at eleven o'clock, I cowered behind the wheelbarrow. I ate some Horlicks powder and then lay down and tried to sleep. When I opened my eyes, a teenager in Joseph's coat of many colours, was standing above me, and beside him a dog. 'Are you all right?' he asked.

'Yes, thank you,' I replied, rising to my feet. In the distance, a man led three white camels. 'Is that your father?' I asked. He nodded, and seeing I was well, ran to him.

That night, when the moon had come up over the mountains of bassalt, I was exhausted and depressed, but it did not take long for me to be cheered. Mick was outside, ordering fish and chips, and singing: 'Everybody loves Saturday night. . . .' When Mick was good he was very, very good. . . .

11

BRIGG FAIR

Nine-thirty the following morning, 26 January, I was charging down a narrow valley, aiming to achieve a record thirty miles in one day. Ahead, a dust cloud heralded a Peugeot saloon. The previous evening, I had written a report on the loss of the trailer and here was a chance to post it. When the car had stopped, a comic Arab, from a pantomime of *The Arabian Nights*, popped out. A fat, humorously clumsy Ali Baba bounced at me, and a black youth, in threadbare European dress, trailed behind like a nomad's dog. Ali Baba took hold of the letter and asked me to wait for a few moments. A second vehicle, a Land Rover, arrived. Though wearing a green boiler suit and a black head-wrap, there was no question about the authority of the figure who alighted. He, the leader, was followed by an awkwardly tall Arab in grey robes, with pin-points for eyes and sickle for nose.

The middle-aged leader, tall, dark and thin, with genial blue eyes, introduced himself, 'Where've you been? I've been expecting you for a long time. You wrote to me, remember? I'm the Chief of Police at In Salah and Acting Chief of Police for Tamanrasset. Do you need anything?'

'I wouldn't refuse some bread and perhaps a carrot.' Orders were shouted in Arabic and the boy brought bread and such food as I never knew existed – butter, still strangely solid, wrapped in thick brown paper, fresh olives, tangerines, onions and tomatoes, and it was all a gift.

The boy brought wood and lit a fire off the *piste* among the rocks, while the chief, Ali Baba, and I photographed each other. The chief then brought a plastic bowl of meat which he carried to the fire – a strange way to make a cup of tea. We sat on the ground and chatted while he took two burning brands from the fire and kindled another fire six feet away. By now the first was boiling tea in an enamel kettle. The boy poured it into tea-glasses, like tiny beer mugs, and then tipping it back into the pot, poured it out again, repeating the process many times and finishing with the liquid back in the pot on the fire.

The chief was wielding his dagger with alacrity, carving the meat into inch cubes and laying them in rows on a plastic jerry-can. Ali Baba leaned over and hacked off golf balls of meat which he tossed into the flames. He fished them out smoking, laid them on a flat stone, and tried to beat the charcoal off them with a stick but succeeded only in knocking them into the sand. A further attempt ended in his having to eat meat covered in charcoal and sand. The chief put the pieces he had cut on to six skewers, but would not cook them until the fire had become smokeless embers.

It was now eleven o'clock and my chance of walking thirty miles had slipped away. Furthermore, I had been waiting for one and a half hours and there was still no sign of tea or kebabs. Each man was finding his own amusement. The chief was meddling with my compass, while Ali Baba tuned into French and Arab stations on his radio and the tall man with the sickle nose lay on the stony ground, sleeping. The chief then swapped the compass for a camera and filmed the sleeper as he gently roused him with his foot. The boy took a stone and broke a cake of sugar into the glasses. The tea was powerfully strong, sweet and mildly mint flavoured but I drank one cup after another.

The second fire, now looking dead, was fanned into redness by my host, who had laid the skewers an inch above it. Ten minutes later I was eating the first fresh meat I had tasted for six weeks. It was camel – tasty as best beef and tender as chicken.

The boy put a cooking pot on the fire, diced an onion and fried it in Mazola corn oil. He added Italian tomato purée, water, salt, meat and macaroni. He stopped preparations for a moment when ordered to get the chief's radio, which dwarfed Ali Baba's in size and power. Both radios played different stations at the same time, with everyone, including me, enjoying it all.

All five of us ate from the same pot, the chief with fingers, the rest of us with spoons. When we had picked the bones, the chief smashed them with rocks, sucking out the marrow and wiping the grease from his bandit moustache with the back of his hand. He walked a few yards away, dropped his boiler suit, squatted, and returned to wash his hands. The meal was over. Begging my leave three hours after stopping, I took the compass from around my neck and hung it round the chief's.

More flies than usual followed. I was almost used to them by now. They could play around my nostrils and the corners of my eyes but I could neither bear to breathe them in nor have them feed on the sores around my nose and ears. Sometimes they were a pleasant distraction: they walked over my glasses and I watched them trapped between the lenses of my clip-on sun-glasses and those of my spectacles. The distance between the lenses was greater at the centre and the flies would run in blurred circles trying to escape. Dozens took rides under the brim of my hat and on my right shoulder, sheltering from the wind. I was the dirtiest, smelliest creature they could find. That afternoon, a young Tuareg rode up on his camel to greet me. He was swathed in an indigo head-wrap and a voluminous blue *gandura*. Though he was covered in flies, they did not bother him – apart from his hands and feet, only a narrow slit across his eyes was exposed. As we chatted, the flies that hummed around him and his camel diminished, transferring their loyalty to me.

I feared to take my 'retinue' to camp. There was a strong head wind and so I walked back a few hundred yards from the wheelbarrow and up a bank. Then, jiving wildly, I knocked the flies into a swarm and raced downhill into the wind, away from the flies, back to the wheelbarrow.

The following day should have been pleasant – Tadjmout was due with a promise on the map of a military base, food, fuel and water, but I was inexplicably melancholy. Un-English brown cliffs to the left poked sadly through mountains of grit, like rotten teeth through gums. I did not realize I was missing my homeland until I remembered the tune of Delius' *Brigg Fair*, which I had been trying to think of for days. I met enough characters that day, though, for me to have written *The Canterbury Tales* and one of them in particular jollied me out of moping.

A middle-aged Italian and a young Belgian were mending a puncture on their Citroën. The Belgian, a small, scruffy student, barely visible through a matted beard and hair, spoke in American English. 'We've had eight punctures since Tam. Man, dis life is really someting. I've been aaall over. I've 'eard 'bout you. You're nuts! If you want to walk, trow way all dis junk,' he said, slapping the wheelbarrow. 'You don't need it. You don't need nuttin'. Leave it here and get stuff from de people. They won't let you starve out here. It's crazy. Anybody can live out here. But I like what you're doing, walking. Walking's great. I did it in the Ivory Coast for two whole days. It was great but I got blisters, so I quit.' He was right about the impossibility of starving; later that day German, Italian and British pilgrims made offerings of fruit.

The trail hugged the foot of the ridge to the left, where blackened rock contorted into a fantasia of creatures; beneath a sleeping elephant, the dwarf palms of Tadjmout fanned out over its tin shack, palm-leaf hut and petrol-pumps. Tuaregs shouted greetings from their repose on grass mats, and children ran alongside, lightening my load with their smiles.

We could find no military base at Tadjmout, nor food for sale, but I was given bread by a lorry driver and water from the well. It did not matter that there were no shops; having reached Tadjmout, I could take supplies from the Land Rover. We camped round the next bend, and after Mick had treated me to a plate of his spaghetti bolognese, I did my laundry. With underpants on my head as protection from the night air, I washed my denim cap , while Paddy fitted the repaired spoked wheel. We worked hard and long and I had less than six hours in bed.

The Belgians had told me of sand for the twenty-six miles from Tadjmout to Arak, but the next morning I found the going easy, along a narrow valley between the steep sides of low, barren hills. I had been prepared for the worst, but was slowed down only by reporters. Two French men and a female photographer wanted my story, but I told them I would have to turn them down. My contract would not allow me to talk to them.

In the October before the expedition, reporters had not left me alone. A number of the daily newspapers had run my story and then the *Sun* had wanted its turn. I had agreed to pose for its photographer at the seaside, until Derek Cattani, a freelance photographer from London, had rung one Tuesday evening. With his journalist partner, John Lawless, he had offered to do a feature for the *Sunday Times*, but only if I was prepared to cancel my arrangement with the *Sun*. He had argued that an article in the *Sunday Times* was more likely to bring me the Land Rover and sponsorship I needed. I had been persuaded, but came to regret breaking the arrangement, and effectively my word, with the other newspaper. John, Derek and I got on well together, however, and we drew up a contract for them to be my press agents. Instead of my being hounded by reporters, they disseminated the information, leaving me free to work on preparation. John and Derek were true professionals, but when we were together we were always laughing. It is hard to take yourself seriously while prancing around at the seaside in a robe, pushing what looks like an ice-cream cart, even if the resulting photograph is about to hit the world press. It was even more difficult for me to look serious when I was being photographed jogging through the back streets. Trigger-happy Derek was unable to keep up with me so he was being pushed by John in Susan's pram, that was until the wheel fell off.

After a few minutes with the French reporters at Tadjmout, I posed for a photograph, on the understanding that they would contact John and Derek before publishing it. As the camera clicked, a sand devil, or whirlwind, crossed the *piste*, tearing up the ground, spiralling it into the clouds and bounding westward over the rocks and out of sight.

Round the next bend, a German car whose occupants had greeted me the previous day, was hobbling home with broken shock absorbers. The young driver and his elderly mother were more concerned for my welfare than their own. Seeing my clip-on sun-glasses held together by tape, they gave me another pair and asked if I needed anything else. Their breakdown helped me to take my mind off myself, and I made good time that day.

Flies came in pursuit – nine flew into my mouth in less than an hour, twenty-three drank from the blood and antiseptic cream on my left hand, and others tantalized my eyes, nose and ears. Their number was always in proportion to the surrounding vegetation. There were now many bushes – at least one every ten yards – and four ragged children ran from among them. There was no sight of homes or adults. They had happy faces and unshod feet, and chased me, carrying basketwork which they hoped I would buy. I might have done so but for their flies. Instead, I watched their delight wane as I pushed further and faster than they, and was sobered by the irony of neglecting those whom the walk was designed to help.

Arak hid in a gorge of the same name. I lunched before the town on a bend on the edge of a twenty foot drop. I was tired of dust and lorries and figured that vehicles would corner too slowly to raise dust, or else land in the river-bed. I figured wrongly. A juggernaut thundered round at full speed on a magic carpet of dust. I was covered from boots to hat.

Arak had a hotel and a restaurant, I had been told, and I was looking forward to a shower and a meal. A plaque on the side of the gorge announced the town and round the bend was a low, brick building, like a public convenience, a grass hut and a tree-shaded table marked, 'Café'. A black African and his teenage daughter stood by the table which was laid with inverted tea glasses. Underneath the table was a bucket of muddy washing-up water with tea-leaves floating on top. This was Arak?

The trail followed the river-bed through the gorge. Five doves walked side by side ahead of me. Each time I caught them up they flew forward fifty yards and continued walking in the same formation, keeping me company in this manner for several minutes.

We camped that night near a clump of thorn-trees on the sand of the dung-strewn river-bed at the bottom of the gorge. In honour of Arak, I ate a helping of Mick's meat and potato hash and then spent the evening cleaning and replenishing. The wheelbarrow was a sticky mess and the lockers damaged by rattling cans. To prevent further damage and to help with future cleaning, I lined the lockers with cardboard from compo boxes.

Paddy discovered that the gorge had snapped three of my newly mended spokes. The metal brackets he had made to fasten them to the rim were too weak, so, as we were near a place of safety, he began making and fitting all eight spokes with stronger ones, working at the vice which he had clamped to the front bumper of the Land Rover. He sawed the metal which he had salvaged from cars into strips, six inches long and an inch and a half wide. Each strip then had four equally spaced holes drilled into it, and was bent into a right angle to make the bracket. The brackets were then put into place against the spoke and under the inside of the rim. Brackets, spokes and rim had to be drilled before they could be bolted together – a total of sixty-four holes.

At half-past eleven, when I went to bed, Paddy was still working under a bright moon. I woke and fell asleep again at half-past one to the whirr of his hand-drill. At five, I stood beneath the stars inspecting his completed work.

Mornings were always beautiful. Flies never came out in the cold. Today, I pulled away in the darkness before they stirred, but then the sun, red as blood, ballooned up over the crags to my left and excited the swarms. The first of many brought its tickling feet to my festering ear at eight-fifteen.

The wadi ran along the bed of the gorge. It looked as if it had not seen water for centuries and was silted up with wind-blown dust, grit and sand. There were occasional thorn-trees and shrubs without leaves 'growing' not on the edge of the wadi but within it. The *piste* ran parallel to it but occasionally crossed it or even ran along its bed. From Arak to Tamanrasset, the *piste* was effectively a dirt road, not engineered in modern times but worn by the feet of man and beast over millenia.

The sides of the gorge were irregular. In some places, it might have been possible to scramble up them over a cascade of boulders. In other places, they were sheer. Lack of geological expertise and a mind focussed on other things prevented my knowing of what type of rock the gorge was formed, but most of it was blackened by the sun: constant sunshine draws minerals to the surface, producing a black, laquered effect or 'desert varnish'.

As the *piste* climbed up the gorge, the wheelbarrow pushed back against me stubbornly and I felt faint and sickly. My father's voice echoed through the canyon. 'Now listen here, I don't want any more of this nonsense. Settle down. You've a wife and family to think of.' But that was not his style; what I had heard was a cry from my own heart. Camels, rocks and trees passed eyes fogged by thirst and self-pity. I could hear ghostly chimes as if my ears were full of water.

Joan knew about thirst too – we had both been caught without water in Africa. It had happened in the hot season when we had decided to walk just seven miles from a leprosy hospital to Maiduguri. We were on holiday, taking a break from the mission school, and preferred the exercise to getting a lift. There was a dirt road but we took a short cut across the bush instead. We were not very fit and had no water with us. By noon it had grown so hot that it felt as if we were surrounded by dozens of electric fires. After a mile, we were thirsty; after another three, Joan was lying on the ground, sobbing. She could go no further. I dared not leave her. There were no distinctive features in that part of the bush and it might have taken an army to find her, so I forced myself to be angry. I dragged her to her feet and bullied her for a further hour and a half until we reached safety.

Now, in my imagination, I strove to reach Joan, walking into Kano along a tarred road. Cars and passenger lorries passed as the conurbation grew denser. She appeared by the side of the road twenty yards ahead. I dropped the wheelbarrow, leapt over the shafts, and as I ran to her she and Kano retreated.

I was brought back to reality with a jolt – another two spokes snapped. I crouched mournfully to fix them with wire, but an hour later all eight of them went as the wheel collapsed with an almighty bang. The sun was almost down, so I made camp in the canyon where I was and waited for the lads to find me. The *piste* was no longer following the bed of the gorge but ran part way up it along the left side. The steep, rocky slope to the bottom was to the right, beyond which was the other face of the gorge about a hundred yards away. It was a place of animated shadows and echoes. The lighted candles made the shadows of boulders dance, and when I threw the billycan inside the locker, the metallic thud came back at me from the darkness of the chasm. I enjoyed the surroundings and felt more likely to frighten than to be frightened but was disappointed that the rules would have to be bent again. They dictated that I should have abandoned the wheelbarrow, carried supplies on my back and retrieved it repaired at the next well. Without a trailer to carry the wheelbarrow, Paddy, when he had driven back to find me, had to change the wheel on the spot. He then went off to rejoin Mick at the place where they had camped.

The steel wheel was, he had said, irreparable without welding gear, so the aluminium wheel with the loose rim *had* to get me to Taman-rasset. I had not felt too well all day and woke up during the night with a fever. At home, I later discovered, Susan, our three-year-old, had also woken, distressed that she had dreamt she was playing on my grave. My mother had also had a disturbing dream, which involved firemen.

In the morning, the *piste* climbed on to a plateau on which hillocks and crags made it impossible to see for more than a few hundred yards. Between the areas of higher ground, there were boulders and much sand but the constancy of the traffic – perhaps half a dozen vehicles a day – kept sand off the *piste*. That morning, I came across a broken-down lorry, set back from the road, guarded by the teenage son of the café proprietor from Arak. He invited me to drink tea with him in his tent, a lean-to of canvas stretched from the side of the vehicle. It was stifling inside, stank of sour milk, and was infested with flies. He proudly invited me to sit on a pile of old rugs, where I shared his bread and he my sardines.

12

HOT TODDY

With my swarming entourage and attendant filth I paraded into camp amid friendly jeers of disgust. We were two hundred yards from the well of Meniet and the lads had bathed. After a celebration scrub, I settled down to cook. It was too windy outside and I was comfortably drowsy and preferred the warmth of the tent. I lay, fully-clothed, leaning on my left elbow, writing and listening to a can of Hunter's meat pudding dancing in the pan. It was dark, the torchlight no more than an oily smear across the page, so I lit a candle.

Hunter's meat puddings took twenty-five minutes to steam, too long for my liking, and I was forever prodding them before their time. This night was different. Absorbed in writing, I had left the pudding unchecked for twenty minutes, and at some time the burner had gone out. The pudding was cold.

I was lying with my head at the blind end of the tent, and my feet towards the zipped flaps. The gas cylinder on the stove was empty but I always kept a spare one in the tent, so I began to fit one where I was. I normally leaned outside to do this, but I was now so irritated by the cold pudding, the pangs of hunger, and the thought of waiting twenty-five minutes for a meal that was already late, that I forgot myself. The old cylinder was off and a new one almost on, but the washer I had made from a car tyre was out of place, so I adjusted it with my thumb. A rush of liquefied gas sprayed my hands and face. For a second, no more, I tried to push the washer back in place, but it had split.

The spray hit the candle, ignited, and burst over me with the force of a flame-thrower. I was alive with fire. I saw a mental picture of Joan, the children and my parents, with mouths and eyes open in horror. A presence of mind and a strength not my own took over. I was thrown to the flaps faster than I could think and was clawing, scratching and kicking. Fire raced around the tent and I was burning. There was no getting under the canvas because of the sewn-in groundsheet, and the zips were jammed. Mick was shouting frantically, 'Geoff, Geoff, get out! For God's sake get out!' There was no reply. I could not breathe the inflamed air. Nor could I see; my eyelids were shutting out the heat, but I felt the horizontal zip give a few inches. I fought, fought, fought, but the gap was too small. Behind me was the roaring canister, all around me pain, and inside me a battle to stop straining lungs from inhaling fire.

Paddy, who had been sitting in the cab writing, jumped out. His first thought was to rip open the tent with a knife (though he later said that, even if he had had a blade in his hand, there would have been no time to use it).

There was a slit in the horizontal zip. With a tug on the vertical one I would be through, but the nylon of the zips was melting. There was not enough time; I was passing out. I had no thoughts of God, nor of heaven, nor of my sins and past life. My mind was being rocketed from my body into the ever enlarging faces of the family-group photograph. I was possessed by their look of terror. Though I was unable to breathe, the sight of them brought a great surge of adrenalin. I tugged at the zip like a maniac until it gave a little and my head rammed itself through the narrow opening and gasped cold air.

My legs moved like pistons and I shot under the fly sheet, coming into the darkness like a sprinter from the starting blocks. Mick was in front of me, wide-eyed, his face lit up by the flames. 'I'll never know how you got out,' he said. 'There was nothing I could do. Look at it.'

Orange flames ten feet high were crackling up into the night sky, blowing near the other tent. Mick came to his senses, and ran to uproot it and pull it clear. Paddy was shovelling sand on to the blaze, but within half a minute it had burned itself out.

I doused my smouldering clothing, and the lads made sure nothing else was alight. A torch beam showed the metal tent-poles still standing, one of them bent in the heat, but not even ash remained of the tent, sleeping-bag, groundsheet, clothes and towels. Two one-gallon plastic jars full of water were now a molten smear in the sand, and the cassette recorder, electrical thermometer and medical supplies were unrecognizable. My boots, outside the tent, were scorched, and their laces were burnt to ash.

The three of us were stunned as we looked at the remains. 'It's a pity it has to end up like this,' said Mick.

'What d'you mean, end up like this? I'm going on,' I said.

'You can't be serious.'

'I've not got this far to give up now.'

'Was there anything of value in there?' asked Paddy. I then realized that my chances of finishing the walk had been left in the tent.

'My passport, traveller's cheques, and air ticket,' I said. Paddy rummaged around and brought a shovelfull of smoking papers out of the sand. The vital documents had been rolled up next to my Bible, inside a ream of writing paper. The writing paper had burned through, so had half the Bible. Their ashes blew off the shovel, leaving the documents intact, but with charred margins. The traveller's cheques had burnt to within one eighth of an inch of the serial number, but they, with the ticket and passport, were still valid. I had no idea what to say. I was unspeakably happy.

'Oh, chuffed to Naffy breaks, chuffed to Naffy breaks,' said Mick. 'Those old ladies must have been on their knees this morning.'

'They really were, Mick. They really were.' Whether I was still hungry or just wanted something to chew, I don't remember, but I asked Mick for a meal. I climbed arthritically into the cab. Mick gave me two painkilling tablets, and then, silent and deep in thought, he sat stirring a pan of goulash for me. Paddy cleared the back of the Land Rover for my bed and made me a hot toddy.

Shock has always seemed rather bogus to me, an excuse for self-pity. Much of it was in my case, but it was beyond my control to lift an arm without its trembling or a leg without my becoming breathless.

I was also in pain. The only exposed parts had been my hands and face. The denim cap, which had caught fire, had given some protection. My glasses had saved my eyes, though I had lost the lashes and sustained a large blister over the left lid. The skin's leathery texture and the ability to perspire instantly was its own protection. I felt as if fire was still smouldering over my hands and face, which were covered with tiny blisters resembling the pimples on orange peel. My ear looked like a mutation, while blisters covered my temple, cheek and wrist. From inside, my face was an inflexible mask, stiff as cardboard.

I swallowed two more painkilling tablets with my last mouthful of whisky as Mick climbed in with the food. Shock demanded that we dwell on the accident, dissect it and examine it, even celebrate it. So we did, with wine saved for the half-way mark. It was not disaster but triumph, not what was lost but what had been saved that mattered.

Bed was a blanket, two coats and a squeeze between boxes. Bravado had gone to sleep with the lads. Now alone, I was terrified of being trapped in the Land Rover and of half a ton of equipment falling through the roof. Worse was the thought of what would have happened to Joan and the children if I had died. Lips mumbled thanks to God, both as I fell asleep and when I woke later. I could hardly believe I was alive. It was fitting that my scheduled Bible reading that morning began, 'If God be for us, who can be against us?' The feeling of foreboding which had come as a result of the vision of myself and of the dream of the policeman had now gone. I felt as if evil had done its worst, as if a black cloud that had hung over me had disappeared. The dream I had had about Joan still had me by the throat though.

At seven, Mick and I were standing by the cab-door, drinking tea. He looked sick. 'Ugh, Geoff, those burns are horrible. Let me drive you to the hospital at Tam.'

'All they'll do is dress them and tell me to come back in ten days. If you fix them today, I'll walk to Tam and the hospital can check 'em.' At my request, Mick photographed what was left of the tent, and went on to dress me up with powder and bandage and photograph the result. He hated publicity photographs because, he said, they distorted reality.

Paddy had been driving a stake in the ground to support the clothes-line. He walked cheerfully over to us, holding out a finger he had split open with the sledge-hammer. 'Well done, Paddy,' I said. 'Hold it out and Mick'll take your picture.' Paddy pretended to like the idea. Mick could see no humour in it, and after a verbal blast, stormed off to get the first-aid box.

We planned a day of salvaging, restocking and washing. The documents, tent-pegs, cutlery, cooking pot, half a Bible and camera had survived. The camera had been hiding in a case of thick hide behind a water-bottle, well away from the stove. The outer case and film were destroyed, but the inner case, lens and shutter were undamaged, so I could still take pictures. Mercifully, I had given a traveller earlier volumes of the log to post just a few days before, so it did not take me long to reconstruct the notes that had been burnt. Furthermore, we had replacements in the Land Rover for all the destroyed kit other than the robe, tent, sleeping-bag and electric thermometer.

Sticking up and out from the front of the wheelbarrow was a bracket about two feet long. It was designed to hold the mast, but as I no longer used the sail, one end of it was unattached and vibrated annoyingly when I was on the move. As the tent-poles were now useless, I put one of them where the mast should have been in order to hold the bracket still. I had in my suitcase a Union Jack, about the size of two handkerchiefs, so I tied it to the top of the tent-pole.

Towards noon, a Land Rover, with a footprint painted on its side, arrived. Clive Foot, a construction engineer, and his wife, Pamela, needed an oil-seal for their brakes. Paddy gave them one and helped them fit it. In gratitude they gave us half a bottle of whisky and an eight millimetre film which they had shot of the scene of the fire.

The flies took their leave with the sun, but as it grew dark the winter wind blew a snowstorm of small, grey moths over us. We sheltered behind the Land Rover, drinking around the petrol stove. Four candles pulled kamikaze moths out of the darkness. The singed ones twitched and flapped on the ground. Others stuck to their targets soaking up hot wax and giving a crackling flame. We kept hands over the rims of our mugs to keep out intruders. Paddy put the kettle on again. 'Well, I'm gonna have a hot toddy. Hows about you twos?'

'Deal me in,' I said. 'Why not use the tea-glasses I got in Adrar? They're on top of the Rover, in my case.' Paddy sprang over the bonnet and on to the roof, throwing down the tea-glasses. Paddy knew the kit well, right down to the inside of my suitcase.

The whisky, sugar and hot water was a luxury, but luxuries were of more importance than what are normally considered necessities. The tramp who spends the last of his money on a glass of beer has my sympathy. But for missing my family I could have gone on for ever eating dry oats, stale bread, dehydrated potato, and tinned vegetables. I could have lived without decent clothes, bathing or sleeping in a bed. It was the luxuries that I missed – good music or things I rarely touched at home, like dressed crab or chocolate gateau with cream. The warming glass was my compensation.

The Land Rover was now my permanent bed. This compromise was the only alternative to giving up, but I kept to carrying all my water and supplies, between points of safety. At noon on the first day back on the road, a jeep drew alongside and a French accent demanded, 'Two large cones, please.' This was not the first time that someone had seen the similarity between the wheelbarrow and an ice-cream cart. Down stepped a young man dressed for a cool evening in Paris, in a black velvet suit and white shirt. He was typical of the French we met. The British were, by comparison, dishevelled.

The fire altered days as well as nights for a time. I became timid, frightened of exertion and easily daunted, but through it I gained the sympathy of many. I was no longer the poppy seller helping intangible victims, but the bandaged, blood-stained soldier, fresh from the war. Though I refused some gifts, by the time evening came that day, sentiment had heaped up tangerines, onions, garlic, apples, carrots, dates, jam, bread, evaporated milk, condensed milk, canned fish, stew, peas, biscuits, coffee powder, file paper, nuts and bolts, a bottle of beer and a cigarette. I never saw another day like it. I usually shared my bounty with the lads and for many days after that they welcomed me to camp by asking, 'What have you bummed for us today?'

I had taken to leaving camp just before dawn. Next morning, the sun pulled the covers off a distant black dome of rock bigger than St Paul's Cathedral. Nearer, it divided into two giant snails, nose to nose. Before them, on the plain, a small, square room, painted white, was drawn up at the corners into turrets which flew red-and-green flags. It was the shrine of the Holy Man of Moulay, around which travellers are advised to drive three times in order to ensure their safety. The attendant was waiting with free tea for all who did this for the first time. I never met anyone who claimed to have ignored the custom, though I did hear of a clergyman who did so and went on to lose his convoy of seven vehicles.

I walked past, to impassioned shouts from those at the shrine, and turned my nose towards In Ecker, two days away. Ahead of me, a giant white bird, its wings edged with black, rested on the thermals, like a pointer nailed to the sky. Minutes later, a raven landed at my feet and chatted in the bass tones of an electronic organ.

It was a land of granite monoliths and sand. In Ecker had its own mound like that of Moulay, but beneath it, I was told, was a French nuclear research station, and behind, an army base. The rock was hedged by a roll of barbed wire, low enough for a school boy to jump. It was a sombre place, with its barbed wire, black rock, soldiers, and the recent graves of three anonymous travellers, crudely dug by the wayside and marked with one simple cross and scratchings in the earth which read, 'Followers of the trail'.

In Ecker to In Amguel was an easy day's walk across a dump for thousands of oil drums, mountains of rubbish, tin hats, kitchen sinks and concrete blocks. Paddy loved it and scavenged all day.

The hill beyond the dump afforded a pleasant view of valley, green with trees, through which the *piste* dipped. At the top of the hill, I gave in to childishness. Beside the track, a lorry tyre was asking to be rolled down the hill, but after struggling to get it upright, I lost the inclination. The rubber was stripped away on what had been the underside, exposing hair-thin wires, which were now sticking into the fingers of my left hand.

Those needles prevented the tyre from ravaging the concealed village of In Amguel. In the valley, on both sides of the *piste*, houses of brown earth hid behind high fences made from palm-leaf matting. I could smell dung, smoke and decaying vegetation. In front of me, on the *piste*, a goat, gaunt and still, blinked away the flies, while chickens scratched the earth. A group of children raced past, wearing the same sort of dresses and shorts that might be seen on the streets of Salford. A woman wearing heavy, black robes hurried barefoot into her yard and out of sight, while a man in a long, white shirt came to shake my hand and greet me in a language I did not understand. He smelt of horses.

In Amguel was a smelly place, inhabited by smelly, barefooted people. In Amguel was goats and mud huts, mosquitoes and houseflies. Then again, In Amguel was people, and it was also palms and shade, a ditch running with water, a farmyard of animal noises and animal smells, with chickens scratching the sand. In Amguel was lived in; it was beautiful.

A white mini-Citroën bounced past, scattering the chickens and goats before halting. A tall, blond young man approached, with a blonde girl following. She was shorter, rounder and with her hair in a pony-tail. 'I'm Ed and this is Jane. We're from Holland. At last we've found you. We've been following your tracks for over a day.' In five minutes we were old friends and had arranged to camp together. Another baby Citroën rolled up, and a Swiss couple, Lucas and Eva, got out, and then they all went off to find the lads, who had camped on the other side of the village.

The three vehicles were to the right of the track beyond the village, in the mountain pass. The Citroëns' detachable front seats were positioned around a pile of wood laid for a fire. 'I'm sure we can buy a chicken in In Amguel. Why don't we have a barbecue?' I mooted. The motion carried, Paddy drove Lucas and me back to where there had been chickens, but now there were none to be seen. There was movement in one of the compounds, so we shouted, '*Bon soir*'. A Tuareg, near to old age, opened a section of the matting that served as a doorway.

'Chickens? No, there are no chickens in this village.' He went inside and we called to a woman over the next fence. She spoke no French so Lucas clucked and I flapped my elbows and scraped the ground with my foot. But no, there were no chickens in In Amguel. I began to think I had imagined them until the woman offered us some eggs. The old man from next door came with more.

'Yes, we want eggs but we also want a chicken.'

'There are no chickens here.' Just then a squawk came from behind the house.

'There, there we heard it! That's what we want!' But they would not admit to having chickens even when offered more than double the English price for them.

It was dark when we returned. The six of them sat round the camp-fire, Mick and Jane preparing the food. Mick was a good cook, and had brought a variety of herbs and spices to liven the tins of army mince. One day he hoped to be a hotelier.

After bathing behind some rocks and washing my clothes, I joined the circle. Ed sat on a jerry-can and pushed me into his armchair. We feasted on spaghetti bolognese and were entertained by Janis Joplin and Elvis Presley. Then, as I wrote up the log, Ed passed round the last of his liquor, a little white rum with a trace of brandy.

The Hoggar mountains rise to just less than ten thousand feet. They are a range of five hundred million year old sandstone and granite, through which long-extinct volcanoes burst, leaving cones, peaks, volcanic plugs and bassalt. In places, the range resembles the Alps but more usually it looks dusty and eroded, like a blackened moonscape.

For the next three and a half days, the last seventy-nine miles to Tamanrasset hurdled the northern part of the range, over the Tropic of

Cancer, and down past the airport to the macadam, five miles before the town. I was now managing twenty-six miles a day, but the journey from In Amguel was a catalogue of groans. The Land Rover had split another rim and the double-burner gas stove which I had used since the fire was leaking. I accidentally rubbed the skin and blisters off the back of my hand, and my bandaged left ear hurt and was growing deaf. It was too cold without a sleeping-bag and I was usually awake by four o'clock and up by five, spending twelve hours on the *piste*. Then there was the cooking, washing, sewing and writing to do. I wrote:

Bandaged leg . . . nasty swollen vein . . . uphill . . . too tired . . . couldn't move . . . went in daze . . . ear and nose hurting a lot . . . flies on fork . . . jam, bread . . . had to knock flies off before every mouthful . . . 35 flies on water bottle, 12 on bandage . . . had to put DDT on face, sweated it off . . . put on repellent, worked for half an hour . . . hot day, ate pinch of salt, tasted good, ate more. M & P – 'Geoff, you're covered in flies.' Thousands all over me.

That same day, when relieving myself every fly left me in preference for my dung. I sacrificed principles for comfort. Rather than cover it and regain the swarms, I left them free to breed.

It was not all bad news. It had only taken three or four days to recover from the shock of the fire, and, for the last hundred miles to Taman-rasset, if I had not hurried I might have enjoyed myself. Physically I was strong. I had been transformed into a pushing machine – a skeleton with calf and stomach muscles.

The day before reaching Tamanrasset, I had found an alternative to the leaking stove and had begun collecting wood which had spilled off lorries. Three sticks, a foot long and an inch in diameter, were sufficient for preparing a meal. They were placed on the ground with ends touching, like three equally spaced spokes with a handful of sand removed from under the hub. They were lit at the centre and burned with a single flame which could be extinguished by withdrawing the sticks. The cooking pot rested on three stones placed between them. Paddy had joined the hunt for wood and after cooking, we sat around a camp-fire swapping stories. Thereafter, I rarely used the stove.

My mind was far away from collecting wood as I hit the tarmac on 9 February. The Tamanrasset Plain spanned twelve miles, surrounded by peaks. The town was in the middle of it, five miles away, at the other end of the road. This was the last town before the Niger border, which was another two hundred and fifty miles south.

I stopped at midday, two miles before the town to smarten up and

114

Practising on Morecambe Sands prior to departure for the Sahara
(Photograph Derek Cattani)

At times it was as difficult to keep the Chinese sailing wheelbarrow upright as it was to push it. This photograph was taken on the dirt track near Reggane. The shells embedded in the ground not far from here (inset) were over a hundred million years old

Left: An inhabitant of Adrar, the first town on the route, poses for the camera in the town square

Right: The small settlement at Arak *(Photograph Ed Troe)*

Below: Mick and Paddy near In Guezzam

Right: Inspecting the scene of devastation following the tent-fire near Meniet

Below: A caravan of three camels making its way through the varied terrain between Arlit and Agadez

Left: This photograph of me was taken by Paddy

Below: A view of the lower reaches of the Hoggar mountains, showing part of the long and difficult descent (6,000 ft in 40 miles) from Tamanrasset

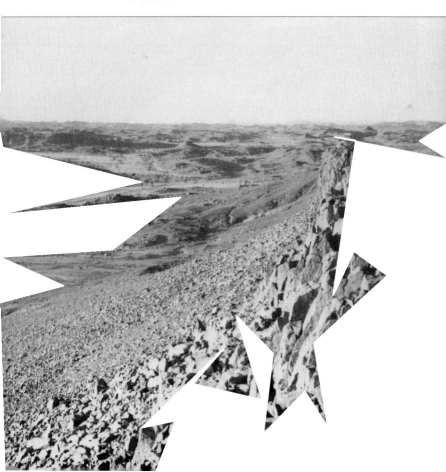

I was in good spirits as I headed south not far from Agadez. Soon before, a village chief had insisted on giving me vegetables and money, with the wish, 'May God give you strength!'

powder myself with DDT. The first sign of Tamanrasset was a hoarding to the left. On the right, houses grew up from the stuff of the ground. Mick and Paddy had found a camp site and Paddy had driven back to meet me. 'Just walk on in front and I'll follow and give you a toot when you have to turn. The camp site's quite nice. It's clean and there are grass huts to sleep in. There's a shower and toilets.'

The road became an avenue of trees in front of the mud façades of houses and shops. There were people everywhere: Arabs, Tuaregs, Africans and Europeans. Before long, they converged around me and brought me to a halt. Who I was, where I was from and what I was doing, they all knew. An Arab mechanic, oiled and boiler-suited, explained to the crowd the reason for my bandages. 'Tired?' one man asked.

'Not a bit. I've only walked thirteen miles today.' Cameras clicked and Paddy sounded his impatience on the horn. The crowd parted, and the flies, now gone, were replaced by a more amiable following. The town had come out to see. Paddy overtook and led me past the post office, two small hotels and cement rendered offices. No cloak of modesty could hide my pride. I beamed at everyone. I was half-way to Kano. We turned right through the town, into what was marked as a hotel, and saw the straw bungalows of the camp site.

— 13 —

MOVIE STARS

Somewhere beyond the roofs of the straw bungalows, through the trees, guns fired. Ed handed me a mug of coffee and Jane pushed me into the shower with soap, towel and clean clothes. 'Hurry up, you have fifteen minutes.'

'What's the rush?'

'You're going to a wedding!' Outside, an Italian doctor whom I had met two days earlier was preparing to treat my burns. He took longer 'scrubbing up' than I did. He and Renzo, his brother-in-law, were touring with two French hitch-hikers, Christiane and Nicole. I was to go to the wedding with the four of them.

We moved down alleys against the flow of the hubbub to its source, a back-street gathering. Drummers and dancers, all armed Tuareg men, leapt with Cossack fury, aimed their loaded muskets and fired. The dust settled in silence. The bullets were embedded in the ground and the dancers resting. The doctor led us through them into a yard where we took off our shoes before entering a carpeted but unfurnished room. The mud walls had no windows but there was light enough. Tuareg men sat cross-legged, holding their feet and chatting through their mufflers.

The doctor, a balding little man of fifty, spoke only Italian and a few words of cinema French. He reached out, pulled the veil from a young Tuareg and nudged Nicole. Neither she, the Tuaregs, nor I understood Italian, but we all knew that he said, 'Look at him, Nicole. He's not bad-looking. Why not settle here – he'd send your father ten camels and give you lots of children.' The room laughed and the young man covered his smile with his blue wrap.

Nicole was a pretty nineteen-year-old from Marseilles. She wore a sweater but no bra. The doctor deliberately moved his eyes from the Tuareg to Nicole's bust, one breast of which he covered with his hat and tried to lift. The company warmed to the doctor, all mufflers were down, and Renzo handed out his cigarettes. Two enormous bowls of couscous were carried in. The company divided around the bowls and ate. Waiters brought cooked lamb from which they pulled small pieces with their fingers. They circled each group of cross-legged diners, slopping bits of meat into the cavities we had made in the couscous with our spoons.

There were no women present, apart from Nicole, and we saw neither bride nor groom. We heard that the groom had gone off to his intended brother-in-law's to win his consent by offering him a pair of shoes. The brother-in-law would refuse, but each day of the wedding, the groom would offer a better pair until the seventh, when they would be accepted.

I was glad to leave the wedding. I had arrived in Tamanrasset like a holiday camper weary with travel, disappointed that I had to join in the games immediately. I had wanted to be lazy, to chat to the campers, to go for a stroll in the evening, and retire early. But, after the wedding, I was whizzed off to the hotel bar, then back to camp, and again to the bar, before a socializing supper around the camp-fire.

Ed and Jane entertained the doctor's party, Eva, Lucas and ourselves to rice, sauce and kebabs. Ahmed, the lonely camp attendant, leaned on a distant tree and looked on, his face and robe flickering in and out of vision with the vicissitudes of the fire. His wife had left him and he was not up to cooking much. He was welcomed into the circle.

The food and company were rich, but too much for me, and I became ill. I went to bed in the straw hut and slept covered by Mick's duffle-coat. The hut had two rooms and a common vestibule. I slept in one room and Mick and Paddy in the other. It was too cold for sleep, but at one o'clock Paddy crept in before he went to bed and threw over me the duffle-coat he had been wearing.

It gave me sleep until eight o'clock; I woke feeling much better, though I still had diarrhoea. The doctor ordered me to rest, but I sneaked off to see if I had any mail. Mick was already in the post office, as were other Europeans. The clerk looked up. 'Sorry, Mr Goldsmith, none for you.'

'There are. I can see them, dozens of them!' The clerk ignored him. Mick protested loudly in English, to the amusement of the Europeans present, until the mail drawer was opened for somebody else. Mick shouted again, saying that he could see a pile of envelopes from his father. This time his pleas were heard and he pushed toward me, sorting his catch.

'Bugger! No visas! Not a bloody thing!'

'You'd better send a telegram,' I said.

'Yeah, I will, but let's go and have a beer first.'

'Go across to the bar. I'll join you when I've got my mail.' There were three letters, one each from my sister and parents, and a bumper one from Joan. I walked across the street to the forecourt of the hotel, which was furnished with round tables shaded by parasols. Europeans and westernized Arabs drank beer and Coca-Cola while Tuaregs hawked leatherwork and ornamental weapons from table to table. I drew a chair up to the beer Mick had bought for me, and opened Joan's letter.

I did not understand what I was reading at first. She had developed a crush on Mike, one of our friends, and was emotionally involved in a big way. Mike had often looked after our children, taken them to the park and put them in the bath – things that I had been too busy to do. Now that I was away, he had continued to help.

There was, however, much in the letter to show that she loved me and that she had no intention of becoming involved with him. She had told the friends with whom she was living about her feelings so that they could keep an eye on her. Nevertheless, the depth of those feelings seemed so strong that I wondered how she could contain them. The dream I had had at Aulef had already half come true – Mike was tall, dark and young. The trip was no longer about hardship or danger: it was about uncertainty, and I was powerless to do anything. The visas, my marriage, and the expedition all hung in the balance.

Mick read humorous bits from his sister's letter and I laughed, though I had not heard. With Joan's letter, the lack of visas, and the broken wheel to think of, I went back to the bar for another bottle of distraction.

That evening, the doctor threw a dinner party for us, which helped me to forget. There was one outsider, Hector, a loud Walter Mitty from Nigeria. We sat on the sand, in the doctor's hut, backs to the wall, dining on soup and macaroni. Hector and the doctor had no mutual language but by shouting, waving arms and pulling faces, they were carrying on a discussion about Colonel Gadafi and General Amin. The doctor smiled as he talked, and his eyes twinkled. He was a master of silent comedy. Hector became heated by the scorn the doctor poured over Amin.

'Jeeeesus Christ!' bellowed Hector, his white eyes like headlamps in the dark. 'Jeeeesus Christ!' Suddenly he remembered that I was a clergyman, glanced across, embarrassed, flicked a smile, and uttered in pious tones, 'Oh yes, Jesus Christ, blessed Lord, save us and help us.'

It was a night of hilarity, with songs and poems from Hector and a performance from the silent movie stars, the doctor and Nicole. It was a night in which to forget, but eight hours later, sobriety returned with the dawn. Ed and Jane were making breakfast in the back of their van. 'Hello Geoff! Would you like some coffee?'

'That'd be nice, thanks, Ed.' Jane was sitting inside the back of the vehicle. Ed was outside, leaning in.

'What's the visa situation?' asked Ed.

'Grim. There's no news. We've sent a telegram, but there's no chance of a reply yet.'

'Can't they try to get into Niger without a visa?'

'They're under orders not to. We've done everything we can. We met a man from Niger immigration in the bar yesterday and he's gonna have a go for us, but he doesn't hold out much hope.'

'What about the Algerian reporter who promised to help?'

'Here's your coffee. Be careful – it's hot.'

'Thanks.' I took the mug.

'Yes, what about the reporter?' asked Jane.

'He's disappeared. Got cold feet if you ask me. "Cold feet" is an expression meaning . . .'

'Yes, I know what it means.' We drank our coffee and Jane ate a crispbread.

'Look. I've discussed it with Mick and Paddy, and we think it best that I go on without them. It's at least ten days to the border. If there are no visas by then, they'll drive down and give me supplies for Niger. What I want to know is, well, will you take their place from here?'

'Yes, we will,' Ed said, without hesitation.

'You don't have to make up your mind now,' I said. 'Talk it over with Jane. Think about it. It'll be really boring and horrible.'

'We've talked it over already. We were going to offer. When do we leave?'

'Tomorrow.' We had a lot to do and began immediately, going first to buy vegetables, sardines, bread, and a robe of thin white cotton to replace the one destroyed in the fire. We toured the police and immigration departments and I ended up at the hospital for a booster cholera injection which I needed for entry into Niger and Nigeria.

A man in a white laboratory coat led me to what he said was the waiting room. I opened the door and saw a chair and table by the window, a household refrigerator in one corner and a Tuareg woman, fully clothed, in bed. 'Pardon, madame,' I said, and backed out. My escort gone, I found another who took me to the same room. The woman was now sitting up, making dressings, and patting together lint and cotton wool with her hands. This was the hospital to which I would have come but for the Italian doctor, and I wondered whether those were the 'sterile' dressings that would have been used for my burns. Not only preservation of my life and documents, but even aftercare had been thrown in with the same miracle.

A middle-aged Algerian breezed in, his white doctor's coat unbuttoned. He walked to the refrigerator and found it empty except for a small packet wrapped in the pages of a magazine – I thought it might be butter. 'Now let me see. Cholera vaccine?' he said, ponderously tapping the refrigerator door, 'Cholera vaccine, cholera vaccine..No, no, I don't think so. No, no, we have no cholera vaccine. Buy some from the drugstore and bring it to me.' But the drugstore had none either. Entry into Niger and Nigeria was now in jeopardy, but I had no alternative other than to carry on and see what would happen.

As darkness claimed the sky, we laid aside preparations for the next day and began to cook a meal. The doctor's party and the Swiss were camping in the mountains, giving medical treatment to the nomads. Jane was cutting meat up into a pot and I offered help. 'There's nothing much to do, Geoff. Go and enjoy yourself. You won't be able to tomorrow. Take Paddy with you and if you find Mick bring him back at seven for supper.'

The bar beckoned us back along a boulevard of dim street-lights and small illuminated signs. Mick was on the hotel patio, sitting under a wall-lamp with three English airmen, Cliff, Steve and Sandy, who had touched down that day on their return from the Zaire River Expedition.

Mick invited them to eat, and so we sauntered back to eke out the spaghetti with a few quick cans of Mick's army stew. We ate out in the open, near the vehicles. Mick and I had been getting on well for a long time, when Ahmed, the janitor, wandered over. Ahmed always got himself noticed when food was about. Mick spotted this and reacted. Ahmed appealed to Mick, crouching in front of him and pointing to his mouth. 'My tooth hurts. Please give me some medicine.'

'No! Go away! The doctor will be back tomorrow.'

'Don't be so heartless,' I said. 'A pain-killer won't cost anything.'

'You know what these gollies are like. They'll do anything for medicine. Anyway, the doctor put some tincture on it,' he retorted sharply.

'But that was twelve hours ago!' I said. Mick put his plate angrily on the bonnet, brought a tablet, and told Ahmed how to take it. Paddy echoed my thoughts,

'Isn't that a water-purifying tablet?'

'Hey Mick,' I yelled, 'what d'you think you're playing at? You can't give him a chlorine tablet!' He remained composed while talking to Ahmed and then erupted.

'Look Geoff, think what you like! Do what you like! I don't care! And you can write *that* in your little book.' Every day I had made notes with the intention of writing a book, and Mick had taken this as a threat. I made no reply, though angry. We had never had a row and I had no wish to endanger relations by having one now, and anyway his feelings were understandable. I knew that if I kept cool it would blow over. Incidents between Mick and me were diminishing. Sometimes I wondered whether he realized he was ragging me at all. He would flare up and a second later it was forgotten.

We had no wood, so we bought some from Ahmed, and Cliff made a fire with it. Our attention was soon drawn from the flames to an amber light in the sky. It darted in straight lines, made circles, and stopped for a few minutes at a time. We left the fire for a better view. 'No, it's not a chopper. Not an aircraft at all, nor a weather balloon,' said Steve. The airmen had seen many strange things in the sky and were the first to lose interest and return to the fire.

Steve George, the RAF pilot, was the most talkative. He spoke French and Arabic and seemed to be enjoying Tamanrasset. Cliff Taylor, the army pilot, was a little older and an amiable father figure, while Sandy Donald, a Scottish aircraft mechanic from the same regiment as Paddy, was full of entertaining stories about the forces.

They had flown their Beaver, built in 1932, from Zaire, on their way home from the expedition. Frequent refuelling was necessary. When circling their previous stop, Kano, ground control had warned that they had no diplomatic clearance. The airmen assured them that they had. What they did have was a blank sheet of note paper from the British Embassy, Kinshase. Still airborne, Steve scribbled a note from an imaginary official confirming their clearance. They were given the benefit of the doubt and had twenty-four hours in Kano, but were told that if they returned without clearance, they would be arrested. Kano was, as they described it, in terms unpublishable for a clergyman, a serviceman's paradise. In the space of an hour, Kano became as much Mick's and Paddy's objective as mine.

From Nigeria, they had flown to Tamanrasset, to find that they had no clearance for Algeria either. They were arrested and had their passports confiscated; subsequently they were allowed to go free, but only on the condition that they were out of the country by six o'clock on Wednesday, the following evening. On full tanks they could reach only northern Algeria or Kano. In either case they faced arrest. This brought home to Mick and Paddy the danger they themselves were in. They still had no clearance for Algeria and were masquerading as civilians.

There could have been gloom, but instead we had a ball. They were like screen soldiers, at their best when the situation was worst and I was buoyed up. I slipped away to see how Ahmed was reacting to the tablet. His was the only circular hut on the site and he was sitting inside chatting to old men of the town. 'How's your tooth, Ahmed?'

'Oh, it's much better.'

'Do you feel sick?'

'No. I'm well. The medicine is very good.' I returned to within earshot of the party, loaded the wheelbarrow and wrote a long report.

Less than four hours later I was up. So were Ed, Jane, Steve, Cliff and Sandy, who had come from the hotel to see me off. At dawn, we walked to the police station on the edge of the town, where travellers had to report before leaving for the border, but it was shut, so we photographed ourselves by the signs which forbade us to do so. By nine o'clock my passport had been stamped, and the six of us began to walk along the two hundred and fifty-two mile trail to In Guezzam and the Niger border. The others would turn back after a mile or so.

For two years, since I had bought my first map of the Sahara, Tamanrasset to In Guezzam had been the bogey. I had told Hawker Siddeley that a wheelbarrow designed to cope with this leg would manage the rest. I had trained and planned for this, the longest section, knowing that all others would be easy by comparison. On paper, I could just do it if everything ran smoothly. I needed an uneventful descent from the mountains, no delays, no breakdowns, no sickness and no sand until almost at In Guezzam, when the wheelbarrow would be lighter. A breakdown was likely – I was using the damaged aluminium wheel with the loose rim as we had been unable to get the one with the steel spokes welded.

The six of us strolled along the trail, closing our eyes to the coming ordeal and to the impending arrest, and generated a blind, sentimental optimism. 'You watch. Those stupid bastards at the police station will think we're trying to abscond with you.' They joked me along the first mile, helping me to put the approaching dangers out of mind.

The Union Jack flapped to the fore. All was silent. I stopped and turned. They were two hundred yards behind, watching me. They waved. I waved and did not look back again.

14

OFFICERS' MESS

My companions were soon replaced by that familiar but disagreeable crowd of followers – flies, in their thousands. I no longer minded, except when eating, as Ed had given me a head-net.

I had not gone far when a lorry appeared. Four Algerians got out and stood in my way, refusing to let me pass. 'There is no water for four hundred kilometres,' they said, 'and there are bandits with guns. You must go back.' It took me ten minutes to argue my way forward.

The *piste* crossed the shale plateau but after a few miles abruptly began the forty-mile descent from the Hoggar range. The view from the top was of a range of hills and extinct volcanoes tumbling down the mountain. They looked like a family of sleeping dinosaurs whose fawn and brown backs were covered with scales of blackened boulders and broken rock. At two hundred kilograms, the wheelbarrow was heavier than ever, and the hills too steep to climb or descend in a straight line. The zigzag method was the only way up and over forty miles of roller-coaster. One driver who passed told me that he had been in first and second gear for three hours. It had been weeks since the wheelbarrow had fallen from my hands but it now happened every few minutes and it was almost too heavy to right. The heat was stifling and I drank twenty-two pints of water in twenty-four hours. For two and a half days, the *piste* mounted one brontosaurus' back after another, draining my strength and my will. Never had it been so tough. Joan's letter and the dream, which the distractions of Tamanrasset had helped me to forget, drained me further. I wanted to go home but lacked the courage. I prayed for an honourable discharge, for the wheel to break irreparably.

A note in my diary asked whether it would take more courage to go on or to give in. I did not know, but felt that to do either demanded more guts than I had. I ended up asking whether it was important to be courageous at all.

On the third day the descent was complete, and the terrain now reminded me of the shallow hills and salmon-pink expanses of sand between Aulef el Arab and In Salah. None the less, the going was easier than it had been over the hills and I tried to forget the misery of the past two days. I had been depressed, and, like a beach-ball held under water, surfaced with force. My spirits lifted. Five hours' sleep was all I took that night, and I was well into the fourth day's walk by dawn. I managed twenty-six miles, but it was not all good news. I had eaten the last of my sweets and oats. My other food was low too, and I had only seven gallons of water for the remaining one hundred and seventy miles. I would have to aim at twenty-five miles a day and ration myself to one gallon, but I knew that one bad stretch of sand, or a breakdown, could mean a quick return home.

All was well on the fifth day until there was a bang like a hammer-blow and I was pitched to the ground. The wheel rim had split and sprung out, jamming against the chassis. One of the bolts had sheared from where the rim, which had been made in two pieces, was fastened to a backing plate. I was carrying no tool-kit, Ed would be another three hours, and other help was unlikely. We were only seeing a couple of vehicles a day in these parts. This could be the end.

I took my hat in my hand and began a dance, singing 'Slow Boat to China'. There seemed nothing else to do. Almost instantly a Citroën, like Ed's, broke the horizon. Two French gymnasts, carrying a lot of muscle and wearing only shorts, stopped and examined the rim. 'No, no. The bolts have not sheared,' said one, shaking his head. 'The threads are OK, but you have an English nut on a French bolt.' He brought nuts from his tool box and fitted them in seconds.

Somewhere, some old lady had been on her knees. With the kind of help I had just received, the trip might be possible without Paddy. Leaving the lads behind would not be easy, but I had to be prepared for it. I pictured them coming to wave me across the border. They would not see Kano, just Niger from behind a fence. Two weeks and they might be shivering under Salford's grey chill, telling Joan they had left me well. I blamed the army. I was not surprised by military inefficiency and had been aware of it from the first day of the expedition, when I had flown to Gibraltar.

* * *

I had been due to rendezvous with Mick and Paddy, who had taken the Land Rover there on a munitions ship. We were to catch the ferry to Tangier the following day. Though I had been told that I would be escorted from the airport to accommodation in the officers' mess at the 1st Battalion Queen's Regiment, there was no one to meet me. I tried to telephone the army without success, so after a long delay I took a cab two miles up and around the Rock to the barracks overlooking the sea. I climbed up the concrete steps to the guardroom's reception window and saw three corporals inside. While two of them chatted about the times that were had when the border with Spain had been open, the other attended to me. 'My name's Howard. I've a room booked in the officers' mess.'

'I'm sorry, we're not expecting anyone. You must be at the wrong place.'

'Are you the 1st Battalion Queen's?'

'Yes.'

'I'm sure this is the place. It's been arranged by signal from Bulford Camp. I embark for North Africa tomorrow with two soldiers.'

'You *must* have the wrong place. None of *our* lads are going anywhere.'

'They're not *your* lads. One's REME, the other's RA, and they've stayed here overnight.'

'There's no one staying here. I'd be the first to know. Which regiment are you from?'

'I'm a civilian.'

'I think you'd better leave.'

'Phone the duty officer and he'll confirm everything.'

'I can't phone him. It's after five o'clock.'

'What would you do if you were under attack?'

'God knows!'

'Could I leave my case?'

'It's against regulations. I'm sorry you'll have to go.'

'Would you ring for a taxi for me?'

'I'm sorry, I can't do that either.' I turned my back, picked up the case, and began the two-mile descent to the town. I could have been in Gibraltar for a month and still not met the lads. By chance, however, within half a mile I hailed what I thought was a taxi but which turned out to be a soldier's car. Paddy was on the back seat on his way to the pub. He got out and walked with me back up the hill, past the guardroom, and into the barracks where he and Mick were staying.

I slept in their room, on the bare springs of a bed, with a borrowed pillow and blanket. I had learnt that the lads were to sail to Tangier in the afternoon on a civilian ferry and that they had not booked for me because, contrary to my knowledge and our agreed plans, the army had told them I was flying to Algeria directly. Paddy immediately rushed me off to get a ferry ticket but I was told that all ferries were fully booked for the next three days. After a tour of travel agents, I was back at the main ticket-office, letting the manager assume I was military. 'There's no question of my not getting a ticket,' I explained. 'If I don't go, the whole exercise is off.' The ticket was issued without further questions.

As we were driving out of the barracks to catch the ferry, the major who was to have been my host hailed me. 'Good to meet you, Reverend,' he said, greeting me through the passenger-door window. Would you like to come to the mess? We have a room for you.'

* * *

My thoughts turned from Gibraltar to the spare inner tubes the army had supplied, patched too much to be of any use; to the petrol stove that leaked; to a second one with a faulty valve; and to the trailer, written off before we left.

I was not in the frame of mind to appreciate what the army had done, stepping in to save the expedition. I had forgotten the long hours worked and the many favours done by soldiers of all ranks just to get me on the road. I spent the afternoon fretting about the lads' visas, angry at the army's slackness, and then the doctor and his party drew up. I asked about their time in the mountains, but Renzo replied, 'Geoff, Geoff! Mick and Paddy have their visas. A telegram came. They'll be driving down in a day or two. They have welded your wheel and they have petrol for Ed.' The doctor let his party walk a victory mile with me before scooping them up and taking them south to Niger.

There was now increased urgency. I *had* to get to In Guezzam, but I doubted whether the wheel would hold. The honeycomb in-fill was so battered that it was no longer round, and the load was bouncing with every turn. Shortage of water would not allow me to slow down, so I pressed on, hoping it would hold, and singing, 'Goodbye Tamanrasset, farewell In Sha-la, it's a long, long way to get to Kano . . .', and I wondered whether Joan would be there.

We camped on sand, by the shell of a Lotus No. 6. It had been stripped of everything and sand-blasted to bare metal. I ate soya protein and potato near the tent I had borrowed from Mick and Paddy. They would have it back when they returned, and I would resume sleeping in the Land Rover. When I had finished eating, we saw headlights and heard an engine labouring not far away. It cut out and a minute later an Algerian came wading through the darkness and sand to our camp-fire. He carried a torch, two empty fuel-cans and a bundle of banknotes, and asked to buy ten litres of petrol. We could only give him the dregs from the jerry-cans, as the Citroën's tank was only a third full.

After a further day and a half, the petrol tank was almost empty. Things had been going well for me. I had been managing twenty-five miles a day, and the hardships were minor. I had had to eat dehydrated potato powder straight from the packet for breakfast and lunch, and my ear, still raw from the burns, had bled during the night and stuck to my jacket. Otherwise everything was fine, that was until the wheel rim sprang open again. The new nuts had not held. The wheelbarrow was thrown forward, with its nose in the sand.

Ed had loaned me a spanner and I was able to make a repair of sorts, but after half an hour I had to do it again. The wheel had become misshapen, and the rising and falling of the load put extra stress on the bolts. I now had to move so slowly for fear of further damage that I could not expect to manage anything like twenty-five miles.

Mick and Paddy should have arrived the day before and unless they turned up soon to change the wheel, I would run out of water before In Guezzam. I was gripped by despair, shouting into the wind, 'Mick, Paddy, where are you?' Then I heard a noise I knew well: the cream-coloured Land Rover, lumbering, wallowing, ploughing, on, on, on – five, four, three, two, one hundred yards away. I jumped, I shouted, I grovelled. 'Thank you! Thank you! Thank you!' But where were all its jerry-cans? The roof-rack? Who was that driving? Where were Mick and Paddy? It had got to be Mick and Paddy! Please God!

There was nothing so cruel as that Land Rover with the Swiss number-plates. If Mick and Paddy did not arrive by the next morning, I would have to beg petrol for Ed. I might be forced to finish the walk without the wheelbarrow – I would leave it as an offering to the desert. Perhaps that would be a fitting end; it was better for an old ship to come to its end on the rocks than in the breaker's yard, and better for the wheelbarrow to lie half-buried in the sand, like the dead camels and wrecked cars I had seen. It would become sand-blasted, glinting aluminium, marking the way – better than corroding in the garden at home.

I lunched on dry potato powder, my eyes looking north. I recognized a speck on the horizon, the cream-coloured Land Rover, jerry-cans, roof-rack, Mick, Paddy and all. I whooped, I danced, I shouted. 'Thank you! Thank you! Thank you!' Paddy had welded the steel wheel and added four more spokes of steel piping. He fitted it, the total hold-up being no longer than for a normal lunch.

Evening camp was gloriously familiar. We pooled our wood and gathered round its warmth. Paddy fed sticks to the fire, and Ed, peanuts to a gerbil. 'Can you get to Arlit by March the first, Geoff?' asked Mick. Paddy and I conferred.

'I'll have a go. Twenty-five miles a day gets us there on February twenty-fifth. But why March the first?'

'Norwich City are in the League Cup Final, and if you get to Arlit in time for me to hear a bit of it on the World Service, I'll stand you both as much as you can eat and drink all day.'

We had not originally intended to pass through Arlit, to the south-east, as the map had shown a frightening amount of sand. We had hoped to go south through In Abangarit but had changed our minds. The Belgian conference interpreters had told us that it was firm all the way to Arlit, and others had told us that the small amount of sand was worth enduring. Arlit had a restaurant, swimming-pool and supermarket; two hundred French people lived there, workers at a uranium mine.

The next day the Citroën was often, and the Land Rover occasionally, stuck. Ed and Jane were weak with diarrhoea, and my legs refused to move, so I flung them forward as if they were artificial. Sometimes I saw two faceless children. I had forgotten what Susan and Sam looked like. I was too tired to stand, too proud to stop, but somehow I managed twenty-six miles. A gritty gale made me put on goggles. The smog-mask had been destroyed in the fire, so I breathed over my shoulder like a swimmer. In my imagination I heard an orchestra playing *La Calinda*.

At camp, just before dark, a car stopped. Out of it stepped a tall Algerian in a grey suit, wearing white plastic shoes and no socks. His wife, a veiled ball of white cotton fabric, was with him. A little man with a dark suit, a smile, and inquisitive fingers followed. He opened the wheelbarrow and took out Mick's cassette recorder. 'You sell? How much?'

'Not for sale,' I said.

'You have a lot of wood. Where you get it?'

'I found it.'

'What's that you're cooking?'

'It's made from beans but tastes like meat.' The woman picked up a piece of dried soya protein while Ed watched 'Fingers' search out a camera from the Citroën.

'How much I pay?' he asked in English. It was Ed's spare camera, a cheap model. Films for it were not available in Algeria, and he had used his last, but he haggled with the man until he got three times the price he had paid for it in Holland.

As twilight waned and we settled with our food, a gerbil foraged in the rubbish pit. 'You know,' said Mick, 'I'm sure that's the same gerbil we've seen every day. You think you'll be a hero when you get back, Geoff, but wait until they hear about the mouse who crossed the Sahara at forty k's a day.'

Forty kilometres, twenty-five miles, was less than our average for the next three days, bringing In Guezzam to within seventeen miles on 21 February, the eve of my birthday. I had enough water – three pints – but I lay in the Land Rover, hungry. In the darkness, I fingered Joan's birthday present to me, hoping it was chocolate. Through the wrapping, I felt an irregular shape, twice as big as my fist. I pulled at the paper guiltily, almost wishing it would not tear; I was opening it a day early. There were two gifts, and as the wrapping came apart, one of them fell into my lap. The other was a small cardboard box with a waxy rounded shape poking from it. This was surely something to eat! I switched on the torch expecting to find an Easter egg, but it was a bar of soap in a decorative box, and in my lap, a scrubbing brush!

─── *15* ───
HAPPY BIRTHDAY!

In Guezzam was seventeen miles away and I would remain hungry until I got there. I was out of food. I galloped until around midday, when a strip of square houses appeared like a broken cliff along the horizon – In Guezzam. No signpost marked its boundary, only a dead camel. It had tucked its head under its haunches and died, beaten by the last mile. But *I* could make it; I still had a toothmug of water left. Drawing nearer, the town was no longer a two-dimensional strip: its houses were set back a hundred yards either side of the track. 'Happy Birthday, Geoff!' said a continental voice. A tall Swede, whom I had met in Tamanrasset, had stopped and was holding out his hand. 'Here's a present.' He left a sticky, brown rectangle on my palm. I had my chocolate after all.

In Guezzam had many houses with broken walls and without roofs. Urchins played games around me. One of them leapt from a snake. I panicked, crashing to a halt. Two more steps and I would have needed the serum I was carrying. The boys squealed with delight and mocked, pushing wheelbarrows of their own imagination beside me. The snake was a rope. They laughed and danced in circles until a rock the size of a cricket ball came from a doorway and scattered them. A soldier followed and dispersed them further with rapid-fire Arabic.

Tuaregs, billowed in blue, Arabs, and two bronzed Frenchmen clustered as I took a drink. 'Hi, remember me? I passed you at Tadjmout. How long's it taken you from Tam?' asked one of the French.

'Ten days and four hours.'

'I think we'll get a wheelbarrow. It took us eight days and we still can't go on. Sand in the engine, the fuel, everywhere.'

The children had regrouped – an Arab swung his foot, catching a young rump. 'Leave them!' I yelled.

'Don't worry. He's their teacher,' said the Frenchman.

Before the Second World War, I was told, we would have celebrated here on champagne and French cuisine. Now there was neither shop, post office, nor filling station, only a few yards of sand-drifted cobblestones leading to the barbed wire frontier. Two soldiers in green rags slouched against the barrier. One, with torn canvas boots, left his oily machine gun and took my passport. 'Please wait the other side of the gate till we've stamped your papers.'

The last yard of Algeria slipped from under my feet. The hard times seemed to have happened to somebody else. I had met warmth and friendship, no bandits, and no thieves, but people who had known how to give. I remembered the little Belgian with the matted beard, near Tadjmout, and his, 'Dey won't let you starve out here. It's crazy.' Behind us was Arab Algeria, ahead black Niger, different languages, cultures and foods, only the wandering Tuareg at home in both.

On the other side there were a few trees and a well where Mick and Jane were washing themselves. 'Come and try this, Geoff.'

'No thanks, Mick. I'll get some water and wash tonight.'

'Come on! It's beautiful, warm and clear.'

'I can't afford the time. Kano, remember?'

'Oh, for God's sake, forget that for a bit. You've just walked two hundred and fifty miles and you can't stop for a bath!'

The Niger frontier post was eighteen miles ahead at Assamaka. I took on water and biscuits and lumbered over the bank ahead. The configuration of hillocks, crags and small dunes was like that of a rough sea. It was tough for all of us. Mick, Paddy, Ed and Jane overtook me, but later I saw their tracks among footprints and shovelled sand.

After a further hour, the landscape resembled Southport beach with the tide out – mile after mile of sand, flat as a lake. When I first spotted the Land Rover and Citroën, they looked like little boats anchored a mile away. Mick and Jane were in the galley preparing a birthday meal, while Paddy kept the kettle singing. I imagined that the wheelbarrow was a small craft sailing out to rendezvous with them.

I was fearful of the reception I would get after having turned down Mick's earlier invitation to bathe. I felt like shouting, 'I can't come. There's pox on board.' Eleven days' sweat looked like engine oil. The wheelbarrow was just as dirty and my eating utensils worse, having remained unwashed since Tamanrasset.

The sand dragged like a current and altered my angle of approach. I had been heading for their starboard side but was carried round towards their stern. The three little crafts were the only mark on the undisturbed golden expanse. When I was ten yards away from him, Paddy poured coffee into a Ministry of Defence green plastic mug, and handed it to me as I drew alongside. 'What kept you?' asked Mick, trying to conceal a smile. He had not expected me to make such good time. It had not been so bad for me – the wheelbarrow had been almost empty.

I drank the coffee, took my new bar of soap and scrubbed myself sore. A pinker, shinier me, in soft, clean clothes, joined the circle for rice and chicken. Only wine was missing. I had tried to buy some in Tamanrasset but the hotel was out of stock. Mick let us eat half our meal before he got up to go into the cab. He came back with a bottle of Algerian 'Burgundy'. 'Happy Birthday, Geoff! From all of us,' he said. Paddy sprang up and threw down my tea-glasses from the Land Rover roof.

'None for me,' said Ed, nursing his belly. 'I couldn't take it.'

'None for me either,' added Paddy. 'You know I can't stand the stuff.'

'Have a heart you lot. What's the use of wine if nobody'll share it?' I said.

'Oh, I'm not going to be miserable,' said Paddy. 'I'll drink your health with a can of beer I've been saving.' I turned to Jane and to Mick. 'Grab a glass. I know you two won't refuse.'

'Only a little, Geoff,' said Mick. 'I think I'm getting the craps, like Ed.' With these excuses they made sure I enjoyed myself. It seemed years since we had shared a meal on the trail. But it was only at In Amguel, almost three weeks ago, the night we had met Ed and Jane. And tonight looked like being our last time with them.

Provided we got safely into Niger, they would drive on. It was an evening for sentiment, for talking about Norwich City and the League Cup, for remembering Ed's holiday in Poland, and for planning what we would do in Kano.

'When I get to Kano,' said Mick, 'I'm gonna buy a new suit, sit in the bar of the Kano Club and pick up a bit of black. Sometime I'm gonna go to Kano market and buy some of that fancy silverware, and I'm gonna buy a goatskin bag to keep the water cool for driving back, and I'm gonna buy sacks of fruit and enough veg to see us home.'

'When I get to Kano,' said Ed, 'I'm going to drive at seventy miles an hour all day long on those roads.'

'You can do what you like,' blurted Jane, 'I'm going to get out of this heat and find a swimming-pool.'

'When I get to Kano,' I mused, 'I'm gonna climb into a big silver bird and when you're all hot and sweaty, driving back, I'll be sipping iced cocktails.'

Paddy doodled in the sand with a stick. 'Anyway, it's not far now, only seven hundred and forty-odd miles.'

'Not as far as that as the crow flies,' I said. 'Just over four hundred.' Kano seemed a stride away. I fancied I could smell it, and I wondered whether the flies that day had commuted from it.

It had been a happy, happy birthday, and when I crawled off to bed to complete it with a recorded birthday message from Joan, I noticed faint lights in the south, the aura of a town. Not Kano, surely? No, though I might have happily deceived myself; it was Assamaka, the Niger frontier, eight miles away. But it was Kano and Nigeria that filled my thoughts as I fell asleep.

* * *

Joan and I had spent the first year of our marriage in Nigeria, and we had become fond of that country. When passing through customs at Kano, Joan had been carrying a few red roses, a gift from my mother. One of the officials said, 'Those plastic roses look real.'

'They are real,' said Joan.

'They are plastic!' he insisted, and he pointed over his shoulder with his thumb. The sign read: 'It Is An Offence To Bring Fruit And Plants Into The Country.'

'They are plastic!' he said. Nigerians were a welcoming people. We had made many friends there. One of them, Lydia, had only one garment, a tattered dress, in which to live and sleep. On washday, she found it hard to borrow anything to wear because so many other people were in the same predicament. Yet she was generous, twice presenting us with a chicken when she could rarely afford meat. Her own daily food was gruel made from earthy-tasting Guinea corn.

There was Bulus, whose father earned £80 a year as a cook at a secondary school. Bulus had passed the entrance examination for the same school, but his father could not afford the £40 fee to send him there. There was Degi, who had tuberculosis. He used to sell the drugs he was given to buy food. Garba should have been in a mental hospital, but there wasn't one, nor any money to send him if there had been. Instead, he was prevented from running amok by an iron staple which clamped his leg to a heavy log. He could just drag the log far enough from his hut for him to perform his natural functions.

They had been friends, not clients. All of them, except Garba, visited our home and we theirs. We shared their food, jokes and, to a small extent, their family life. I was crossing the desert in order to help people like them. Indeed, it had been while we were in Nigeria that the idea had come about. Sometimes, when I was supervising students in the library, I flipped open an atlas and looked at the overland route to home. I had thought about walking it, but the Sahara seemed too great a barrier – almost twice the size of the USA, twice as far from north to south as Manchester is from the south of France. The compulsion to make the journey grew once we had flown home. That was almost six years before.

* * *

It was now Sunday 23 February, the day after my birthday, the sixty-second day of my journey, and I was still part-way between the

Algerian and Niger frontier posts. I woke early to pray but missed having somebody to pray with. It had not bothered me whether my companions had the same interest in music or art as me, but I wanted them to share my faith, weak as it was.

Ahead, Assamaka split the horizon, a silhouette rippling in the heat between yellow sand and blue sky. A pylon, tree, lorry and buildings grew and separated into their distinct shapes. I had been warned of the sand and I had made sure that the wheelbarrow was almost empty. The small load was placed at the rear to take weight off the sinking wheel and put it on to my feet.

The pylon became a derrick, with unlit electric lamps at the top and workmen below. From my angle of approach, the 'town' looked like an English farm complex. There were small breeze-block buildings and a larger one like a barn, next to which the Land Rover and Citroën were parked.

A figure was walking towards me across the hot sand but it seemed to take him a long time to get near. He was a round Idi Amin of a man in a navy-blue boiler suit, carrying a piece of paper – the keys to Niger and to the next six hundred and thirty-three miles. Ed's and Jane's papers were in order and so were mine, except for the cholera vaccination certificate. But had clearance for Mick and Paddy got from the Niger Foreign Office through the tangle of the security forces?

My stomach nervously craved attention. The fat man welcomed me cheerfully and escorted me to his office. His face darkened as we approached. 'Where is your licence-plate, log-book and insurance for this thing?'

'They don't issue them in my country.'

'Well, they do here, and you cannot enter Niger without them.'

When he saw my look of panic, he laughed, put a broad arm around my shoulders and led me into a shack. There was a heap of camel saddles in the corner, and a table and chair in the middle of the room. 'And these two men,' he said, sitting behind the table, 'they didn't tell me they were military. I have clearance for them too.' He filled out my travelling permit and squinted at me through the windowless gloom. 'It says here you're a priest. Are you sure? You don't look like a priest.'

'I don't feel like a priest, at the moment.'

'You know there are two routes to Agadez? You must go via Arlit and report to the military there.'

'I've heard that that route is tough.'

'It's two hundred and ten kilometres. The first fifty have a lot of sand but it's all right after that. How long will it take you?'

'Five days.'

'Good. Today I will signal our chief.' He tapped out a message on the bare table with his index finger and thumb. 'Then all along the route the army will be watching out for you. Are you married with children?' I nodded. He shook his head gently, smiled and put his hands flat against his cheek in the charade for sleep. 'Do you dream of them?'

'Often, but usually when I'm awake.'

'They must be very anxious, but after Arlit their fears are over.' He took me by the arm through the blinding doorway of light, like men entering a furnace. The sun was high and the world glowed white like an overexposed photograph. I clipped on my sun-glasses. He gripped my right shoulder and raised an arm. 'Arlit is over there.' He was pointing at a black dot about half a mile away. 'There are oil drums like that every kilometre. When you get to the first you can see the second, and so on. Take plenty of water and have courage.'

16
CUP FINAL

A mirage lapped beyond the first oil drum. There was nothing to see other than an expanse of dazzling yellow under the sky. Hot and inhospitable. My heart thumped so hard as I wrestled that I thought I might die. The wheelbarrow was fully laden. I was forced to rest several times before the first oil drum, and when I reached it, Assamaka seemed only an arm's length over my shoulder. I was sure it could not be this bad for long.

Before I had reached the next oil drum, Ed and Jane stopped to say goodbye. It seemed that we should have had something profound to say, but we talked only of the weather, sand and of meeting in England in the autumn. Ed handed me ten pounds sterling. 'Take this.'

'What for?'

'For our food. You've given us a lot since we met.'

'Don't be silly. You were with us for my benefit. I can't take your money.'

'It wasn't your food and it's not your money. It all belongs to the charity. Please take it for those poor people.' I accepted it gratefully, shook his hand and gave Jane a peck on the cheek, though I wanted to hug them both. They got in the car, but Ed got out again, holding a thermometer. 'Here, this is of more use to you than me. When I see the temperature I may go crazy.'

'Thanks.' I paused. 'Till autumn then.'

'Till autumn,' I never saw their brave Citroën again. When they had gone and I began to flag, I saw in my imagination six angels, eight feet tall, pulling the wheelbarrow with golden cords. Even with their help I was forced to rest again, and when I did, I took the temperature under the shade of the wheelbarrow: 100 degrees Fahrenheit at five in the afternoon. When we camped by the twenty-third oil drum at six-thirty, it was 87 degrees.

Next day was worse in every respect. I swore at the wheelbarrow, kicked it and dragged it by the scruff of its neck, cursing the Belgian couple who had said this way was easy. I drank twelve pints and only urinated a dribble. Mick and Paddy rolled up in the afternoon. 'Keep it up, Geoff,' said Mick. 'Just think of that silver bird. When you're up there with your iced cocktails, we'll still be here, sweating it out.' Mick's encouragement and the thought of that silver bird kept me going.

Two vehicles stopped before nightfall, the first a Toyota truck with a young French driver, taking supplies to the frontier post. 'Hello. Your Dutch friends in the Citroën asked me to see if you were all right.'

'I'm OK, but how are they?'

'They're not far ahead, perhaps twenty-five kilometres. I pulled them out of the sand.'

'Is there much of it?'

'No, not after the sixtieth oil drum, then it's hard and flat.' The second vehicle was a caravanette, carrying a black guide, with tribal scars on his cheeks, and two middle-aged female missionaries from the Congo.

'Did you see the Dutch in a Citroën?'

'Yes, about thirty miles away. They were stuck.' Poor Ed and Jane. 'But your other friends are OK. They're not far away.' Their guide asked to try the wheelbarrow. He took the shafts and pushed.

'It won't move. There is something under the wheel,' he said.

'Only sand,' I said.

'But the car moves easily.' He pushed again, grimacing, but the wheelbarrow fell. 'It's not easy,' he said, shaking his head. He was right, except that where pebbles patterned the sand I made reasonable progress, though by the end of the second day, Assamaka was only thirty miles behind.

I had seen no wood since the border, and I might have had to burn some kit or have no supper, but at camp there was a wooden crate leaning on the forty-eighth oil drum, like Abraham's ram caught in the thicket. It was a cool, moonlit 70 degrees and I was enjoying my meat pudding. 'I'm sorry about progress, Mick, but we'll be OK. I'll increase to twenty-one miles a day. We'll get to Arlit for the final.'

'Oh, NFI, Geoff, NFI. You can't help it,' said Mick.

'You know, those two German women made me feel quite randy,' said Paddy.

'You must be in a bad way. They were nearly as old as my grannie and twice as ugly,' I said.

'I'm serious!'

'I bet that golly guide's been through the pair of 'em,' said Mick.

'Give over. They're missionaries. They're in a different world.'

'They've probably raped him. You can tell they were a pair of frustrated spinsters. I wouldn't like to imagine where that golly's had his big lips,' said Mick. They enjoyed teasing me.

'And what a face!' said Paddy. 'Did you see those tribal markings?

There's a better tread on his face than on our tyres. And as for those women – when I shook hands, I felt weak at the knees.'

'You can't be serious,' I said.

'You've got to get what you can, when you can, and not bother what it's wrapped up in,' said Mick. Paddy smashed some more wood and a gerbil climbed on my foot. I gently tipped him off and went to bed.

I rose with enthusiasm, racing along islands of pebbles gaining momentum to cross to the next, but after two hours I hit a soft, ploughed field. The huge tyres of military vehicles had dug a criss-cross pattern of deep furrows. I left the wheelbarrow to test the ground and mark the way with my foot. I then meandered backwards, jerking the whellbarrow one horrific mile in three hours. Then at half-past one, the bearing jammed and I could go no further. I lay on the ground, my head and shoulders under the wheelbarrow, escaping from the heat. Even so, the thermometer showed it to be 110 degrees Fahrenheit in that bit of shade. Half an hour later, Paddy came and made a repair. On I went, expecting firmer ground over each hill as promised by the Frenchman, the border chief, and the Belgians, but I was always disappointed. I ended up on the ground like a discarded marionette. Weeping, shouting and beating the wheelbarrow was all part of the routine now.

Next, there was a dune in my path. The shallows had been enough. I could not manage a tidal wave two hundred yards across. I whimpered like a child, 'I can't do it. I can't do it. It's cruel,' then shouted, 'You swines! You swines! You filthy Belgian swines!' I climbed up on to my small craft and prayed for a lorry to take me and the wheelbarrow to Arlit. I took a long drink and remembered the words, 'Don't expect me to cover the sun or flatten the dunes.' I lay down, my torso under the shade of the wheelbarrow, and said, 'I give up. I'm going home,' and I meant it. But while I was waiting for a lorry, I began to think of Douglas Ford, a nine-year-old, back home. One night, at the boys' club, he had looked up into my eyes and said, 'My dad says you're daft. You'll never do it!' For the sake of Douglas Ford and his dad, I got up and had another go, jerking backwards inches at a time.

I groaned 'The Song of the Volga Boatman' and every 'Yo Ho Heave Ho' meant three inches. When I got to the top of the dune, the thought of an Englishman wearing Nigerian clothes, singing a Russian song, dragging a Chinese wheelbarrow over a sand dune, made me laugh a little. The laugh crescendoed to hysteria. There was nothing funny any longer. Inside I hurt, but my body was laughing uncontrollably. I had gone mad, I thought. Tears ran down my face. My legs withered, throwing me back on my haunches, then forward face down. I melted into convulsions like hearty sobs.

There was deep sand underfoot for the rest of the day. When I saw the

Land Rover in the evening, I was overjoyed but had to struggle round an arc half a mile wide, round impossibly deep sand, to reach it. When it was dark, the Frenchman drew up in the Toyota truck and walked to our fire.

'What's this?' I said, pointing angrily at the sand.

'What's what?'

'This sand! You said there was no sand after sixty kilometres!'

'Oh, this is nothing,' he grinned.

'But it *is* something to me! I've not got eight gears and four-wheel drive! Is there much more ahead?'

'No, you've finished with it now, definitely.' I wanted to believe him, but I knew he did not notice sand, skating over everything at seventy miles an hour. He got back into his truck and revved up, stuck up to his spinning axles. It was the best five minutes of the day.

In the morning, I saw that there was some truth in what the Frenchman had said. The Savannah *was* on its way. I was crossing the starkest of hills, like skin shaved bald, but now and then, tufts of dried grass hid like porcupines among the rocks. As I passed one of them, a jerboa bolted from it like a miniature kangaroo, the ground exploding with each jump. Later, I picked up the horns of a gazelle, then saw thirteen camels on the brow of a hill ahead. Every one of them was still, every eye on me until a brown bull pushed through the pack and stood between us. His nose was held high, his legs and neck stiff. I advanced until at twenty yards they circled at a gallop, two grey juveniles trailing behind, until they were facing me again fifty yards away. They charged again blindly, stopping to my left. I put down the wheelbarrow and spoke to them kindly.

It was a delightful day with nineteen miles put behind us, but it was too good to last. Next morning my diarrhoea was worse and I spent most of the first three hours squatting. A wind sprang up, and being too ill to fight it, I tipped the wheelbarrow on its side, and fell asleep behind it. At about two o'clock, I woke up, shivering, to hear a voice shouting, 'Hey, Mr Wheelbarrow Man!' I pulled myself up to see two vanloads of English people clamouring to take photographs. I paraded drunkenly with the wheelbarrow before their lenses and then lay down again.

After an hour, Mick and Paddy arrived. Though I had walked only five miles that day, we made camp and I went straight to bed. While I slept, my fingers became locked in a half-clenched position like claws. It happened every night and sometimes during the day when I forgetfully closed my hand. It had been caused by gripping the narrow shafts over a sustained period. I had had thick handles put on the ends of the shafts when they had been made in order to prevent the problem, but I had found that I could not control the wheelbarrow unless I held the shafts where they were narrow, nearer the lockers. The index fingers and thumbs were not badly affected, though, and I was able to 'snap' open the locked fingers on one hand with the free ones on the other.

At dawn, while the Norwich City and Aston Villa teams slept, gaining strength for their battle, mine had already begun. Paddy might have been dreaming of the feast we would miss, but for me the delay was more serious. Arlit was forty-seven miles away and I had little food and water left. The town had to arrive the following day or it never would.

By the time of the kick off, Arlit was thirty miles away, but I could see a huge tower at the mine there. Waves of heat drifted ripples along it like a whip being cracked in slow motion. Then the tower ran from right to left and back, becoming shorter and fatter. It was not part of the mine, after all, but a mirage-distorted grey-green Land Rover, with white jerry-cans on top. I knew it well. It was Renzo and the doctor, looking thinner and greyer. There was something wrong. We embraced solemnly. 'I expected you ten days ago.' I said.

'The back axle broke in Agadez,' answered Renzo. 'We couldn't get it mended there. It took us four days to get back to Arlit and as long again for the repair.' I whistled.

'That must have been costly,' I said.

'Very costly. But how about you?'

'I've got diarrhoea, but not badly.' I said. The doctor walked deliberately to the back of the vehicle and lifted out his giant medicine chest and opened it.

'See,' said Renzo, as the doctor shook empty bottles. 'Nothing left.'

'Oh, I wasn't asking for medicine. We've got plenty. When you see Mick and Paddy ask them for some.' Moments later they were on their way, leaving me with a note from Ed and Jane, whom they had seen in Arlit:

Dear Geoff, Mick and Paddy,

We have been thinking of you a lot out there between Assamaka and Arlit. The man in the Toyota truck does the whole journey in three hours. It took us three days. It was horrible. But for the man in the Toyota we would still be there. We were stuck for half a day in a sand dune. There were snake tracks everywhere. Jane was crying and we were almost in despair. But now the worst is over. When we get to civilisation we'll sell the car and fly home.

Good luck till the autumn.

Ed and Jane

At twenty-past five, I was climbing a gentle slope when I saw Paddy coming to meet me, red-faced, and wearing shorts and a knotted handkerchief. 'Hi there! You've nearly done eighteen,' he said. 'We're only a quarter of a mile away.' He strolled with me, casting a concerned eye at the wheel, which was wobbling from side to side, due to a worn bearing. When we got to the Land Rover, Mick's radio was on the bonnet receiving the last twenty minutes of the League Cup Final from the BBC World Service. Mick was slumped drunkenly on a jerry-can against the vehicle, beside the remnants of a carton of lager. Round his neck and waist were Norwich City scarves and four more flapped from the Land Rover. His jowls hung and his eyes were fixed. His shouts came through half a dozen thorn-trees, mingling with the roar of Wembley. 'What's the score?' I shouted.

'We're winning, nil–nil.'

'They need encouraging! Shout a bit louder!' On I pushed, until, when the sun had dropped to eye-level, Paddy drove up to my right and Mick stuck out his head.

'Have you seen any Villa supporters? We lost one–nil. A penalty ten minutes from the end.'

'How much further?' cut in Paddy.

'Make it twenty-one.' At camp I prepared the last of my food, dehydrated potato and soya protein. Mick was already tented while Paddy and I sat by the fire, watching the stars and what we thought was the glow of Arlit twenty-six miles away.

'When d'you reckon we'll get there? Monday?'

'No, tomorrow. I'm out of grub. Even if I only do fifteen miles by sunset, I'll keep on and follow the lights.'

Next morning, 2 March, I woke hungry and found myself shaking the empty food containers for the third time, just in case. I decided to race and not stop in spite of an opposing wind and the soft going. Pain was tempered by day-dreams of Arlit's restaurant and swimming-pool.

There was little else in Arlit, not even on a Sunday when the mine was shut. There, it was a day for indolence, swimming or visiting friends or the French Club. Maurice and Jean, whom we met later, often went south to hunt gazelle, but today they were off for a drive out towards Assamaka and a picnic, with the hope of seeing the mad Englishman.

The first sightseers, two men, arrived at ten o'clock and were followed by families and a minibusload of children brought by the priest. Carload after carload wanted me to chat but I declined and wobbled hungrily on, as they unfolded picnic tables and put out iced drinks and sandwiches. They pointed their cameras and asked me to pose, but I dared not stop.

The *knowledge* that a town was near was rarely a boost. It was the *sight* of it that counted, whether it was two or twenty miles away. At the first glimpse of the mine's flat-topped slag-heaps, I was sure that the worst, the very worst, was over. Kano was in the bag.

I skipped between the mine and the airfield, along a four-mile dual carriageway surfaced with red clay, curving down to the right, towards the town. On the way, the mine's manager, Pascal Witzgal, met me, and said that I could have a shower at his home and stay the night. Then I was swept along by a flotilla of lorries, cars, mopeds and bicycles, while children in the minibus waved their handkerchiefs and drivers sounded their horns. I stopped at the edge of the town, where the Land Rover and a crowd were waiting. They cheered as a young woman slinked from among them. She was clean, fresh and shapely, striding deliberately and gracefully towards me. She wore a floral dress, was a lovely twenty-two-year-old, smelt as sweet as bathtime and carried in her hand an ice-cold can of beer. She smiled and pulled the ring, letting froth erupt over her manicured fingers, run down the can and mingle with beads of condensation. I put down the wheelbarrow, got from between the shafts and accepted the offering at arm's length, ashamed of myself. My mouth was foul, my lip bleeding, and my body and unshaven face covered with a paste of sour sweat and grime. I drank from the can and momentarily forgot the girl, until I felt her arm around me. This was Arlit, the fight was over, and my legs were refusing to hold me. My right side seemed embarrassingly stuck to her, but I was enjoying every moment. Then her long, blonde hair blew across my face, its fine strands running through my grubby claw as I combed it away.

I wanted to look at her again, so I drank from the can and glanced out of the corner of my eye. She was still smiling and I smiled too. What a hero I felt and how I was enjoying her affection, until somebody embraced me from the other side. Perhaps this one was a brunette! I looked to my left and saw that it was a tall man with a beard. He had seen the delight the young woman had brought me and looked put out. 'I am her husband!' he said aggressively.

They had given a friend their camera and had come to stand with me to have their photograph taken. I had misinterpreted the young woman's actions and had not seen the man. Then the others came in ones and twos for a photographed embrace.

17

SWINGING SAHEL

We followed Pascal through unmade streets, to report to the army. Tuaregs, Europeans and West Africans jostled round us, and the Land Rover trailed behind. Two little black boys, their legs white with dust, darted into the mêlée, almost colliding with Pascal and stopping me in my tracks. I felt distant from it all. I was moving my limbs by remote control. A young Frenchman in a floral shirt embraced me as I tried to keep my balance. 'I am Maurice,' he said, squeezing my arm. 'What a man you are! So strong! You have conquered!' I was glad to get to the military headquarters and leave his affections outside.

The building itself was indistinguishable from the mud and breeze-block provision stores except for a sign on the lintel. Inside there were an electric light, a filing cabinet and a desk, behind which sat a slightly dishevelled black African. His military jacket was on the back of his chair, his sleeves rolled up, and cap cocked back in the heat. He leaned away from his desk and grinned a broad, African grin. 'We were expecting you five days ago. What kept you?'

'A bit of sand,' I said, trying my best to sound like Robert Mitchum with a French accent. His eyes smiled. He was thinking of other things.

'Have you a tape-recorder I could buy?'

'Sorry, we are only carrying essentials.'

'You're tired. Call in tomorrow and we'll have a chat.' I set off towards Pascal's, pausing only to look at two cheetahs behind a chain-link fence. The wheel lurched from side to side, jarring against the frame and throwing the one hundred kilogram load haphazardly. I could not hold on much longer.

When we got to Pascal's prefabricated bungalow, a mist had blown across my senses, though I do remember the air-conditioning making me cold. People stood and applauded. There was a ringing in my ears and I felt as if I was under water. Someone put a bouquet of chrysanthemums in my arms, and another gave me champagne. I raised my glass and took a sip. They applauded again and led me to a sofa, but I refused to sit because I was so dirty. They gently pushed me and I sank into the sage-green upholstery. Everyone was talking at once above the sound of a Fats Domino record. Maurice and another man, Jean, were arranging for Mick and Paddy to stay with them. Another, the only one speaking English, said that they were going to take Paddy to the mine tomorrow and weld the wheel. 'You can't weld aluminium,' I kept saying. The tone of his reply was deliberately soothing.

'It will be all right. It will be all right. We have aluminium welding.' Someone twice added tots of Johnny Walker to my glass. I refused water with it, saying that for sixty days I had drunk water without whisky. Now I would try it the other way round.

I went for a shower, rinsing my clothes at the same time. Ahmed, the house boy, would wash them thoroughly the next day. For an hour, I drunkenly watched the endless red dust swirl out of my socks and listened to concerned French men knocking on the shower-door and enquiring after my welfare. Then, when the crowd had gone home, I emerged to beat the dust out of my jacket.

Every day I had woken up sticky and gone to bed sticky with dried sweat, and my clothes had had a greasy dampness. But now, though shabby, they were newly changed and as snug as flannellette sheets. I put on a tie and set out for the club curling my toes, trying not to step out of my battered suede shoes. The soles were split and I had ditched the laces when they had been fouled with diarrhoea.

The streets were dark and empty but here and there windows shone bright with electric light. Sand was underfoot and buildings all around, but my nose detected moist foliage and chlorinated swimming-pools.

Sometimes, in the safety of my bed, the horror of the fire had returned. Now, in an Arlit street, while Mick and Paddy talked with Pascal, I shuddered in terror as I remembered the last nine days. Now that they were over and I was full of alcohol, I could allow myself to fear. Pictures filled my head: wastes so dazzling that even with dark glasses, my eyes were slits; cold water as hot as tea, and shafts I could not touch except when they were bandaged; as I staggered, the wheelbarrow, mocking me like some large, playful animal, always wanting me to wrestle.

Then the door of the club swung open and the cocktail bar and immaculately laid tables invited us inside.

* * *

I got up at eight o'clock with a fearful hangover. After a ham salad and a can of lager at the club, I had returned to the bungalow and vomited in, and, much to Mick's disgust, around the lavatory pan. I apologized to Pascal, but he blamed himself for giving me alcohol when I had been so tired and had hardly eaten for twenty-four hours.

After a wash and shave, I went to the breakfast table, where I sat holding my head with one hand and my stomach with the other. Pascal's wife came in and flung back the curtains. The glare made my eyeballs feel as if they were being squeezed with pliers. She dumped a coffee-pot in front of me, sending shock waves up from my forearm to my temples.

She was a self-assertive, efficient woman, aged about forty. Pascal had insisted on Christian names from the start, but she was always 'Madame Witzgal'. She gestured at the bread and honey on the table, 'If you need more, then ask Ahmed.'

I ate one and a half baguettes with honey, and drank two pots of sweet, black coffee. Then I sat outside by their small swimming-pool. Madame was pegging out my washing. 'You must thank Ahmed for doing my washing,' I said.

'It is no trouble to him,' she said. 'We have a machine.'

'Your garden is quite lovely,' I said, admiring the flowers. 'Who looks after it?'

'I do most of it, but it doesn't take much work. Five years ago there was nothing here,' she said, keeping one hand on the line and pointing with a peg. 'That sapling was only a seed. All I do is put plenty of water on it.'

'Is your water rationed?'

'No, there is no shortage in Arlit. We have a borehole.' Wells were drying up, and herds and people were dying, while water was being sprinkled on gardens, filling swimming-pools, and running washing-machines. A Tuareg well could not compete with a thousand metre borehole which gradually lowers the water-table.

The miners had had water on demand at home, so, to keep them happy, they were given the same provision here. For a similar reason, the mining company ran a typical French store. Later in the morning, Mick and I were taken there by Madame. From its rough exterior, the store might have been a Tuareg coffee-house. We kicked the hot sand off our shoes and pushed the heavily sprung door.

I was blinded for a moment, as if entering a cave. There were no windows, only fluorescent tubes, giving a dimmer, more civilized light. Then, except for the whirr of the air-conditioning, we could have been in a Parisian shop on a winter evening. Cold dampness radiated from the tiles and there were the smells of cheeses and cooked meats. Cans, packets and bottles were shelved from floor to ceiling. Not even in Nigeria had I seen anything like this. There was a butcher's counter and one with fresh cheeses, pâtés, continental sausage, bacon and ham. The range of beer, wines and spirits was as good as at the off-licence at home. No wonder two air shipments a week were needed!

I bought two cartons of groceries and arrived home in time to meet Pascal and Paddy coming from the mine for lunch. We tucked into tomatoes, sausage and bread. Every time I stopped eating, Pascal said, 'Geoff, *mangez!*' I ate twice as much as anyone else, forgetting the French custom of serving several small courses. Ahmed now brought in a cold lamb salad, of which I managed two helpings with bread. I undid the top of my shorts and slumped back, thinking I had finished, when, to the amusement of everyone, Ahmed put a plate of steak, chips and beans in front of me. Pascal impishly coaxed me to eat not only that but also an apple, a banana, and some cheese and biscuits.

The afternoon was spent scouring billycans, scrubbing kit and talking to Pascal's five-year-old daughter, who had been at kindergarten all morning. I loaded the wheelbarrow with the jam, chillis, pâté and various tins I had bought, and went out with Pascal, wearing a pair of brogues – he had insisted I borrow them. The French ambassador had flown in to visit the mine and we were going to a reception he was throwing at the club.

After he had made a short speech, there was a free-for-all around the food and drinks. Maurice, my admirer of the day before, was occupied behind the bar. No alcohol was served, not that I minded. I was to begin the one hundred and forty-seven miles to Agadez at dawn. However, the confectionery had considerable appeal. Fame of my appetite had reached the priest, a witty, beetle-browed little man of about fifty who spoke excellent English. We were standing conveniently near the cream-filled lemon buns. Now and then he would drop one of them on my plate with the words, 'A cake a mile, eh, Geoff?'

The miners and their wives came over to meet me but I got the impression that they barely knew the priest. 'Are they good Catholics here?' I asked him.

'I get eight or less to mass, and two of those are Africans.'

The ambassador, a tall man with a suit to match his silver-grey hair, was being introduced to the workers by the mine's top man, Colonel Noël. Pascal trailed at their heels. Then I saw him leave the entourage with the urgency of a court messenger and weave towards me. 'Geoff,' he called from a few yards away. 'The ambassador wishes to speak with you.' Here was my chance to challenge him about the morality of boreholes. I turned to the priest to excuse myself and felt a slight impact on my paper plate. The priest's eyes twinkled, 'A cake a mile, eh, Geoff?'

* * *

No brighter than a ripe fruit, the fat sun sat on the house tops, too heavy to rise. Past the cheetahs' enclosure, a tennis-court, a building site, and I lifted a hand to return a farewell. There was now no play in the bearing and I was able to speed over the friable ground.

The town festered on in a tumour of shanties. Packing-cases, cardboard and plastic bags held together with gravity, nails and string. Women were cooking in large tin cans over open fires, and others were spreading washing over their makeshift homes. These were not olive-skinned nomads, but black town-dwellers from the south in search of work. The people, dogs and smoke from the breakfast fires moved with languor and were tinted gold by the early sun. A man in clean shirt and trousers crawled from a cardboard hovel. His clothes had been pressed, I guessed, on layers of newspaper with a charcoal iron.

An old man wearing a blanket and leaning on a staff was hurrying, as best he could, from among the dwellings. 'Good morning,' I shouted in his language, genuflecting. He beamed, and shook his fist in the manner of a Hausa greeting. Still smiling, he lifted his blanket and squatted among the rocks.

At ten o'clock, I put *my* blanket on the hot wheelbarrow and sat down to eat a small loaf, dipping it into a tin of jam. It was already 100° Fahrenheit and there was no wind. The sky was a milky blue, and to the south was a single fleck of cloud. Nothing stirred on the mid-brown plains except the quivering heat haze and lapping mirages which taunted the dry ground. Not a bird in the sky, not one scuttling lizard, just a leafless thorn-bush half-buried in the sand. It was as if I had never known anything else. It had become mine. Yet, after today, I might never see the open desert again. By nightfall I would have crossed the tree line.

No need now to pick up every scrap of wood on the way. Twenty-six miles south of Arlit there was more than enough. As I gathered it from the stony ground, and from among patches of yellow stubble, grass-hoppers, resembling bits of straw, darted from my path, like sparks from a fire. The trees were no bigger than shrubs, and their few leaves leathery and covered in dust, like the rubber plant at home.

I kindled a fire not far from where the lads were slumped on jerry-cans with their backs to the Land Rover. Mick looked as if he had run a race. He was red-faced and awash with sweat. 'Ugh! All that food and booze! No good in this heat. Jean and Maurice did us proud today. When I get to Kano, I'm gonna stay in the pool.' I was writing, making use of the fading light while my rice was cooking. 'You know, Geoff,' said Mick, 'you're wrong about Jean and Maurice. They're not a pair of queers.'

'I didn't say they were,' I said.

'That's what you meant, but they're not you know. They're really nice blokes.'

'I know they're nice blokes, very nice blokes, but Maurice was all over me.'

'All French fellas are like that. Neither of them made a pass at us did they, Paddy? Anyway, look what they've given us,' he said, pointing to a carton of groceries and four cans of lager.

'That's got nothing to do with it. Anyway, how do we divide four cans of lager into three?'

'It was just for us two,' said Paddy, 'but we'll share it with you.'

'Don't be daft,' I said.

'NFI,' said Mick. 'Take a can of my lager. I've had enough to last me to Kano.'

By now it was almost dark. The rice had boiled dry, so I stirred in a tin of peas and another of sardines. Paddy put down his map, filled the blackened kettle from the jerry-can on which he had been sitting, put the kettle on the fire and sat down again. I rested my hot aluminium dish on top of the notes on my lap and began to eat. Mick got up, went into the cab, came out with a torch and crawled into the tent. 'NFI,' he said, 'I'm having an early night.'

''Night, Mick,' we said.

'Bloody 'ell, it's warm in here,' said Mick.

'Geoff,' said Paddy, 'how was the barrow?'

'Solid as a rock.'

'It was fascinating at the mine. They've got equipment I've never seen before. They sprayed the worn spindle with metal, and then turned it down on a lathe. Aluminium welding, too!'

'Those plates they've welded to the rim surprised me. Hawker Siddeley said that if the aluminium wheel bust it couldn't be repaired in Africa. It's as strong now as when it was built.' The kettle began to whistle.

'Throw us your mug,' said Paddy. 'How long d'you reckon to Agadez? A week? Eight days?'

'Not if I can help it. Five more, I reckon. And after that it'll be a piece of cake. The rest's bush.'

At one-thirty, I was up with diarrhoea. I watched the rising yellow moon, and listened to the sound of small animals and insects. Then I could not sleep: I had little flesh to cushion my bones from the steel floor, and I could not stop thinking of Joan – there had been no mail at Arlit.

Getting to her in order to sort things out between us had become my only goal. Nothing else much mattered. Not even the rules, which were becoming a farce. I had never intended to accept food and drink off travellers, but now, quite regularly, I was given a sandwich by a Frenchman, or a lager by an Australian.

Hygiene had gone by the board, too. My socks would stay on my feet for days and nights. I rarely washed, not even after the toilet. At first it was because I was short of water, but now I just did not care. Nothing mattered so long as I got to Kano as fast as possible. Each day, I would try to go harder, further, faster than the day before. I was living off my nerves and there was little rest. I would not get one inch nearer Joan with my feet up.

I even skimped my devotions. Listening to tape-recorded sermons, reading my Bible, and praying had been little more than mechanical acts. I had been playing a role, doing what I expected of myself, but in reality I had retreated from God. I knew that if I had got too close I would have heard things I did not wish to hear, though I never felt that he was far away. It was as if he was tailing me in the way I had originally hoped the Land Rover would. He was within sight and helping distance but not usually near enough to talk to. I kept him away unless I needed him.

* * *

It was to be two and a half years before I would want God on his terms rather than my own, when, after serving a second curacy, I asked the bishop for an inner-city parish. I was made incumbent of St Ambrose's Church, Pendleton, Salford. It lay between dockland and the newly-built shopping precinct. Four thousand parishoners lived in one quarter of a square mile of concrete flats and terraced houses, which were used for *Coronation Street* location shots.

The terraced houses were occupied by old Salfordians. Unemployment there was about average for the north, but among the flats hardly anyone worked, and the flats themselves had been ripped apart by the angry young, watched by the apathetic old. Rubbish chutes had been set alight and stairways fouled. The hand rails could never be touched for fear of touching the unthinkable. Almost everyone in those flats had applied for a transfer. After massive input by two community associations and many community workers – there were sixteen in the area when I arrived – there was little sense of community other than that generated by opposition to the city council.

The large church building had suffered from a leaky roof, pigeons, and dry rot, leaving the congregation in debt. Three energetic incumbents and a band of tireless lay folk had served the church lovingly through the post-war years, but as soon as one problem had been overcome, another had arisen. Mid-week activities with children were thriving, but the number of adults in church on Sundays was about two dozen. Yet, though the parish was a wilderness in anticipation, it was not one on realization. I had thought a successful church to be one which had sound buildings, money in the bank, and a large congregation. I wanted success in those terms, but what I found was the happiness of being where I believed God wanted me to be, and of being a working partner with caring, unpretentious people.

* * *

The next day of my walk took me over sparsely-wooded hills and across dried up streams. That morning the driver of a truck stopped to greet me. This small beetle-browed man, wearing a black turban and baggy Moroccan trousers, was the 'cake-a-mile' priest. It warmed my heart to see him.

Later, the French consul from Zinder and his oriental wife drove up. They too had been at the ambassador's reception. He gave me a can of lager, invited me to dinner when I passed through town, and practised his English. 'God save our gracious king' was his limit. When they had gone, Joan's face looked down on me from the sky and I imagined a plaintive tenor voice to be singing the intermezzo from Delius' *Hassan*.

Gourds, looking like grapefruits, were growing on vines by the *piste*. Cardinal birds and green parrots were in the trees, while a train of seventy-two camels strode purposefully north by the side of the *piste*. These were not nomads' ambling beasts, but the heavy haulage of the Sahara, piled with bales and hessian sacks. There were no women, children, dogs or flocks, just six Tuaregs riding high in their saddles and wrapped up as if for winter in their blue *ganduras* and bandannas. Each man wore a broadsword, dagger and spear and carried a riding crop. There were herdsmen too, people who said they were from the 'Busu' tribe, though I never saw the name written down. These coffee-coloured people were tall and good-looking, with slender noses, thin lips and bright eyes.

I arrived at camp to see one of them, not twenty yards away, standing high in the red saddle of his camel, poised to hurl his spear. His tanned brow was tense, and his black robe, water-skin, and sword, hung motionless. The camel moved with the stealth of a chameleon, one limb at a time. I put down the shafts and thoughtlessly shouted a greeting. The rider ignored me but the camel froze like a bronze horse, with one foot held high. Then a black hornbill, startled by my voice, beat its ungainly wings and escaped from among the bushes and over the trees. The rider saluted me with his spear and trotted away.

After supper, we gathered round the fire, waiting for the kettle and listening to crickets and the far-off bray of a donkey. There was no moon, but the sky was alive with stars. Paddy was repairing his torch, and Mick was playing tiddlywinks with grasshoppers, touching their tails with a straw. 'I'm sick of all this tea,' he said.

'You've gotta drink something,' I said, looking up from my papers.

'I could do with a cold pint,' he said, drinking from an imaginary glass. 'It'd slide down my throat in one.'

'I'd settle for cold milk,' I said.

'You can't get milk in the Hebs,' said Paddy.

'I'm gonna have ice in *all* my drinks when I get back,' said Mick. Mick touched the tail of a grasshopper and it jumped straight into the fire. 'Oh, yes!' he whooped. 'D'you see that! Bull's-eye!'

'Don't be tight,' I said.

'They've as much right to live as you, Mick,' added Paddy.

'Give over,' Mick said. 'Here's another.' The fortunate creature missed the flames and landed at my feet. I took a twig to encourage it to leap out of harm's way.

'Come on little fellow,' I said. 'Go and play in the bush.' Instead, it leapt backwards, straight into the flames. We laughed and laughed.

The many insects were a delight and it was unthinkable to kill any except the houseflies. That night, when I had gone to bed, I took hold of something that was tickling my ear. It was a harmless praying mantis, so I put it back. It stayed there until I had gone to sleep.

The desert was encroaching on this region and its population was forced to rely on travellers for life support. On my way next morning, I gave water to a family whose well had run dry. Others wanted tea-bags, food, water containers and medicine. A boy with a deep infected cut above the eye asked for antiseptic cream.

About midday, an American missionary, Dr Weisback, with his son Daniel, met me on their way north. They were working in a remote area and had been for supplies. Apart from him, I saw no evidence of permanent medical help for the bush and desert dwellers of Niger.

At a quarter to four, the lads arrived stripped to their waists, Paddy wearing his knotted handkerchief. Mick spat on the ground.

'How far have I come?' I asked.

'Twenty-two,' said Mick, turning from me and spitting again.

'I'll do another six,' I said.

'Ugh!' said Mick. 'I saw a kind of grapefruit growing by the *piste* and I took a bite.'

'You twit,' I said, unable to hold my laughter. 'That was a gourd. That'd even pucker the mouth of a goat.' He spat again, grinning this time.

'I was telling Paddy,' he said. 'I bet Geoff's eaten dozens of these. He'll eat anything.'

At camp, a Busu girl of about sixteen was crouching barefoot, tending two pots on Mick's fire. She wore a blue skirt and white blouse and had long straight hair. Now and then Mick walked to her to inspect the stew. I gathered sticks and began to cook soya protein. The girl's wide eyes followed us everywhere. Mick sat on a jerry-can and lit a cigarette. 'How'd you like to take her in the tent for half an hour, Geoff?' he asked. He turned to her and spoke as one might to a baby or animal. 'I know what you want. You want my tulip.' She returned his smile, not understanding. He brought three china plates, put out Paddy's meal and then asked the girl, 'Do you want some?'

'*Kina son abinci*?' I asked.

'*Ae,*' she said.

'She says she would,' I said. As she ate, her eyes never left us.

'I reckon she wants one of us,' said Mick.

'You've got a one-track mind,' I said.

'These gollies are all alike. They can't get enough of it.' Mick had begun to wash the plates when she spoke to him. '*Ina son sibili.*'

'She wants some soap,' I said, after hesitating. She had not used the word for soap that I was used to. Then, as it was almost dark, she took her soap and rode away on her donkey.

The following day, there were frequent settlements, all dependent on travellers for their economy. Small boys sat on stacks of firewood they were hoping to sell. Little girls chased me with what I thought were dried cow-pats, but turned out to be goats' cheese, or *chucku*. Two men in grubby robes of thin white cotton joined me, opening the lockers and meddling with the kit.

At lunch-time, I stopped in a clearing about the size of a cricket field. The perimeter was densely wooded by trees with rubber-like leaves. A young man approached with a teenage girl, her face painted with rouge. 'Would you like her?' he asked. She hung her head and giggled. 'Pay me and you can take her into the hut,' he said. The girl smiled. I dipped a piece of bread into the jam and ate it. Then a donkey galloped across the open ground, raising dust.

'No thank you,' I said.

'If you don't want me,' she flirted, 'at least give me some bread.' I broke some for her and left immediately, to the sound of their laughter. I set a fast pace and completed a record thirty miles by evening.

We camped in a river-bed under overhanging trees. I was cooking *chucku* and chillies when I noticed two young Busu women talking to Mick. They each wore a *zeni* – a dress improvised from two yards of brightly printed cotton fabric, similar to the sort of robe a woman might improvise from a towel when coming from the shower. They were beautiful, with shining hair and white teeth. They gave Mick an avocado-like fruit. 'Hey Geoff, this is good news. You drink it. It's like coconut milk.' They stayed until twilight, leaving us to speculate why they had come. Mick was washing up and I was dining on goats' cheese fondu. 'I reckon they wanted one of us,' said Mick.

'For heaven's sake! They're all after it according to you!' I snapped.

'Maybe they are!' he replied with a hopeful grin.

* * *

It was 8 March, my seventy-fifth day, and I had walked almost fifteen hundred miles. I hoped to maintain twenty-five miles a day, and get to Kano by the end of March. At half-past eight, long after I had left, Mick was writing a letter. Paddy got up, had breakfast and went for his morning walk. He explored the bush until he came to a tree, the roots of which had lost their grip, and which was leaning over the river-bed. Two goats were browsing nearby on the yellow tufts. The billy nudged the nanny with his snout. She skipped away but he trotted after. These creatures, less than half the size of their European cousins, raced in a wide circle like small dogs, then scrambled on to the overhanging tree. The closer Billy got, the further Nanny went along the narrowing trunk, until in his excitement, Billy missed his footing and fell unhurt on to the pebbles.

Paddy headed back towards camp, but met the two young women cooking outside their grass hut. Their husband, an older man, came out and made signs for Paddy first to take one of the wives, and then the other, inside. Paddy shook his head and sauntered back under the sparse shade.

I had been passing through a forest where the trees were gnarled like moorland oaks, but by late morning it had thinned into scrub. There had been a few huts, little boys on stacks of wood, women pounding millet and men making grass mats. Similar mats were mounted on poles at the next village and used as homes without walls.

Villagers sat in the shade plaiting straw into rope. This was the first purely black African village I had come across on the expedition. The grass-mat homes were tucked under palm-trees, as were hand-watered plots of tomatoes and onions. The last time I had seen vegetables cultivated was at In Salah, one quarter of the way across. Today, one quarter of the journey remained.

The old chief, whose teeth were stained yellow from eating tobacco flowers, leaned on his staff and led his people to greet me. He wore a long, white cotton robe with voluminous sleeves. I left the wheelbarrow and met him half-way. We clasped hands and I bowed at the knee, greeting him in Hausa. He replied in French.

'You speak French?' I asked.

'Yes – I was in the army.' Then he shouted over his shoulder in a language I did not understand, and a small boy brought me a carrier-bag of tomatoes and onions.

'Keep these for your children,' I protested.

'They are yours,' he said, taking my hand and pressing into it two hundred Niger francs.

'I cannot accept,' I said firmly. Then I did something I had never done in front of a stranger. I took off my money belt and showed him more money than he could earn in a year. His kind eyes caught mine. They were begging me not to spurn his gift. I saw in them a sadness and wisdom gained from a long life of hardship.

'We have heard,' he said quietly, 'that you are doing this walk for our people. Do not be proud. Allow us to help you.' I expressed my gratitude, tucked his money into my belt, and walked to the wheelbarrow. He shouted after me, 'May God give you strength!'

I faced him, shook my fist, and replied, 'And to you also, my father.'

At three o'clock, two Toyota trucks stopped, and a Dutch couple got out of each. 'So we've finally met you!' said one of the men in an American accent. 'Everyone between here and Kano's been telling us to watch out for you. I'm Hank. How are you doing?'

'Not too bad. The worst's over.'

'Don't be too sure,' he said. 'The other side of Agadez is hell.'

'I thought it was bush all the way to Kano.'

'It is, sort of, but there's a forest of thorn-trees growing out of pure sand. It's tough, I can tell you. We've been told it's the worst part of the whole crossing. I wish you luck.'

'It sounds as if I'll need it,' I said.

'Make sure you get well rested at the camp site,' said Hank.

'Camp site?' I said.

'Yes, there's a camp site six miles this side of Agadez,' he said.

'We'll watch out for it,' I said.

'Make sure you do. It's the only one this side of Kano,' he said.

'Were you working there?' I asked.

'Where? Kano? No, we only passed through. We've come from Kinshase,' said Hank.

'Zaire? I don't suppose you saw anything of the Zaire River Expedition?' I asked.

'Yeah, we had one of the men living with us for three months.'

'Did you meet the airmen, Steve, Cliff and Sandy?'

'I don't believe it! Steve George lived with us, and we got to know Cliff and Sandy pretty well.' I was telling them about the airmen's time in Kano and Tamanrasset when Hank said, 'Sorry for being so rude, but this is Luke.'

'Hi,' I said. 'Are you from Kinshase as well?'

'No, we're from Kano, but we did meet a Dutch couple who said they knew you, Ed and Jane.'

'Ed and Jane! They were like family to me. How are they?'

'They had a bad time with the car getting stuck, and they have both been ill with dysentery. They're trying to sell their car so they can fly home.'

'You know,' I said, turning to Hank, 'our meeting is a bigger coincidence than you think. These people we're talking about, Ed and Jane, knew Steve, Cliff and Sandy. They cooked a meal for them in Tam.'

After exchanging clichés about it being a small world, Hank asked me if I needed anything.

'Only jam, if you can spare any.'

'Jam? Oh, jelly! I can fix that,' said Hank, climbing into his truck and handing me a half-pound tin.

'Thanks,' I said, examining the familiar golden bloom.

'Army compo?' I suggested. Hank smiled and said,

'Say thanks to the Zaire River Expedition!'

— 18 —
AGADEZ

By four-thirty the next day, 9 March, I had arrived at the camp site and was sitting on the patio in clean shirt and trousers, writing my sixth letter. I had taken a shower and paid a young African the price of a loaf to do my laundry. Mick, across the table, had just finished a letter home. 'Another beer, Geoff?'

'Thanks, Mick,' I said, giving my empty bottle a shake.

The site was run by a German couple in their late fifties and had a colonial air about it. It was shaded by trees and had a small concrete swimming-pool filled from an adjacent well by a petrol-driven pump. We had camped by the pool, not many yards from the bar, restaurant, toilets and showers. The showers were open to the sky, with an overhead water-bucket and pull-chain. It had not been easy washing my feet while hanging on to keep the water flowing.

Mick returned, two green bottles in one hand, a cigarette in the other. He sat down and pushed a bottle towards me. 'They're serving steak dinners at seven o'clock. 750 francs each.'

'One pound twenty! Not bad!'

'You've gotta notify them before five and pay in advance.'

'Nip over, Mick, and book for the three of us.'

As lamps were being lit across the camp, we went into the restaurant. A dozen or so Europeans were quietly chatting at the long refectory tables. Above, three paraffin pressure lamps hissed, filling the room with a pale, green light. After home-made beef and vegetable soup, steak, mash and salad were served. Paddy poked at his. Mick spoke up for him. 'This isn't potato!'

'Nobody said it was,' I said. 'It's yam. Quite a good one.' Paddy began to eat with caution but soon acquired the taste. After pancakes, we headed back to the Land Rover.

We had developed a morbid preoccupation with the end of the walk. The subjects, 'not long now', 'visas for Nigeria', 'the swimming-pool in Kano', 'ice-cold drinks', and 'the Kano Club', were raised in almost every conversation. They were the same greasy cards dealt out in every hand, but instead of groaning at the sight of them we clutched them as if they were aces.

I was, typically, sitting on a jerry-can, writing a letter. 'Anyone fancy some wine?' asked Mick.

'Not for me, thanks,' answered Paddy.

'I couldn't see you drink alone,' I said. Paddy opened a bottle of lager and crawled into his tent.

'Goodnight, you twos. Sweet dreams.'

'Night, Paddy.'

'Could we use your tea-glasses, Geoff?' asked Mick.

'Help yourself.' Mick pulled the cork, drew up a jerry-can, put the bottle on the ground between us and handed me a full glass. 'Cheers, Mick!' I said, taking a sip. 'Mmm! This *is* nice. What is it?'

'Burgundy – real Burgundy, not the Algerian stuff. Not long now, eh, Geoff?'

'Only about three weeks unless we get held up south of Agadez.'

'I can't wait to get off the damned *piste*.'

'Once we're on tarmac, it'll only take six days to Kano.'

'I can't wait,' said Mick. 'I'm gonna give it the big lips at the Kano Club, then jump in the pool and stay there all day. I hope those cowboys at Bulford have pulled their fingers out. If there are no visas for us, someone's gonna swing.'

'It'll be fine. I'm sending regular reports. They know where I am and I've given them the earliest date I expect to be at the border. I'm sure it'll be OK.'

'I'm not so sure. They made a balls-up in Gib, and we had to pass through Algeria without clearance, *and* they almost left us in the lurch at Tam.'

'We got here in the end, though. It'll sort itself out.'

'I hope so. You're almost six weeks ahead of schedule and I'm not so sure they appreciate that.'

'Well they ought to. I've written to them often enough. Anyway, it was their schedule, not mine. You don't want me to go any slower do you?'

'The sooner you get off that *piste*, the better. More wine?'

'Cheers.'

* * *

I was too short of breath to breathe through my nose, so I held my tongue up to the roof of my mouth to keep out the flies. The green head-net gave me such an awesome appearance that I would not wear it walking into town. By eight o'clock, I had covered the six miles from the camp site to Agadez post office and collected my mail. I met Mick and Paddy at the police station, where we waited two hours for clearance to leave for Zinder.

As I moved through town, six little boys latched onto me. They wore only shorts and their skin was dusty. 'Ina hanyan Zinder?' I said, asking them the way out of town. They led me southwards through the unmade streets and past concrete and mud buildings – shops without windows and houses with windows but no glass. Vendors were on every corner, urchins with sweets on brightly-coloured enamel trays, old women sitting beside heaps of yams or cooking over open fires. I bought sweets and a couple of dozen kwosai – small beancakes fried in oil – and shared them with my guides. They turned back in ones and twos until two miles out of town only one small pair of bare feet ran with me. Suddenly, they raced forward and the boy put out an arm, bringing me to a halt. 'Zinder!' he said, pointing.

I had known the way since leaving town, but I opened the locker and gave him two more kwosai. He chased after me, shouting furiously, and swinging on my right arm. He was speaking too fast but I got the message. He had not brought me this far to be paid with beancakes! I argued that it was his choice to come so far. I had only asked him to point me in the right direction. We haggled until, in despair, his eyes filled with tears. I dipped into my pocket and pulled out the price of a few more beancakes. His face brightened and, I confess, so did mine.

The headwind was strong and I was glad to put my feet up when Mick and Paddy drew up in the early afternoon. Mick put his face up to mine and stared at me; I thought he was going to pick an argument but he was looking at my sun-glasses. 'Those lenses are terribly scuffed, Geoff.'

'A lot of grit has been ground into 'em since Tadjmout.'

'I'm surprised you can see.'

'I can't. It's like walking in fog. It's even worse when the sun's low.'

'I've not got any clip-ons but I've an ordinary pair you can have.' They were large enough to fit over my own frames, so from then on I wore both pairs at the same time.

Joan's third letter had been awaiting me at Agadez but I had left it unopened until after supper. She urged me not to give up. She knew how many times I had been on the point of coming home – she had my letters and the completed volumes of the log. She had told both Mike, on whom she had the crush, and his fiancée about her emotions. It had not had quite the desired effect though. She thought it would draw the sting, but instead, she found out that he had a crush on her. Joan's words were full of assurance, but I wondered how much longer she could hold on. She had not let the relationship develop, nor had she any desire to do so, but I was disturbed to read, first that the crisis was over, and then that she had sat holding Mike's hand for an hour, talking about their desire to put God first. Her desire not to develop the relationship did not seem to fit in with holding hands. I was deeply sorry for myself. I could not appreciate the strain that my neglect and absence had put on Joan.

There were eighteen other letters, prompted mostly by the fire. The fact that so many had arrived showed that people knew I was ahead of schedule. Hopefully, the army did too. The letters from friends read like sermons. 'Why on earth did you cook in your tent? . . . Aren't you stupid . . . You nearly left a widow.' Page after page, all the same.

The next two days, I managed fifty miles along the bush track in spite of illness, but on the third, the *piste* turned to sand. It divided into many strands through a forest of thorn-bushes, just as Hank had promised. The wheelbarrow, now as heavy as two dead men, and as hard to move, conspired against me with the ground. The harder I pushed, the harder they pushed back. I resorted to techniques developed further north, pushing from as near the horizontal as I could get, turning round and leaping backwards, jerking inches at a time. The heat was inescapable. For seven hours a day it was over 100 degrees Fahrenheit in the shade, except that I was not in the shade.

I was looking forward to reaching Tomboutega that afternoon. It was shown on a map that had a scale of twenty-two miles to an inch and promised to be more than a hamlet. It was, in fact, three huts, a well and six people. The old man there filled my containers for me with brown water, and asked me to stay, but I declined. What I could put behind me today I would not have to face tomorrow.

I had not gone far when the lads arrived. I eased myself onto the locker. 'Look at the poor bugger,' said Mick to Paddy. 'He's done for.'

'Quite right. I'm knackered,' I said.

'Just think of that silver bird, Geoff. When you're up there with your iced drinks, we'll be sweating it out. I could do with a cold pint right now,' he said, wiping the sweat from his face, and holding up his imaginary glass. 'It'd slide down my throat in one! Nothing's cold here. Look at that.' He pointed to a goatskin *guerba*, plump with water, hanging from the side of the Land Rover. 'It's useless. I bought it in Agadez. It's supposed to keep the water cool! It's warmer, if anything, and it's leaking like a tap. You're doing OK, though, Geoff, in spite of the *piste*: nineteen point four.'

'Well, make it twenty-five, but don't expect me too early.'

As evening came, bush travellers resumed their journeys. A Fulani woman, whose weeping I had heard drifting through the bush before I saw her, was carrying firewood and four calabash dishes on her head. 'Give me a drink and some money for food,' she wailed. 'I have lost everything.' I poured water into her dish and gave her enough money to buy a few loaves. Soon after, a boy came on a donkey, followed by a man on foot. They both begged water, bread and medicines.

They were a mild nuisance. I had to remind myself that these were the ones for whom I was doing the walk. If I did not care for them individually, then how could I claim to care for them collectively?

It would be easy to gather sponsorship money and send it to some agency, but I found my generosity stretched when asked to share the last of my bread. It was easier to give in ways that cost nothing, stale bread when I had fresh, and medicines I would never need, like those people who only give their scrap or surplus, their silver foil or loose change, but leave their bank balances untouched.

Near Beni Abbes, in December, we had had ten degrees of frost and seen icicles hanging from a water-tower. In Niger, the temperature rarely fell below 80° Fahrenheit even at night. The north of the Sahara had had wide daily extremes of temperature; in the south, it was always hot. The climatic difference was not surprising, since we had been in Beni Abbes in December, and furthermore, we were now as far south of there as Manchester is from the Arctic Circle.

At nine o'clock that evening, it was 86 degrees Fahrenheit but we still sat round the fire as if it were winter. It gave free light, was a focus, and boiled the kettle. We replaced lost body fluids with endless mugs of tea. That night I drank eight. Paddy was studying the map, Mick was throwing sticks into the fire and I was completing a report. With Kano not far away, I still did not know the lads. They hid themselves behind caricatures; I guessed that their jokes and their style of conversation had been rehearsed and proven in their billets and on exercises. The presentation of a façade makes it easy, I suppose, when a man is posted. One set of mates is exchanged for another without emotion. The new man knows he will be instantly accepted. The caricature is well tried. Why should any soldier get to know his real comrade when either one of them might be moved next week? Mick hid himself behind his jokes, Paddy behind his silence.

Mick threw another stick in the fire. 'Hey, Geoff! Good news on the radio today. City have signed Martin Peters, England beat West Germany, and John Conteh has kept his world title. Not bad for one day, eh?'

'Yeah, especially about John Conteh. I've met him. I was on Euston Station waiting for Thames Television to pick me up and he was right next to me. He's massive. He looked more like a heavyweight.'

'Did you talk to him?' asked Paddy.

'Yeah. I've always despised autograph hunters, but the temptation was too great. I've got a weakness for boxing.'

'More tea?' asked Mick, lifting the boiling kettle.

'Please,' I said, dropping a tea-bag into my mug.

'I'd swap this tea for a cold pint any day. Roll on Kano. Not long now, eh, Geoff? Three weeks and I'll be in that pool.' Delight spread across Mick's face.

'I think it'll be even quicker than that, Mick. Easter I reckon. Seventeen days. I've written and told Joan that the earliest possible date is Thursday, March twenty-seventh, so we're reasonably on target. I'm hoping she can get her free ticket so she can fly out on the Wednesday and meet us near the border.'

'Are you still planning on having her camp with us for the last few days?' asked Paddy.

'If you don't mind. I'd like her to know a little bit of what it's been like,' I said.

'I don't mind,' said Mick. 'At least there'll be someone else to give a hand with the cooking. But I hope that Bulford's got those visas.'

'In all three letters, Joan says she's been constantly badgering them and they keep saying that it's all in hand and that there's plenty of time. I'm more worried about my cholera jab. It only lasts six months and I had it done in August. They're pretty sticky on that sort of thing in Nigeria. My visa's run out, too. That only lasts three months from the date of issue, but I suppose having got so far we'll get in – even if we have to sneak!'

In Clayton, Manchester, two miles from my boyhood home, there had been an offal merchants and glue-makers, known locally as 'the knacker's yard'. Its putrid smell pervaded the district, turning stomachs and lingering in the clothes. Hardly the smell to expect here. Yet, next morning, when I had been on the *piste* for three hours, it was in the wind. I thought it was a decaying carcass. Then there was a noise I could not christen, a rumbling and rustling that came from no particular direction, followed by bleating. Hundreds of sheep were plodding through the trees, churning the sand with their hooves and being herded from behind by three men in long nightshirts.

When the sheep had passed downwind, the men greeted me, allowing the herd to forage. They recognized me and wanted to chat, so I took my mid-morning snack. The oldest loaf was gooey and yellow inside and smelt rancid. I offered it to the men, keeping the best loaf for myself. They broke it into sticky pieces and ate it unperturbed. 'We saw you in Arlit,' said one of them.

'Arlit! You got here quickly,' I said.

'No,' he laughed. 'We came by lorry. You are the quick one. You are here two days quicker than the herdsmen.'

'How far am I from the next village?' I asked.

'It's just here,' he said pointing. 'About a kilometre. It's called Abelama.'

'Is there much sand? This thing,' I said, gripping the wheel, 'doesn't like sand.'

'Keep to your right. It's not as bad.'

The *piste* led into the sandy village-square, which was edged by tall, spreading trees and low buildings. The African's ability to sit under a tree and watch the world go by gained my admiration. I cast an envious eye under the shade. Two old men were going through the rigmarole of a lengthy greeting. Then three young and beautiful Fulani women were sitting half-naked on a grass mat, plaiting each other's hair. They had just bathed and oiled their skins. One of them was telling a story so funny that she was barely able to get the words out, then all three fell about, convulsed with laughter.

Further on sat a large woman, dressed in the style of the city. Brightly printed cotton, wrapped round and round, finished with a whorl of the same material on the top of the head. This imperious woman ran the show. She was the chief's wife and village entrepreneur.

On the mat in front of her were boiled sweets, arranged in handfulls, rows of tomatoes and cola nuts, and packets of cigarettes. Her manservant was sitting on his heels behind her. I left the wheelbarrow in the sunshine and crouched to greet her. 'Good morning, madam teacher!' – not strictly the correct Hausa greeting, but in the bush anyone with education is called 'teacher'.

'Good morning,' she said, enjoying the flattery.

'How much are the tomatoes?'

'One *dela* for two.'

'I'll take twelve. How much are the sweets?'

'One *dela* for two.'

'Forty please, and how much are the cola nuts?'

'Three *dela*s each.'

'*Kai*! That's expensive! Only four of those.' The servant began to gather my order into a heap. 'Have you any *kwosai*?' I asked. She nodded. 'Twenty,' I said.

She spoke abruptly to her lackey. He jumped up, his tartan Bermuda shorts slipping perilously low, revealing three inches of rear cleavage. He scurried through the trees into a doorway. 'I'd like two kilos of beans as well,' I said, knowing that if she sold beancakes she would also sell beans. I handed her a plastic bag and watched her stand, inconvenienced, before she slipped on her sandals, tightened her skirt, and tiptoed over the exposed tree roots. The man reappeared first, carrying the *kwosai* on a brightly coloured enamel tray, followed by the woman with the black-eyed beans.

Hooves had churned the village-square into powder and I was finding it difficult to get going when a troupe of small boys descended like chattering monkeys. For a few coppers they tugged along with me to the end of the village.

An hour on into the bush, the muted sound of an engine was coming from the *piste*, but I saw something only three feet high, with no wheels, gliding between the trees, carrying sacks of cement, and half a dozen men. It was like a hovercraft but raised no dust, and had no skirt, no pilot, and no steering mechanism. It was something out of science fiction, not a shiny, new vehicle made by space engineers in this century, but something from an inter-galactic junkyard of the future. This craft was a long wooden crate and had seen better days. Yet it kept its course and missed the trees as if by magic. I doubted my sanity before realising it was the top of a lorry. The *piste* was so worn that the rest of it was obscured.

I had avoided the *piste* by dodging in and out of the thorn-trees, but the wheel, like the lorries, cut its own trench. It was the hell that Hank had promised. Sandy gullies, ten feet deep, crossed my path every few miles, each one robbing me of time and strength. The bearing, repaired at Arlit, began to tighten and act like a brake. It had become so hot that the grease was thinning and draining away. And just to annoy me, there were tufts of dried grass bristling with tiny golden burrs which scratched my legs and stuck in their hundreds to my socks and robe. Tuaregs carry tweezers to remove them from their skin and clothes.

When our Land Rover drew up, Paddy was riding 'shot-gun' on the roof-rack. He climbed down and pumped some grease into the bearing. 'What d'you reckon to this, then, Geoff?' asked Mick.

'I've been tempted to use the *piste*. It's knackering up here, but I reckon once I get in it, I'll never get out.'

'It's worse than the underground,' said Mick. 'Paddy's had to stay up there in case we missed you.'

I had managed thirteen miles and arranged to do another five, but at five-thirty I was sitting on the wheelbarrow, deep in the bush by the side of the track, watching the courtship of a pair of crows and adding to the log. Not that I had reached camp; I was unable to – the bearing had jammed, and I had no grease gun. I told myself I was not worried, but I prayed one panicked prayer after another; I did not fancy sleeping on the ground with the snakes and scorpions. Panicked prayers or not, after twenty minutes a lorry came and I was able to borrow a grease gun and add the name for it – *Pom pom griz* – to my knowledge of Hausa.

The sun was low and red through the trees. Mick was stirring a pot, Paddy adjusting the kettle on the fire and I was sitting, wearing only my boots and shorts, too tired to move. 'Pretty tough, today, Geoff?' said Mick.

'The worst since Arlit. Not even one and a half miles an hour.'

'Throw us your mug, Geoff,' said Paddy. Reluctantly, I got to my feet to get it.

'You can eat with us,' said Mick. 'There's a village not far away.'

'You're a good 'un. I don't much feel like cooking.'

'Hello!' said Mick, looking into the bush. 'We've got a visitor.' A Fulani was riding out of the low sun, his sword bouncing by his side and his straw hat dancing to the rhythm of the hooves. He dismounted, carrying a bundle of rag, kicked the donkey back the way it had come, and sat on the ground near me. Many Fulani have straight hair and light-brown skin, but this man was indistinguishable from other black West Africans. He would, though, be proud to be Fulani and feel himself to be superior to his black neighbours. The Fulani are traditionally nomadic cattle people, renowned for the distances they walk with their herds, though this one, like many of them, had settled.

He wore a waistcoat and short leather skirt and had a dagger 'bandaged' to the top of his bare arm. '*Afinijum*,' I said, using up one third of my Fulani vocabulary.

'*Jum*,' he replied.

'What did he say?' asked Mick, stirring his pot of rice.

'He just said, "Hello".'

'Tell him to push off. He'll be snooping into everything we've got.'

'Wait a minute. For all you know we're in his back yard. I'll ask him what he wants.' I turned to the man and asked him in Hausa.

'I'm waiting for a lorry to Agadez. I'm going to sell my butter.' He unwrapped his bundle, revealing a bulging goatskin twice the size of a football. 'See, it's leaking,' he said, running his hand down the seam and showing me his oily fingers. 'Give me one of those.' He pointed his lips towards a jerry-can.

'They don't belong to me, but you can have one of these,' I said, holding up a gallon container.

'Too small,' he said.

'Shift him, Geoff. We'll be eating soon,' said Mick.

'He's waiting for the lorry to Agadez,' I said. Then Mick, with a baffling change of heart, said,

'Ask him if he wants some rice and stew.'

The Fulani ate from the china plate as if he were born to it. When he had finished, he handed it back to Mick, and thanked him in Fulani. While Mick was doing the washing up, the man was showing me a swelling and cut on his shin. 'Give me medicine for my leg. I have a pain here too,' he said, holding his groin, 'and I have a headache and I'm very weak.' I squatted in front of him, in the half-light, with my medical kit.

'Watch,' I said, slowly unscrewing the cap off the antiseptic cream. 'Now you do it.' He took the tube and pulled and pushed at the cap to no effect. 'Watch,' I said, demonstrating with an exaggerated twisting motion. This time he twisted the cap back and forth in rapid succession. 'Watch carefully,' I said, showing him how to let go after each turn. Then I gave him a course of antibiotics. 'When the sun is there,' I said, showing him the pills and pointing east, 'eat one of these.' I pointed overhead and then west, repeating the instruction, and adding, 'Three tablets every day for seven days. If you eat them all at once you may die.' He was repeating what I had said when Mick cut in.

'You must be mad, Geoff, giving him tablets. He'll eat 'em all at once.'

'He's pretty sick,' I said. 'What else can I do?' Mick put his pots and pans in the back of the Land Rover and jumped off the tailboard, flashing his torch towards us. He walked to the Fulani and put his medical kit on the ground in front of him. Paddy was by the fire, watching the kettle.

'Bring some of that hot water in a bowl and my towel, will you, Paddy?' asked Mick. Then, while the Fulani held the torch, Mick bathed and dressed the wound. At about nine o'clock Mick and Paddy went to bed, leaving the Fulani and myself by the fire.

'What's your name?' I asked, making notes as I spoke.

'Abu Bakr.'

'Feeling better, Abu Bakr?'

'Much better. I thank God.' He looked down at the bandage, which glowed white in the darkness.

'How old are you?' I asked.

'Thirty-four,' he chuckled. 'An old man, but I have three young wives. They are twenty, twenty-two and twenty-four years old. And I have five children.'

He lifted his head like an alert animal and listened to the faint sound of a diesel engine. Without a farewell, he picked up his bundle and hobbled to the *piste*. The noise grew louder, ripping through the night. The headlights turned the bush into day and showed up swarms of insects in their beam. The lorry, piled high with cargo and passengers, stopped, its engine still throbbing and its lights ablaze. There was arguing before it roared away, leaving Abu Bakr by the *piste*. He struggled back with his skin of butter.

'Black men are no good!' he said, sitting down. 'We white men are best. There was plenty of room on the lorry. He just didn't want a Fulani!' I beamed my torch on my straw hat – identical to his – hanging on the front of the wheelbarrow. It was a Fulani hat, bought when I was last in Nigeria.

'See,' I said, 'I'm a Fulani too. That hat is my medicine against the sun.' He chuckled again.

'Do you want a little medicine for the night? A woman's medicine? One of my wives?' I remembered the delightful young women who had been plaiting their hair at Abelama.

'No thank you,' I said. 'I have a wife and I will be seeing her soon.'

'We Fulanis are like that,' he said, chuckling even more and breaking into a babble.

At five o'clock next morning, 15 March, I was in bed in the narrow trench between the side of the Land Rover and some stacked boxes. I freed my locked fingers, reached for my torch, Bible and container of rolled oats, and sat up for my devotions and breakfast. Then I scrambled to the tailboard and lowered it quietly so as not to wake the lads, and sat there to put on my boots. They were the ones I had been wearing from Benni Abbes, apart from a few days I had been in training shoes. There was enough sole left on them to get me to Kano. The book of Deuteronomy says that the Children of Israel each wore only one pair of shoes in their desert wanderings. I could believe it.

It was dark and the stars were veiled by thin cloud. Abu Bakr was asleep on the ground, without bed or blanket, his arms protectively round his bundle. I jumped off the tailboard and walked a few yards away to urinate. The sound of snoring was coming from the tent and a cricket sang in a bush near Abu Bakr. I walked to where the fire had been, gathered the charred sticks into a heap, lit them, filled the billycan with water and left it on the flames. I loaded the wheelbarrow with water containers, breakfast cereal box, blanket, Bible, maps and documents, before sitting down with a mug of tea.

Birds had been cooing for some time, but then a crow cawed and flapped across the lightening sky. Abu Bakr sat up anxiously and examined the leaking seam; it was not as bad as he had feared. 'Anilijum,' I said, using up another third of my Fulani vocabulary.

'Jum,' he replied. I threw the mug and billycan loosely into the wheelbarrow and put on the shoulder-strap. 'See you some day,' I said.

'Where are you going?' he asked.

'Kano.'

'Not in the motor?'

'I told you,' I said. 'I'm a Fulani. I walk everywhere.'

19

THIEF IN THE NIGHT

The grey light was ample and there was neither the glare of the low sun nor the heat of the day. After a few minutes, I was greeted by the smell of a badly-kept zoo, where camels and goats were gathered with their herdsmen round a well and wooden drinking-troughs.

The sky lightened gradually, as if controlled by a dimmer-switch, until the sun, bright as running metal, glinted through the trees. I took off my khaki shirt, put Mick's sun-glasses on over my own, and cocked my straw hat down to the left to keep out the glare. As it became hotter, I frequently became stuck and often left the wheelbarrow to look for a firmer parallel route.

By four o'clock, when I had averaged only one mile an hour, the lads drew up in convoy with the blue Land Rover of Mike Johnes and Brian Perryman from Worcestershire. The men were going to camp with us and Brian offered to walk the last four miles with me. He gave me a spirited hand, tugging while I pushed.

We camped in a circle and when the others had eaten we gathered round the fire. Brian had flopped on his camp-bed and I was eating my last Hunter's meat pudding. Mick turned to Brian, 'Do you sleep in the open all the time?'

'Yes,' said Brian. 'It works well.'

'I'm stifled these days,' said Mick, 'especially first thing in the morning when the sun gets up. I'm gonna try it outside. We've got a couple of camp-beds but they're too big for both of 'em to go in the tent.' I finished my meal and began to tidy up the wheelbarrow. 'What brings you two out here? Business?' asked Mick.

'No,' said Mike. 'We've got a business at home, but we're getting away from it. We work hard for two years and then take a long holiday. Last time we sailed the Atlantic.' After a while, Paddy went into the tent, and the other three turned in under the stars. I was still writing:

> . . . terrain terrible, couldn't use *piste*, knocked leg, made lump and hole, bleeding, put on Vaseline. Ate cod livers bought in Arlit – awful. Very hot, water tasting foul. Lorry stuck in deep sand. . . .

By the time I had finished writing the log and a couple of letters, Mick, the only one awake, was smoking and watching the stars. 'Cup of tea, Mick?' I asked.

'Why not? I don't need to go far for a pee.' When I put his tea on the ground near him, he turned towards me, leaning on an elbow,

'Did that Fulani get his lift to Agadez?' I asked.

'Yeah, and I fixed his leg for him. I wanted to have a look at it in daylight so I took the bandage off and bathed it again. It opened right up and I got a splinter out an inch long and loads of pus. He was amazing. He never flinched. He completely trusted me. I'd just dressed it again when the lorry stopped. It was piled high with gollies and I don't know what he told 'em but I ended up bandaging the lot of 'em. Anyway he left really cheerful.'

I wished Mick a comfortable night and climbed into the Land Rover. The kit had been slightly rearranged, and the gap was now so narrow that I could not lie on my back. Burrs had stuck to my blanket and got into my clothes, so I slept badly and was tired even before I began next morning. It was the same debilitating struggle as the day before except that I had borrowed Paddy's grease gun.

About noon, the load seemed to double in weight. The wheel was biting two inches into the ground but that was normal. I took out the grease gun – its casing was hot – and gave the bearing a squirt. Since I had stopped I decided to have lunch there. Out came bread, sardines, a gallon of water and my blanket, protection from the hot metal while I sat.

The sun was out of sight overhead but it glinted in the sardine can, and in the salt that had crystallized out of the dried sweat on my shoulder-harness. There was no shade. The trees were no more than prickly bushes and impossible to get under. At 110° it was as still as an oil painting. The sound of my eating seemed irreverent. There were not even any birds at this time of day – they had more sense – just a few flies drinking from my skin.

It was sweaty work and I drank profusely. When thirsty, I became quickly tired, but if I kept thirst at bay I could work hard. I ignored the advice given me by armchair travellers and old soldiers, that the more you drink, the more thirsty you become. At the first sign of thirst I would drink as much as I could until I began to feel a little sick. After a couple of minutes, I would drink again until the sickness returned, and repeat the process until I could take no more, usually after two or three pints. The nausea soon passed and I could keep going for more than two hours without excessive thirst or fatigue. It worked well, considering the task. I had stopped taking salt tablets early in the walk but had resumed at In Guezzam when I had craved abnormal amounts of salt in my food.

I had a fight on my hands that afternoon. I had seen the lads just after two-thirty, and had told them I could manage another six miles, but four hours later, with the sun nearly gone, there was no sign of camp. Mick and Paddy, anxious for my safety, had already left their tent and were driving north to find me. Fortunately, they did not have to go far; I was only two-thirds of a mile away.

By seven o'clock, I was sitting on a jerry-can by the Land Rover, where I stayed fifteen minutes. After sixteen miles in twelve and a half hours I had never been so tired. I limped around picking up sticks in order to prepare supper. My legs were a mass of scratches and my green socks had become yellow and prickly with burrs. After supper I tried to pick them off but ended up throwing the socks away. I washed my underwear, wrote a couple of letters and entered up the log. My last words were, 'Unless God gives me bread I will have none tomorrow.'

I woke up in a panic, shouting. It was dark and I was trying to sit up, finding it difficult from my cramped position. I had to stop a thief: an African had his head and arm in the back of the Land Rover and had taken hold of a carrier-bag. Unperturbed, he leaned in further and was coming at me. He was going to hit me, but was out of reach. I managed to sit up, but there was nothing that I could use to defend myself. 'OK, OK,' he said in a loud whisper. 'I've brought you some bread.' He dropped the bag and disappeared. To this day I do not know who he was.

At a quarter to ten the next morning, while I was taking a snack, a Fulani led towards me a donkey, on which his wife and baby were riding. A camel, carrying a sack and bundles, walked behind, tethered to the donkey's saddle. I thought it unusual to see a saddle on a donkey. I obliged the man with water, pouring some into his gourd, and then off we went together. I was too slow, so he untethered the camel and tied the wheelbarrow in its place. He now led an animal with each hand. The donkey did half my work while I pushed and steered from behind. After a few minutes, he stopped and unwrapped a calabash bowl containing a muddy paste. 'Millet?' I asked.

'Yes, you take it?' he said, scooping some with his fingers and offering it to me. It looked like clay ready to be thrown onto a wheel.

This incident reminded me of the common cup shared at Holy Communion. I have no idea what diseases folk might bring to it, but we share it because we are one family. Sinner and saint recognize in the sacrament a common need for God's grace and a common acceptance of each other.

So, the Fulani offered me his millet. He was not a Christian, but he was a man for whom God went to the cross. The fact that he did not recognize this, did not mean that God loved him less; though not Christian brothers, we were loved by the same Father. Whether or not he wanted to receive the sacrament with me, this calabash of millet had become the bread and wine. Sharing this food was a sacrament, a recognition not only that God had accepted the Fulani, but also that he had accepted me. How could I receive God's love if I would not acknowledge that God loved this man too. If God loved him, then so must I, and I must eat the millet.

The Fulani was still holding the millet on his fingertips, offering it to me. I shook my head. Idealism had failed me, or rather, I had failed idealism, because of my will to survive. African wells contain all manner of deadly ills and I was doubtful of the water with which the millet had been mixed.

'Have some of my food,' I said. He and his wife accepted bread but looked on the pâté with revulsion.

'What's that?' he asked.

'Meat.'

'What kind?'

'I don't know,' I lied. It was pork and he was Muslim.

We set off again and kept a good pace for half an hour, until we reached Eliki at ten-thirty. There were no houses, just a clearing bordered by broad, leafy trees which gave off a beautiful scent. People and animals were under their shade. Four young men with camels were under one, several families under another and a herd of sheep and their shepherds under another. The Fulani untethered the wheelbarrow. 'It's too warm. We'll carry on when the sun is there,' he said, pointing to three o'clock. He led his animals into the shade, but I was going on. One of the four young men left his camel and came for water, followed by an old man for pills, a woman for matches and another for food – the only one I refused.

Beyond Eliki, there was a respite from sand and thorn-bushes, along an avenue of fragrant trees. About four o'clock, with the *piste* back to its worst, some young Australians, seeing Africa from the back of a lorry, leapt from their vehicle in excitement. 'You've made it,' they shouted. 'The good *piste* is only two or three kilometres away.' People had told me about so called good *piste*s before. I was rude to them, but they thought I was joking and gave me leftover beans and Spam.

It took an hour to reach camp, which was at the brow of a gentle rise, half a mile short of a village. I was gathering sticks while Mick was inspecting his stew. 'What about that, then?' he asked.

'What about what?'

'The *piste*.'

'What about it?' I asked.

'Look along a bit,' he said. After a hundred yards, it narrowed to the width of a road, and looked firm. The young Australians had been right.

At twenty-six miles a day I would be at the border in a week and Kano in eleven days, on Good Friday. In a couple of weeks, I would be asking the bishop for another job. There was kit to sort out and a meal to prepare. We worked under the stars, lifting our heads occasionally to look at the cooking fires in the valley across the bush and listen to the echo of drums.

The next four days took us one hundred and six miles through undulating scrubland, past towns which I barely noticed – Tanout, Sabonkafi, Gézawa and Barkin Bershi – pausing only for water, bread, *kwosai* and sweets. Between them, from the tops of hills, I could see the scorched savannah, stretching unbroken from horizon to horizon and rippling in the heat.

Near Gézawa a Land Rover stopped and out teetered a uniformed young man, reeking of alcohol. His grey jacket was saturated with sweat under his arms and across his back. His children and two wives were in the rear of the vehicle, his subordinate at the wheel. 'Passport!' he snapped. He ran his fingers along its charred edge, asked me questions, and then in an over-friendly manner said, 'Have a beer!'

It was the wrong time for alcohol, but it was not the time to upset an official either, especially a drunken one. He barked an order at his chauffeur, deliberately demeaning him. The man obeyed, unruffled, and placed a tray with two glasses and two cans of beer on the bonnet. I drank quickly in an attempt to get away but no sooner had I finished than I was given another. This time, I turned my glass over, as is the custom, to signal that I had had enough. The chauffeur then brought a briefcase. The offical scrawled a note for me and stamped it, declaring that my effects had been cleared by the customs.

Four days on the 'good' *piste* had burst the split rims and played havoc with my wheel. The bearing was now so worn that there were four inches of play at the rim. Paddy would not put on the other wheel until it was absolutely necessary, even though we had only seventeen miles of *piste* left.

Tomorrow the slog would be over. I had forgotten what a real road was like and imagined that the wheelbarrow would propel itself, taking me effortlessly with it. I could not sleep with excitement and was tempted to get up during the night to get there more quickly. At seven o'clock, when I was rumbling out of camp, Mick rolled over on his camp-bed, took a lighted cigarette from his lips, and said with a grin, 'Get out on that *piste*!' For once I was glad to. I raced over one hill after another, past settlements and fellow travellers. I overtook a boy on a horse and a group of young barefooted women, wearing their best floral wraps and carrying bowls on their heads. They were off to market and were so full of fun that they could barely walk for laughter. I was half-way to Zinder when Mick and Paddy arrived. 'Any problems, Geoff?'

'Only the wheel. I'm going all over the place.'

'Persevere,' said Paddy. 'The other one's not much better. We'll save it. If both of them go, you've had it.'

'Give us your passport, Geoff,' said Mick. 'We'll collect your mail and report to the law.' Soon I had gained on a boy who was carrying a bundle on his head. He put it down, retied it, and carried it in his arms.

'How far to Zinder?' I asked him.

'Very far. I am going there,' he replied. I opened one of the lockers.

'Put your bundle in here,' I said. 'We'll go together.' We climbed a long hill. From the top, we looked down across a plain at the rooftops of Zinder, glinting through a bluish haze, seven miles away. By one o'clock, we had reached the outskirts, where there were breeze-block and mud buildings, and a tumbledown petrol station. Just then, Mick and Paddy came back from the town with letters and a telegram for me.

'Well done! You're home and dry,' said Paddy. I tore open the telegram.

'Two-thirds of a mile to tarmac,' added Mick. 'And, oh, you owe me a couple of quid collection fee.'

'Look at that!' I said, showing them the telegram. It read: 'KANO 26th 0700'.

'Joan's flying into Kano next Wednesday morning at seven o'clock!'

'Let's hope they'll let us across the border to meet her,' said Mick.

'No problem,' I said. 'If we've got this far, we'll get to Kano. Where shall I meet you in Zinder?'

'There's a hotel with a bar almost out of town on the other side. Go over a roundabout. Keep straight on and you can't miss it.'

Reaching tarmac was a non-event. I had celebrated it in advance and now took it for granted, thinking only of reaching Joan. The boy took his bundle and went off to his uncle's. I crossed the shabby little town, stopping under a tree by the hotel. I sat on the wheelbarrow to read Joan's letter, which told me that Nigeria Airways had at last sent her free ticket. They had given me mine the evening before I had left England. By the time it had arrived, I had lost all hope of receiving it and had arranged to return overland. In the confusion, I had forgotten to tell the army my change of plan. Unknown to me, they thought I was still going to drive back with the lads. Joan's letter also told me that Peter Lindeck, the vicar of St George's Church, Kano, had arranged to meet her at the airport, and drive her out to me. She also explained that her crush on

Mike had almost gone. Talking about it with Mike's fiancée and other friends had helped to get it out of her system. I was greatly relieved.

The hotelier, a middle-aged Frenchman, came down the steps and shook hands with me. 'Please come inside,' he said, 'and have a drink on me.'

'I'll stay outside because I'm so filthy,' I explained.

'That doesn't matter. Do come in.'

I ordered a Coca-Cola and sat in an easy chair to finish my mail, talking now and then to the lads. By a quarter to four I had picked up bread and water and was on the road, hoping to make another ten miles. After fifteen minutes I was stopped by two French women in an open saloon car. They were in their mid-thirties and wore sun-glasses and head-squares. The blonde driver switched off the engine and asked, 'Are you tired?'

'A little,' I said.

'Come back to our place.'

'No thank you. I've arranged to meet my friends.'

'Wouldn't you like a shower and a few drinks?'

'I must keep on the road or my friends will miss me.'

'Really, it's not very far,' said the other woman.

'I must be going,' I insisted.

The scene was open and brown, with a few mud dwellings and fields of millet stubble. A long green leaf which was lying on the road writhed when the wheel went over it, and proved to be a chameleon. I reluctantly reversed over the creature's head to put it out of its misery.

A fierce southerly wind picked up and I was hard pressed. Philip and Carol Short and Mrs Doris Kapp of the Sudan Interior Mission were waiting to meet me at camp, having expected me earlier. They were uncomplicated people who neither drank nor smoked and found their enjoyment in simple things. They were transparent; I sensed in them a saintliness which unnerved me. Their Christian service was unspectacular but all the greater for being so. Many people would hear of my venture but they, likely as not, would die in obscurity. Yet their work in Africa was much more valuable than mine. It was work *with* African people, not *for* them.

We talked while I lit a fire. 'I hear you were a missionary yourself once,' said Philip.

'Sort of,' I said, interrupted by Mick who shouted from beside his fire.

'Hey, Geoff, I've got you some beer. It's in the Land Rover.' He was deliberately embarrassing me: he knew that I had been in the hotel bar today and that if I had wanted beer I would have bought it for myself.

'Thanks Mick,' I said, not wishing to debate the issue. I turned back to Philip, 'Yes, I was a short-termer, only out for a year.'

'Who were you serving with?'

'The Sudan United Mission. I was teaching at Gindiri on the Nigerian Plateau.'

When they had gone, Mick said, 'I asked 'em if there was any beer on sale at the border. They said they didn't know. I told them how you enjoyed a drink and how important it was that we got you some.' There was enough truth in what he said for it to needle me, though I tried not to show it.

'Hey, Geoff!' said Mick. 'Are you sure I'll be able to get a suit in Kano?'

'Definitely. It'll be lightweight cloth but you should find something you like.'

'What about souvenirs, Geoff?' asked Paddy. 'What's the best thing to get?'

'Leatherwork or tie-dyed cloth. Neither's too expensive, and both are worth taking home.' I said.

'I can't wait to get in that pool. You'll not get me out,' said Mick with pleasure in his face. 'Cold beer, the pool, girls. I can't wait!'

Southwards stretched an arid plain whose monotony was broken only by a cotton field and a few settlements. By nine-fifteen next morning, I had managed thirteen miles, but I slowed as the sun climbed. I was aching and unnaturally tired.

There were pyramids ahead, at least a dozen, each as high as four double-decker buses – sacks of ground-nuts that nobody would buy. I was becoming progressively more ill and had to punish myself to complete thirty-five miles. Next day I became worse. I had a high temperature, ached all over and once again had diarrhoea. Soon after the small town of Kantché, I was stopped at an unexpected immigration post whose purpose was to catch those who had either sneaked across the border or who were hoping to do so. Mick and Paddy had my documents, so I sent them a note with a northbound vehicle. I scribbled a note to Joan, too, telling her to meet me on Wednesday as arranged. I enclosed in it a letter to Peter Lindeck, the vicar, and asked a south-bound driver to deliver them.

— 20 —

MEET ME ON
WEDNESDAY

When the lads arrived, at long last, Paddy changed the wheel for me. Soon after leaving the checkpoint, they had trouble with their split rim again. I caught them up, and having done sixteen miles, I arranged to camp after another eleven, three miles short of the border.

The new wheel was a great improvement – I could now walk in a straight line – but the illness became worse, and I had to stop every half-hour. I remember little except feeling desperately ill and wishing for four hours that camp would come. When it did, I went straight to bed, but I woke up for a pee at nine o'clock that evening, shivering and drenched with sweat. I was weak and once outside had to hold on to the Land Rover.

Next morning I felt much better but was reminded of how disorientated I had become. As I was setting off, Mick shouted, 'Geoff, where are you going, you silly bugger?'

'Kano,' I said innocently.

'Try the other direction. You'll get there quicker.'

The Niger frontier post was a mud hut with a bench outside. We filled in forms and bought millet pancakes from a woman who was cooking them on a sheet of iron over an open fire. Duly cleared, we began to cross no man's land. For part of the way the road was raised fifteen feet above a marsh. Rice and out-of-season crops were growing beneath swarms of colourful tropical birds. It had the lush, cultivated look of the Italian countryside of Renaissance paintings. The wilderness was behind us: I was a day or two away from Joan; Mick and Paddy were a hundred miles from their dream.

Abruptly, the road opened up into the border village. Along the left of the road were shacks with small tin plaques fastened to their walls: 'Guinness is Good for You', 'Persil Washes Whiter', 'Omo', 'Fanta', and 'Tate & Lyle'. There were mats and tables outside displaying the goods for sale.

The customs and immigration office was twenty yards to my right, with our Land Rover parked outside. Mick met me as I was walking towards it. 'See you at twenty-one, Bolton Road,' he said.

'You're joking! They won't let you in?'

'No visa! No clearance! Nothing! Those buggers in Bulford have made a balls-up.'

I was met on the steps of the immigration office by two men in grey shirts and trousers. 'Welcome,' said one of them. 'We were expecting you yesterday. We heard about you on television.'

'It's good to be here,' I said. 'Are you in charge?'

'No, the senior officer is inside.' We passed through a waiting-room, into an office decorated with road-safety posters and a picture of a policeman declaring, 'The policeman is your friend'.

Behind the desk was an immaculately-dressed man with the good looks of the young Mohammed Ali. We greeted each other and he looked at my passport. 'We can let *you* in,' he said. 'Your expired visa can be extended. But we can't issue your friends with new ones. They'll have to go to Niamey in Niger to get theirs.'

'That's a two thousand mile round trip! I assure you, the British Army has got clearance for them!'

'I'm sorry. There's nothing I can do.'

'What about your radio? Give Kano a call and they'll confirm what I've said.'

'It's broken.'

'Can't you send someone by road?'

'It would take too long and you would get a negative reply.'

'These men have been in the desert three months! You can't send them back!'

'There is nothing I can do.'

Mick and Paddy were waiting for me as I walked out in frustration. 'There's no way we're gonna drive to Niamey and back,' said Mick. 'If we turn round, we're off to Gib.'

'Why don't I see if you can stay here a few days,' I said. 'I'll get to Kano as fast as I can, sort out the visas, and bring them back here. There's a chance I could do it in four days.' I went back inside and put the suggestion to the chief.

'I'm sorry. I don't think it would work,' he said. 'They don't issue visas from Kano. You have to get them from outside the country.'

'I know but I'm sure that Kano has already received external clearance.' There was a short silence.

'OK, OK. This is what we'll do: we keep one of the soldiers here; the other one drives my assistant with the three passports and a letter of recommendation from me to the office in Kano.' He began composing a letter to headquarters and I went out to confer with Mick and Paddy.

'It'll be fine,' I said. 'It's obvious that there's no clearance because the radio's broken. And even if there's nothing at Kano they can send a wire to London.'

'OK,' said Mick to Paddy. 'You drive. I'll stay here and give it the big lips.' Before long the young assistant appeared, stunning in his black military hat and trousers and off-white shirt with gold-braided epaulettes and brass buttons, and carrying a silver-topped cane.

'We'll leave in ten minutes,' he said, entering the customs house.

'There's no point you hanging about Geoff,' said Mick. 'It's eleven o'clock and you've only done five miles. We'll catch you up later.' I said farewell to the chief and pushed the wheelbarrow to a roadside stall, where I bought sweets and a tonic water. Mick leaned against the Land Rover, lit a cigarette and watched me walk down the road and out of sight.

The bush was almost desert, its skyline interrupted now and then by a massive baobab tree. There were many village compounds, each surrounded by a grass-mat fence, but few people were out in the heat.

The Land Rover came up, and Paddy checked if I was all right; I shook his hand and wished him well. The solitude had ended by mid-afternoon, when I reached the town of Daura at the height of a Muslim festival. There were hoards of street-sellers, people cooking meat by the road, and youths with large enamel bowls on their heads who were hawking fruit, bread and pastries. African music came from every direction, played on portable tape-recorders and radios. I bought bread, pastries and mangoes and took on water.

On the far side of town, there was almost no traffic. The road was quiet under a deep-blue sky. Our Land Rover had been gone six hours when I saw it approaching from the south. It slowed down gradually from a long way off, as if Paddy had taken his foot off the accelerator and had not applied the brake, and came to rest just ahead of me, on the other side of the road. The immigration officer jumped out of the door nearest me, and Paddy out of the other. I put down the wheelbarrow. There was no leaping exuberance, no smiles, not even a 'Hello'.

Doors slammed, and then there was only the sound of our boots until we stood face to face in the middle of the road. The immigration officer handed me my passport. Paddy spoke. His voice was quiet and his face was holding back emotion. 'Congratulations,' he said. 'You're OK. Mick and me are being sent back.'

The callous swines! The dirty, filthy, callous British Army swines! Someone at Bulford was going to hang for this! I felt not an ounce of joy at my personal clearance. It was like having passed an exam when my friends had failed.

Paddy helped me get some things out of the Land Rover – a little food, exposed films, letters, a shirt, trousers, a bar of chocolate, a pudding, a tin of pâté, and tea-bags. 'Is that all?' he asked, stuffing my blanket into the locker.

'Yes, except this,' I handed him his grease gun.

'The big chief in Kano was impressed,' said Paddy holding on to the cab-handle, 'but he said his hands were tied. The army hadn't applied for clearance as far as he knew.'

I shook Paddy's hand. 'Tell Mick I'm sorry,' I said, walking with him to the driver's side. He climbed into the cab, started the engine, popped out his ginger mop and managed a smile. 'See you in Salford,' he said.

I walked in an angry daze, my face wet with tears, wishing I could have run a bayonet through the man responsible. At six-thirty, a youth ran from a compound just off the road, and invited me to stay the night. It would soon be dark, and I was weak from the previous day's illness, but grief and anger burned inside me, like coal in a fire-box, driving me on.

At eight o'clock, I ate a can of beans. It was dark except for a bright moon, and the air was still and heavy. A shuffling noise came from behind me. When I turned, I saw an old man approaching on the other side of the road. He was wearing a long shirt and carrying a swag stick. I called out a greeting but he was frightened. 'Would you like some chocolate?' I asked in Hausa. He stood looking at me, so I walked over with half a bar held out in my hand.

'Thank you,' he said, taking it.

'Would you like a tin can?' I asked. He followed me to the wheelbarrow and gladly accepted the unwashed bean can, jagged edges and all. 'Is there a town near here?' I asked.

'Yes.'

'Is it far?'

'Two miles. I'm going there. I'll take you.' He was slow, but my legs felt spindly too.

'Is there somewhere I can stay?'

'I'll take you to the chief.'

At nine o'clock, the road entered an avenue of trees and mud-brick houses. Under the trees, in front of the houses, were traders' stalls, each one glittering with paraffin-lamps, made from evaporated-milk tins. I could smell woodsmoke, meat cooking on sticks, and the scent of trees. I could hear the faint beat of a drum, crickets, a radio playing and villagers talking around the stalls. Small boys danced round me chanting the word for white man – *bature* – in the style of football crowds: 'Ba-too-ree! Ba-too-ree! Ba-too-ree!'

The old man led me to the far end of the village, where there was a road-block. We stopped short of it and he pointed out one of the immigration officials as being the chief. I greeted him and he examined my passport. 'I'm looking for somewhere to stay the night,' I said.

'Sorry, there is nowhere here.'

'I can't go another step. I really am very tired.'

'This is only a village. There is no hotel, and even the school is closed.'

'I'm quite happy to sleep on the ground. I'd be all right down there,' I said, pointing to a broad path just off the road between two raffia fences. 'I couldn't get to the next town. I'm on foot.' He shone his torch into my passport again.

'I realize who you are now. If you are happy to sleep down there, then make yourself at home.'

I pushed the wheelbarrow down the alley, put my blanket on the ground, sat on it and took off my boots. I was entering the day's sorry events in the log when a young villager brought me a tray with a pot of tea, a tin of evaporated milk and a box of sugar cubes. Then more local men came to pay their respects and to ask if I needed anything. At ten minutes to ten I rolled myself in my blanket and wished everyone a goodnight. '*Sai da safi*,' I shouted.

'*Yowa, sai da safi*,' came back through the grass fences and from the men on the road-block.

At a quarter to six the next morning a voice rang through the stillness like an unwelcome alarm clock. The imaum was calling the people to prayer. I read a few verses of Scripture, and finished the pastries from the day before. I bought twelve millet pancakes from a roadside griddle, made an entry in the log, and was away by six-thirty.

The events of yesterday were lightened by the thought that it was Wednesday 26 March. Joan would be touching down in half an hour and would be with me by nine o'clock. We had last seen each other as I went through the barrier at Heathrow Airport. It had been a cool, windy day and was a strained parting. Today, if she would give me the chance, I would begin to put things right.

At half-past eight, a saloon car stopped and a tall, serious-looking European got out. He was alone. 'Hello, I'm Peter Lindeck,' he said. Where was Joan? I remained externally calm but was in turmoil.

'Hello, good to meet you,' I replied.

'I didn't expect you so soon,' he said.

'There's no reason to rest at this stage,' I said.

'I've got some mail for you,' he said, handing me several letters. A glance showed that none was from Joan. 'Where are the two soldiers?'

'There was no clearance for them. They got turned back at the border.' Why had he not mentioned Joan? Perhaps the final, awful details of the

Aulef dream had come true. Whatever the reason for her absence, it should have been the first thing he told me. Was the news so bad that he was finding it difficult? I was frightened to ask and had to harden myself to sound casual. 'I thought you'd be meeting my wife.'

'She wasn't on the plane. I checked the passenger list and she wasn't on that either.'

In the dream, Joan had been lying on a bed with her arms around the young man. Every part of the dream, except this one, had unfolded in her letters, as if she had used my written account of it as a script. Now I was sure it had all come true. Joan had never shown the slightest indication that she would want my place to be filled, but perhaps her pain had been unbearable without someone to lean on.

Peter walked a little way with me. I pretended to like the idea. Now and then he would go back for his car and then walk with me again. He was showing me kindness, but I found his presence a strain. Sometimes a mourner needs to be alone. At midday, Peter left for Kano, promising to return in the morning with some bananas. I told him that I would be glad of them, but I was hurting inside like never before. I wanted to rant, rave and scream: 'Bananas! I don't want your bananas! I want my wife!'

In the town of Kazaure, children helped me to take my mind off things, pressing round me as I ate. When I handed a piece of bread to the smallest child, the rest dived on top of him. Another boy wriggled from the scrummage with the bread held high. I caught him by the wrist, and after giving him a lecture returned it to its owner. He and I ate, watched by twenty pairs of eyes.

I pushed on. When I had met Joan at her school dance, she was sixteen. I arranged a date with her at my school dance two days later, but when I arrived she was not there. After waiting a miserable hour, I resorted to dancing with my sister, hardly taking my eyes off the door. That was a Wednesday, too, 19 December 1962, but unlike today she had eventually arrived. I will never forget catching her eye as she walked in, and the delight I felt.

Even now, I hoped that the pattern would be the same. Perhaps there would be another plane; perhaps she was simply late. I kept my eye on the road, expecting Peter's car to return, but the more I watched, the more depressed I became. I thought of Joan and little else until it became too painful to think. By evening, I had covered thirty-six miles and was almost too weary to stand, but to stop and rest would be to start thinking again, so I kept going.

At the town of Dambarta, the road remained unlit. I was dazzled by the traffic and stumbled on the uneven shoulder of the road. I could not go much further. On the far side of the town, on the left of the road, were lights among the trees and a sign which read, 'Dambarta High School'. I made my way up the tree-lined drive into the quadrangle. An old night-watchman appeared, carrying a paraffin hurricane-lamp. 'Do you speak English?' I asked in Hausa.

'No.'

'Where are the European teachers?' I asked, gambling that there were some who might offer hospitality. He led me along a broad dirt path and pointed to the bungalows. One of them had a light at the window and I knocked at the door. A Nigerian teacher in his twenties answered and eyed me suspiciously. I told him about myself and he examined my passport by the light that fell from the doorway.

'You know that the school is on holiday? Most of the staff, including the head, are away.'

'Ah! The Easter holidays! I should have realized!'

'What exactly do you want?' he asked.

'I just need permission to sleep on the ground somewhere on the compound, a place where I won't be woken by suspicious staff or by thieves.'

'The problem is that I don't speak the language of the night-watchman,' he said. 'I'm from Benin.'

'That's OK. I know a little Hausa and I'll explain to him if you'll trust me.'

We walked back to the quadrangle, chatted to the night-watchman, and arranged with him for me to sleep under a tree. I spread out my blanket and began to read my mail. My mother had written, 'I do hope Joan manages to get to see you . . .'. The teacher came back with tea-bags, coffee, sugar, milk, and a flask of hot water on a tray. He stayed asking me questions until I had drunk the contents of the flask, and then he went away to refill it for me for the morning.

I lay watching the moon through the branches. Mosquitoes were humming – unusual in the dry season; they probably bred in the cesspit. Something was prickling me. When I switched on my torch, I discovered ants, half an inch long, all over me and inside my clothing. A column of them was marching to and from a hole five yards away, over and around me, and up the tree. I sprinkled a line of insect powder around the perimeter of the blanket to encourage them to make a detour. Then I sat flicking them from me to the other side of the cordon. I lay down and looked at my watch. Wednesday had gone.

I woke at a quarter to six and after breakfast left the flask on the teacher's doorstep. Kano was thirty-four miles away and I would be there by nightfall. It was the ninety-fourth day and I would have completed 1,946 miles, less the mile I had ridden near the start – an average, including rest days, of more than twenty miles a day. With Joan on my mind I could take no satisfaction in the achievement.

Peter was due at half-past nine but did not show up. As the morning wore on, my spirits sank to new depths. As hard as I tried not to, I was looking at my watch every few minutes and distressing myself with morbid thoughts. At eleven o'clock, when I was seventeen miles from the town, I decided to go straight to the airport. There was no easy way to find Peter's flat – his address was a box number – so I would telephone England and then fly home.

At eleven-fifteen, when I had given up hope, Peter arrived, stopping a little way ahead. I could not see clearly through the windscreen of his car, but there was a passenger with him, an African. When they got out, I nodded to Peter, still a hundred yards away and paid little attention to his friend, who remained half-hidden on the far side of the car. I sensed that he was a church leader come to welcome me, and to bring greetings from his people. I should have been heartened, but I wanted to tell them that if they really cared they would go away.

My eyes turned to the African. There was something odd. He was wearing a most unusual robe, so short, and his arms and legs were white. What I had thought was a black face was a cine camera in front of a white face. I wanted to cry, to race to her. Later I wrote in the log:

She moves it [the cine camera] down, smiles. I keep on walking towards her. I'm sitting hard on my emotions, keep on, it's ten yards only. I'm eight or nine yards from her. I want to make a fool of myself but just beckon her. I let go of the barrow. We hug. Questions. Why not yesterday? How are the kids? Peter occupies himself. It was as if she's never been away, though her lips felt strangely soft.

She held me from herself. 'Your lip's cracked,' she said. 'There's blood on your teeth.' She held me from her again. 'You look so different, so brown.'

'Does it matter?'

'No,' she said, her eyes full of affection. 'I wondered if it would be the same. I just didn't know until I got here.' I had never been happier. Joan continued walking with me while Peter drove ahead and waited.

'When you didn't come yesterday, I was sure you'd gone off with Mike,' I said.

'Nothing so exciting. The plane was full. Fare-paying passengers had priority. It's the Easter rush. Last night was nearly the same. There were queues of wealthy Nigerian ladies paying pounds for excess baggage. Eventually, I was at the end of a line of people with stand-by tickets. Then, after we should have boarded, I was the only one left and an official told me to hurry on to the plane. I got the very last seat. Oh, I've got a letter for you from Colonel Keest. He's furious that you're leaving Mick and Paddy to drive back alone. He insists you go with them.'

To have left Joan and gone back overland would have been hard to take, but if the lads had been there, I would have been duty-bound. At least one small good had come out of the lads' being turned away – they were spared my company on the way home and I was able to return with my wife.

'Didn't Peter tell you they were refused entry?' I asked.

'Yes, but I thought they might still be at the border.'

'Not a chance. They'll be at Agadez now, Arlit tomorrow. I couldn't catch them if I tried. Anyway, they wouldn't want me with them. It's been hard enough putting up with me these last three months.'

I learned that Peter had booked a room for us at the Sudan Interior Mission guest-house, so when Joan grew tired, I asked him to drive her there for the afternoon. He would bring her back at four o'clock.

As the afternoon wore on, the conurbation became more dense. I passed some road-works. A man was driving a dumper truck and others were busy with their shovels. A tall Nigerian, perhaps the surveyor, wearing a pin-striped suit and gold-framed spectacles, was leaving the site and about to get into his expensive car. He watched me and then walked over. 'Where are you going?' he asked.

'Kano,' I replied.

'Kano? With that thing? You'll never make it!'

21

SILVER BIRD

We walked on into the Kano rush-hour, Joan on the pavement, and I among the traffic. A young man on a moped crawled along the kerb and began to pester her. I was about to act, when we recognized him: he had been one of our students five years before at Gindiri, three hundred miles away.

On we trod, past the Coca-Cola factory, into the suburbs, and finally to the guest-house forecourt. There were no cameras or reporters, just three elderly missionary ladies, with beautiful smiles, standing by the door. They clapped me as if I had scored a four. 'Don't stand there, girls,' I said. 'Put the kettle on.'

Soon we were in our room. 'Hey, we've a shower of our own,' I said, untying my boots. 'Come on, let's get under it.'

'Together?' she smiled. 'I can't do that. I don't know what you'd get up to.'

'You've been married to me for six years and you don't know what I'd get up to?' Together, we happily watched the endless red dust swirl down the plughole, but on this occasion there were no concerned men, French or otherwise, knocking on the door.

Four days later, on Easter Monday, I put on the shoulder-harness for the last time and began the six miles to the airport. My thoughts were no longer paralysed with anxiety about Joan or visas. The way of life to which I had become so attached had gone, but I felt as if there were still some part of me north of Arlit, cursing a cart the Chinese should never have invented. I doubted that I would return. It could never be the same.

* * *

I was still committed to writing a book about it, though, and I began work on it soon after I got back, writing in odd moments. By the time a couple of years had passed, however, my interest had waned, and after I took my first living in 1977, the manuscript lay undisturbed, collecting dust. I became absorbed in the church and my family. Life at the vicarage was one of happy chaos, with people coming and going almost incessantly, while I dashed in and out, doing two or three things at once. It was easy to forget the desert, but in quiet moments, or when speaking about my expedition at meetings of the Townswomen's Guild, nostalgia would get the better of me and I would wish that I was on the *piste* again. I forgot the misery, and like old timers remembering the war, began to view some of the worst moments in my life as some of the best.

In truth, I had missed the desert from my first day home but refused to admit it, even to myself. I had buried my love for it so deeply, for fear it would consume me, that for almost ten years I did not allow myself to admit that I wanted to be back there. Perhaps the desire to return explains why, each spring, I have my hair cut almost to the scalp: in the summer my head feels as it did in the desert. My feet betray me too. I wear boots more often than shoes, and I still prefer thick, green army socks.

Friends were keen to find out how the desert had affected me. 'Have you any more trips planned?' they asked, wanting to know if the expedition had purged my system of adventure. My flippant reply, 'I'm working on a pedal-powered submarine to take me under the polar ice-cap', concealed my inner struggle. It was a different desire from wanting to be back in the Sahara; it was the need for new challenges. I had kept telling myself that I had not caught the wanderlust, but it took me eleven years to admit that I had. It is in my blood with the permanence of malaria. I had suppressed it without knowing, afraid to admit it even to myself – I was half-aware of it, but whenever it popped up into my conscious mind, I restrained myself as might a dried-out alcoholic. An ocean or another desert would not satisfy. Travel would become a drug, and I would need mountains to climb, rivers to navigate, or lost tribes to visit, like those who go from expedition to expedition trying to satisfy the insatiable. My life would have degenerated into indulgence.

As the pressure to engage in more adventure increased, I pulled my old manuscript out of the tin trunk. I would relive the desert in pen and ink. Through writing, I would see the thing more clearly, try to examine my motives and understand what the desert had done to me. Fundraising for the poor was admirable, and I was glad to have raised over £2,000 in sponsorship, but I could have raised more money, more easily, by other means. There is no logical reason why I went to the desert. The answer lies in my psychology: it is not, 'Because the desert is there,' but rather, 'Because I am me.'

In writing, I have conferred a significance on the walk that was not there at the time. With hindsight, the adventure has become an aid to understanding myself and my home environment, something against which to measure them, and an aid to objectivity. It has helped me to find significance in my present position, and to understand that in spite of the urge to go on more major adventures, no good would come if I gave into it. The walk was a lesson, not an achievement. What had I achieved anyway? I could hardly claim to have carried *all* my own food and water across the Sahara Desert, not when the rules had been so arbitrary, and so lax. I could not even claim that it had made me a better or more courageous person. I had said before embarking that I hoped that by facing loss in the desert, I might never fear to lose, by enduring pain, I might never shrink from it, by risking death, I might return prepared to give up my life without grudging, and that, having firmly placed my life in God's hands, I might never want to withhold anything from him.

That was embarrassing talk a couple of years later when I had to give up a sponsored walk because of blisters. The desert did not teach me a thing about endurance. What I was before I went, I was when I returned. I am still a craftsman at making beds of nails for myself but an apprentice at cheerfully lying on them. My life at the vicarage in inner-city Salford is an example. We keep open house and would have it no other way. It gives immense satisfaction but, like sponsored walks and deserts, it is sometimes more than we bargain for. We try to be available to parishioners most of the time. In a city where social workers and doctors are under pressure, and where they go home at tea-time, the clergy are a vital support to the community.

Many of those who call need a listening ear and a prayer, but most come for no more than a cup of tea and a chat. The local school teacher, the thief and the child molester stand in our kitchen on equal terms, drinking their tea. Joan often carries on the housework while one caller or another follows her round, engaging her in conversation. She may be holding Luke, our two-year-old, with one arm, stirring a pot with another, listening to someone's troubles with one ear, and Thomas with the other – Mum, Alfred won't let me have the sellotape.' One Christmas morning, someone arrived at seven-thirty. 'I knew you'd be up. I'm a bit fed up. Could I have a cup of tea?' I left the children unpacking their stockings and put the kettle on. We preserve family unity by eating together at least once a day, but even then we usually have guests. Our vicarage is not unique and my testimony is poor compared with that of neighbouring clergy. The rector of the next parish and his wife have seven children and as well as streams of callers, they sometimes give lodging to the homeless and store their furniture if they have been evicted.

No one can pretend that ours is an easy life, and I frequently have to suppress my irritation. Take, for instance, one Wednesday last January. Joan has had a difficult day. One caller after another has brought her their intense concerns – quite wearing when you have jobs to do. She is now at the cooker, preparing goulash, while Harry, a parishioner, is trying to use the oven. George and Mary Barlow are sitting talking to her. They are happy souls; they cannot read or write but that does not seem to worry them. Ernie and Mrs O'Brien are drinking tea. Alfred is in and out of the door that leads from the kitchen into the garage trailed by his two younger brothers. He has been painting a 'car' he has made with lilac emulsion paint and is appealing to me to stop his brothers from spoiling it. Tom, our four-year-old, has an oil-can to lubricate the wheels. Joan asks me to make sure he does not get the oil on his clothes. Mandy, our twelve-year-old, is at the kitchen table doing her homework. Joan is helping her at a distance, while still preparing the food and trying to talk to George and Mary. She thinks that Mandy is being deliberately obtuse and insolent, and is cross with her. Brian, a church member, is in the kitchen. Today, he has passed his PSV driving test and got himself his first real job in years. He is thrilled and we are happy for him as he tells us about it. Joan screams at Mandy again and Brian runs to help Mandy with her maths. The doorbell rings. A friend of Sam's, our thirteen-year-old, comes in. Brian has left Mandy and gone to the study to use the phone. Harry is getting under Joan's feet trying to put his pies in the oven. The doorbell rings again. It is Debbie, a reporter from the local paper. It rings again. In comes Susan's boyfriend, Chris. We notice a man we have never met before in the hall, introduce ourselves and give him a cup of tea. Joan is still trying to teach Mandy while preparing food and is becoming more and more heated. Tears or rage are not far away. The pain she feels has got to me. I am soaking up her hurt. I want to talk to her but there are people, people, people. She is putting out the food and begins to shout at one of the children. I can take no more. I should have tried to ease the situation for Joan, but I am too bound by my own feelings. I am angry but say calmly, 'I can't take any more. I'm going out.'

'You've no need to bother!' she says. 'Susan, you put the tea out! I'm going.' She goes out of the house. I have never known her do that before and I do not know when she will return, though I have a feeling it will not be long. She needs time to be alone. She has been bombarded by callers all day. The argument is like a storm on the ocean. There are miles of still water beneath, but all I can think of is the storm. I struggle to keep calm. I know it is not serious and that everything will be all right, but I am churned up. I am trying to look after the kids, talk to various adults, and mentally prepare myself for an ecumenical service I am to attend in half an hour. Joan walks back into the house. I put on my cassock, and rush off to the service. I return home at half-past nine, sit at the kitchen table, write this all down, and read it out. We are all able to laugh.

The hysteria we experienced that evening is rare, though we do feel the strain now and then. I whinge here, just as I did in the desert. When I do, it does not take much reflection to realize that ministering in Salford, among warm, unpretentious people has, like walking in the Sahara, brought richness into my life. It is a privilege to have lived in both the desert and the city.

* * *

After weighing in the wheelbarrow at the airport, I met Joan in the lounge and we checked in. My ticket had been so badly charred that the clerk had had to ask her superior if it was still valid. Then, as I was going through immigration clearance, the officer said, 'This visa is out of date!'

'But it was extended at the border!' I said.

'No,' he said, flicking through the pages. 'It has not been extended. You cannot leave the country. I am very sorry.'

'You've got to let me out. My children will be waiting at Heathrow. Please telephone your Kano office. They know it's been extended.' He sighed and groaned.

'No. If I do that, you certainly will be delayed. I will use my discretion.' He stamped my passport and scribbled in it. 'Safe journey.' he said.

We now came to the inspection of our health certificates. I had been unable to be vaccinated against cholera in Kano because it was the Easter weekend. If the official was now to spot the expired certificate, he would not let me through. As the line of people moved forward, every certificate was checked. Joan was in front of me and handed our passports in together. The man opened Joan's first and, seeing her papers in order, handed both passports back, assuming that mine was identical.

The silver bird climbed into the sky. After an hour, I guessed that we might be passing over the yellow speck of Land Rover, somewhere near In Guezzam. I looked out at the ochre expanse and raised my glass.

POSTSCRIPT

Immediately after the expedition, Mick, Paddy and Geoff met for debriefing at Bulford Camp and then in Salford for unloading. Up to the time of printing, Geoff had seen neither of them since. Paddy left the army five months after the expedition and immediately lost contact with Mick. Mick left the army after a further three years.

Geoff has been Rector of the Pendleton Team Ministry in Salford since 1991, and Area Dean since 1986. He and Joan have six children. Mandy was adopted in 1975. Alfred, Thomas and Luke were born naturally to them in 1980, 1982 and 1984. In 1988 Geoff used his experience in travel to take parishioners from his downtown parish on a bus to the Holy Land.

Mick lives in his native Norwich. He has remained single and works for a security firm. Paddy is a painter and decorator in his home town and has married his childhood sweetheart. They have two children. The wheelbarrow is now owned by the National Museum of Science and Industry and kept in a hangar in Wroughton, Wiltshire. It may be viewed on certain bank holidays.

GLOSSARY

chucku	cheese
dela	Niger currency
gandura	voluminous Tuareg robe
guerba	goatskin water-bottle
hassi	spring
kwosai	fried beancakes
reg	stony desert plain
zeni	West African dress improvised from a single piece of cloth